THE HOMESTEAD

THE
HOMESTEAD

Chilton Williamson, Jr.

GROVE WEIDENFELD

New York

Published by Grove Weidenfeld
A division of Wheatland Corporation
841 Broadway
New York, NY 10003-4793

Published in Canada by General Publishing Company, Ltd.

LIBRARY OF CONGRESS CATALOGING-IN-PUBLICATION DATA

Williamson, Chilton.
The homestead / Chilton Williamson, Jr. — 1st ed.
p.   cm.
ISBN 0-8021-1253-6 (alk. paper)
I. Title.
PS3573.I45624H66   1989
813'.54—dc20   89-23599
                                            CIP

Manufactured in the United States of America

Printed on acid-free paper

Designed by Kathryn Parise

First Edition 1990

1   3   5   7   9   10   8   6   4   2

For Brenda and Brendan Roberts,
of course

'Chi v'ha guidati, o che vi fu lucerna,
uscendo fuor della profonda notte
che sempre nera fa la valle inferna?'
—Dante, *Purgatorio*

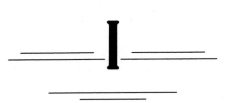

I

so when i saw his hand go under the seat i reached out the boot laying in the bed behind the spare tire and hit him before he could get the gun up and thats the way it has to be because thats the way it happened and cops lawyers judges all of them are interested only in the facts they say so if its truth enough for one family its truth enough for everyone else because wheres the point in scattering truth around like pennies so some appleass can find it and hammer it into a bigger badge for himself

i saw the yellowpainted ford pickup with the company sign on the door coming along the old county road where it starts to get bad less than a quarter of an hour after I'd watched Princess cross the creek a couple hundred yards upstream going along the old cattle trail to the Homestead. I could tell it was Princess on account of the color and the way the hocks turned out and the blind off-front print where Grandy had cut a piece of leather and covered the frog over. Up to then I don't think I had actually believed it, because even though with my own ears I'd heard him brag about it that night when he'd been drinking at the Lone Pine it never had any reality for me. I watched the two of them going uphill away from me, down and up across the clay ridges like a boat with somebody standing in it while the wind blew hard but even too so that the willows laid right over flat not moving and the water was like tea when you blow on it and didn't seem to have any current in it anymore. It was like everything was standing completely still and running away at the same time like a stopped car clock *not lifting the dust where the thunderstorm had wetted it half an hour ago and i threw the traps in the back of the truck and parked it across the road with the creek on one side and the borrow pit on the other and waited while he sat there looking at me from behind the wheel with a kind of slow patient look on his face like i was the pesky kid brother that hed like to wring my neck for me until youre trespassing on private property i said maybe you didnt happen to of seen the sign back there its only six foot tall so im giving you five minutes now to go back three hundred yards before i call the sheriff*

he went on setting there with his arms crossed grinning and looking pretty rough like hed been out partyin the night before and when i was done waiting i reached in the window and flipped off his cap id half figured him for one of those cowards like my brother thats always too proud to fight but he surprised me then rolling on the hard damp clay with his head locked between my head and arm and then him with mine until finally i got him in a double nelson and pitched him and he come back on me swinging one of them big overfed okies slow on his feet but strong like a bull and i ducked and waited and caught him on the chin knocking him onto the fender with the back of his head against the tire and his eyes crossed bleeding and i figured he was down for the count now thinking i could hear the sound of his wristwatch ticking until i saw it was one of those computer watches that dont make a sound like its not human time they are measuring watching his eyelids start to flutter and his face go from white to green to a kind of yellowpink feeling around on the ground with his hands like a

4

blind man before he flopped over onto his belly and begun crawling toward the open door of the truck he had his hand under the seat before i saw it but i had that cowboy boot out in a hurry and swung with it heeldown on the seveninch barrel the sound of it like a woman trying a melon in the supermarket while i hit again and again until finally i threw the boot back in the truck and stood looking down at him thinking I ought to have remembered the last thing he'd want to do was actually shoot me on his way to meet her but there hadn't been time to think and you never know anyway with these goddamn druggies *well jack old man youve done it now*

i left him where he laid and drove back to the highway and called sheriff buckley from the pay phone back of the bar at the lone pine where they had the jukebox turned up so loud i could barely hear my own voice let alone the sheriffs and they told me not to go noplace but wait and the car would meet me outside three deputies in two cars that spreadeagled me on the hood and searched me which was just them doing their job like i had done mine so thats the way its going to be since those are the facts and the truth wouldnt change them at all because the facts are true even if they are not the truth which is why the law is going to have to be satisfied with that and its my word against another guys that they say will probably never speak another word even if he lives so let them believe then that it was never about nothing else than just that seven hundred foot of rightofway for a goddamn pipeline and all i want to know now is is that what it really comes down to anymore bashing white niggers in the head with a cowboy boot or getting shot into space with a peebag and a load of freezedry orangejuice because if it is and the world has got too civilized anymore for courage selfsacrifice and what used to be called honor i dont care they can stick me in jail and throw away the key and i can be dead like captain uncle jo and all the other heroes then like jim bridger said it used to be a man could see forever in this country but anymore nobody wants to look any farther than the end of his own nose

She sat sockfooted at her mother's desk, fidgeting as she stared at the sheet of expensive cream-colored writing paper with the crossed-out block-letter words on it and trying to ignore the heavy roll of the Old Man's chair below. Directly beneath her feet it lurched and swung on little hard wheels as her grandfather, with the determined energy of unchastened age, moved between the row of metal filing cabinets and the massive mahogany desk purchased by him forty-five years ago in Salt Lake City and shipped two hundred miles by rail to Fontenelle before traveling the remaining twenty-six by horse and wagon to the newly built house at Skull Creek. The desk at which she herself worked was much smaller and more delicately proportioned, with an inlaid top of gilt-embossed leather adorned by a monogrammed sterling-silver writing set her mother had brought many years before from New Orleans, an appointment book in leather covers stamped with the initials GSW in gold, a traveling clock in a leather silk-lined case, and a silver-framed portrait photograph of her father wearing a Stetson hat and a red bandanna loosely tied at the throat as he squinted with melancholy eyes at some object apparently far in the distance. Ordinarily she avoided using her mother's writing desk, whose shallow mostly empty drawers had for her the impersonal quality of a piece of motel-room furniture, but today she had gone to it immediately after breakfast, taken a sheet of stationery from the top left drawer, and begun writing. As soon as the telegram was written she would have only to lift the receiver from the arm of the enameled antique telephone and dictate the message to the Western Union office in Fontenelle for urgent transmission to Chipata, Republic of Zambia, the Dark Continent, where her brother had been leading his make-believe life for ten years.

Composing the telegram was an unanticipated amusement, like pasting up a blackmail note from letters clipped out of last Thursday's newspaper or a yellowed telephone directory. She worked with her chin cradled in her hand, sipping cold tea while she spelled out the words in fat capitals as they would appear in the teletyped message and canceled them with a single neat stroke. Sheltered in the kneehole of the desk her woolen feet went on twisting against each other, toe to insole, while she considered the difficulty in recapturing the tone that had been so precisely and uniquely *theirs*. Reason assured her that it made no difference, either he would come or he would not, but it was not primarily reason that concerned her. With a small impatient sound she crossed out the pidgin sentence she had just written, wadded the paper into a tight ball, and took a fresh sheet from the drawer.

In his tobacco-bitten study below crowded with Department of Agriculture reports, veterinary supply catalogues, bound records of the state legislative proceedings, and bales of old newspapers tied up with string, John Clemson Walker lunged again in the chair, and she sat for a moment holding the pencil suspended and hearing the clash of steel drawers as he rifled the cabinets for letters, documents, newspaper clippings marked with scrawled notations—anything which could be transmogrified into an IOU susceptible of immediate presentation by the bearer. Her mother, succumbing as usual to irrelevancy, was in town attending a meeting of her Steering Committee for the Homeless. Pursing her lips in an O of sardonic amusement she printed carefully: JACK CHARGED YESTERDAY WITH ATTEMPTED MURDER FIRST DEGREE STOP HOMEFRONT WHAT YOU WOULD EXPECT STOP YOUR LOVING FAMILY AWAITS YOUR IMMEDIATE RETURN (SIGNED) CLARICE. Then, with her head to one side and the pencil end laid against her nose, she read over what she had written. It sounded better, she thought, but still it was not exactly right.

She rubbed the arch of her right foot along the instep of the left and leaned forward again on her elbow, considering. She took a sip of the tea and held the liquid in her mouth for a moment, as if in its delicate flower-flavor the precise timbre of the past were recoverable. Beyond the tall quarter-pane window, willows and cottonwoods made a protective screen about the house through which she glimpsed in shifting yellow fragments the floodplain of the creek holding at bay the dark blackpointed forest which together they had defied with shouts and armwaving, circling the outbuildings at a gallop and charging across the road and into the meadow with the slingshots and the BB gun (replaced on his twelfth birthday by the Winchester .22 Long Rifle), the tin biscuit boxes filled with BBs, green apples, and smooth round stones from the creek. Flat on their bellies in the redolent sagebrush they had lain staring with hard-screwed eyes toward the palisade of trees for sign of the invasion, Sam holding his finger on the trigger guard while behind them the baby squatted with the ammo boxes until it hurt too much in their ankles and in the small of their backs and Sam stood from behind the bush waving his hat for the all-clear. She scratched out what she had written after the first STOP and wrote above it: YOUR PRESENCE EARNESTLY DESIRED ON THE HOME FRONT. But that was not it either and she wadded that sheet also and took a third one from the drawer.

After ten years she was still furious with her brother. She had never admitted to him outright the proportions of her outrage (the point being that he shouldn't have to be told), even though a full decade had failed to bring him around to loyalty and a sense of his own responsibility. The last time she had seen him—it was three years ago now—his manner had expressed nothing beyond a bland superiority that had made her want to jump up and slap his face. Right now, remembering, she felt her palms tingle with the desire to slap him.

After all, she thought, wetting the corner of the napkin in the tea and pressing it to the swollen throbbing flesh under her eye; after all, why even bother to telegraph? It would seem no more to him than a remote and only faintly disquieting event, like revolution in Nicaragua or a nuclear meltdown in the Ukraine. If he came at all he would come like the International Red Cross, arriving on the scene to snatch disaster from the clumsy hands of the natives and, as the Great White Magician, transform it into salvation before their wondering and grateful eyes. Anyway, she assured herself, as the Old Man made another feint below toward the mobilization of the State of Wyoming on behalf of his younger grandson and sole resident male heir; anyway, I, a woman, can manage as well as or better than any of them—and am proving it!

She rose from the chair suddenly and stood straightbacked behind it, staring through the window like a ghostly general from some long-dead war contemplating again the argument for surrender and finding it, as before, inadmissible. The cataclysm had stripped emotion from her the way lightning peels bark from a tree, exposing the clean hard wood beneath. The afternoon sky was a static yellow blanket and it was as if time had actually stopped for a while except for the creek, which ran smooth and dark beneath a shimmer of broken blue. The water swung against the opposite bank where the trail climbed above it to the Homestead, whose bulging water-stained ceiling and separating log walls stood suddenly before her eyes with the tragic appeal of an abandoned garden, wasted and irretrievable. She put her hand to her face again and winced at the pressure of her fingers against the contusion, thinking: There's two things I've never been, baptized and married, and never will be, either. The travel clock on the desk made a faint almost inaudible spitting sound, like a quietly aroused serpent.

The house seemed to fall backward under the blow, its windows chattering in their frames like loosened teeth as she stood rigid, her hands clenched at her sides, while the shock crashed like thunder in the mountains and was succeeded by a high steady roar. "Damn them!" she cried. If it wasn't the seismographers blowing craters in the ground it was the jets from the U.S. Air Force base up in Great Falls, Montana. Except for the terrible noise, they wouldn't even be real. How can anything be real, she wondered, that moves that fast? *How can anything be real that moves at all?*

For several minutes she went on standing behind the desk, watching a piece of the treeline that appeared to have stepped out overnight from the massed forest behind it. Then abruptly she flung herself into the chair again, seized a pencil, and wrote rapidly and without pause to consider: JACK CHARGED YESTERDAY WITH ATTEMPTED MURDER FIRST DEGREE STOP CANT HOLD THE FORT MUCH LONGER STOP COME ON HOME TO MARLBORO COUNTRY (SIGNED) YOUR SISTER. When she had finished she held the paper out almost at arm's length and read the message over, pursing her lips in satisfaction. Then, after laying it carefully in front of her on the desk, she lifted the telephone receiver and swiftly dialed the Western Union number in Fontenelle. When she was through with the call, Africa still seemed no more real to her than a bad movie.

Without having been a flower child at twenty or a Wall Street insider at thirty—and not to mention being nearly broke at almost forty—I am I realize to every intent and purpose a child of my time. I wasn't born or raised to be one (the opposite, in fact) but by hard work and determination I reinvented myself, though before I had finished shaping the child I was already past becoming a man. My family was the hardest part, while the University of Virginia had mainly a neutral effect; the Army helped a little. Later, it seemed to me that I had watched my entire life unfold itself from that airplane, like one of those clamshells stenciled MADE IN KOREA you drop into a glass of water and a long paper flower opens out from it on a string.

The sound came from all over the sky before concentrating itself in a single invisible spot that suddenly was visible: a black pinpoint just below the soft grayness of the clouds that grew louder and louder without appearing to move until suddenly I could make out the red-and-blue markings of the twin-engine

Piper Cherokee and the wheels hanging like question marks from the belly. I shouted at Mtule to bring the smudge pots and watched as the plane came around and began flying straight again, dropping toward the strip on a low trajectory to touch down in a spread of silver wings and go bumping along between the smudge fires until it rotated abruptly and came trundling back, weaving to avoid the warthog holes. When I made out Patrick Roberts's face behind the windscreen I waved, trying not to look apprehensive. I had the supplies I needed for the rest of the trip and I had told Patrick that I would not expect him until the end of the second week in July. Mtule stood motionless holding his bit of punk to his nose while he watched the plane with somber pale-rimmed eyes. Behind us the suppertime shuffle of the camp had ceased and some unexpectedly thoughtful person had turned off the Rayburn woman's African-war-drums tape, creating a silence punctuated at intervals by the tinkle of ice cubes in cocktail glasses as the engines cut out and the props blurred quickly into focus. In the cockpit Patrick was waving something square and yellow and I began walking forward to meet him as he climbed out on the wing and dropped to the ground as lightly as a leopard, holding the telegram delicately between his thumb and blunt red forefinger. I tore open the back of it and read the message through twice. Then I replaced it in the mutilated envelope, folded the whole thing over, and buttoned it into my shirt pocket. From the edge of the bush a hyena cried once shortly, as if to announce itself. Patrick Roberts said, "They thought at the office you'd want to see that straightaway. Nothing serious, I hope?"

I looked up at the fleecy underbelly of the sky from which the plane had dropped, waiting for the hyena to cry again. I opened the pocket and removed the canary-yellow envelope, which I tore into tiny double bits and cast like ashes on the evening breeze. Patrick thrust his hands into the slash pockets of his flight jacket and gave me an embarrassed look sideways. "That bad, eh?"

"If I was an ancient Roman senator, Pat, you'd be a dead sonofabitch already."

The hyena cried again, closer this time. The filthy bugger, I thought. If he gets any nearer I'll shoot the bastard. In camp the cocktail hour, which had been interrupted by the arrival of the plane, had resumed, to judge from the murmur of conversation and the politely insistent voice of Makhosi handing around the smoked eland and salmon hors d'oeuvres. Through the masculine whiskey-cured voices, strident with triumph at the taking of the fine lion that afternoon, the woman's voice wove itself demurely. Her voice was ever low and sweet, an excellent thing in a Texan. But not compensatory. "The hell with the ancient Romans," I said. "I'll mix us a couple of stiff ones instead."

As we approached camp together the war drums began again, a low insistent uproar just beyond the circle of light. So far the trip had been more like a bad Hollywood movie than a safari. They were a party of Texans from Dallas in the computer-instrument line: big, sunburned, florid men with the cold flat eyes of rattlesnakes or the piss-ant sheriff's deputies, country storekeepers, and crossroads-filling-station attendants their daddies had been. They wore gaudy snapbutton shirts and crisp new Stetsons, talked in loud braying voices blurred by negroid accents, and all of them were crack shots except the woman, who turned out to be interested in the kind of hunting you don't do with a gun. My sister's telegram explained nothing—that was deliberate of course, following the reel-him-in-with-his-own-curiosity technique. Also, explanations weren't really needed, my brother having been presumptively guilty all his life like a mine waiting to have its tripwire kicked. Clarice had been furious with me for ten years, but still she hadn't given up on me, wouldn't cry uncle. After an entire decade she kept on believing she could persuade me finally just to chuck everything I had accomplished in twenty years and accept what she called my responsibilities, of which my brother in her opinion was obviously one. Well, the hell with him I thought: The hell with all of them.

13

The heat of the mopane-wood fire burned through the soles of my desert boots, keeping the chill of the African winter night at bay while I chewed the tender meat in its rich gravy and tried to ignore the conversation of the clients. The hyena cried again from the shadows, almost human-sounding this time. For the past couple of evenings a pack had been skulking in the bush, whooping and screaming after sundown like Indian braves. In *The Adventures of Captain Bonneville, U.S.A.* the Captain describes how at the Rendezvous of 1833 on the Upper Green River where he had rejoined Joseph Walker and his company rabid wolves had attacked the camp and bitten several of the men, who later stripped themselves naked and fled with foaming mouths and gnashing teeth into the wilderness. I am sorry, I thought, for my brother, but every insane man is crazy in exactly the way that he deserves to be. From the corner of my eye I saw Mrs. Rayburn coming toward me in the firelight holding a plate in one hand and a drink in the other. With the drink hand, she balanced herself lightly on my shoulder as she bent to my right ear. "That was absolutely a divine meal, Mr. Walker."

"I'm glad you enjoyed it. Your husband didn't spoil any meat with that shot."

"Oh, but he missed that lion by a couple of miles this afternoon," she said, and I stared at her without answering. In thirty-nine years I have looked over a lot of women without finding one whose final ambition in life was neither to cripple nor destroy her husband. "I wish *you'd* shoot something again," Mrs. Rayburn said. "It's the most beautiful thing, really, watching you shoot a gun."

"I appreciate the compliment, but Jake is pretty quick off the mark himself and he isn't paying me to fill his permits for him." Somewhere in the American Southwest—perhaps that corner of the Arizona desert where they had reconstructed the London Bridge—she had acquired a Palm Springs imitation of an English accent.

"Oh," the woman said, rattling the ice in her glass, "I'm

certain he wouldn't mind if you filled just a few! Jake is so easily bored—like all us Texans, you know." She gave me an arch smile and felt in the pocket of her blouse for a cigarette, while Ganeko waited with the lighter and afterward refilled our glasses. When she turned to me again her expression was coy as she laid a light hand on my arm. "I've been just dying all week to ask you a question. A personal question I mean. Do you mind awfully?"

"Not at all," I lied, withdrawing the arm.

"We—I mean, my husband and I—all of us—have been wondering how, with your name, you don't sound like a Texan. You *are* from Texas, aren't you?"

"Sam Houston was a cousin of an ancestor of mine, Joseph Walker, one of the earliest white explorers of the Rocky Mountains and the Far West. I've been in the Dallas–Fort Worth airport a couple of times changing planes. I grew up on a sheep and cattle ranch in southwestern Wyoming."

"Honestly? Wyoming? Is that a place?"

"It used to be the best place." Before, that is, the penetration of civilization into those hitherto magnificent parts.

"I thought it was just one of those huge vacant lots you fly over between San Francisco and New York that the people in the East want to dump garbage in. What are you doing in Africa then?"

"On the whole, I prefer barbarism." I tapped her glass with a monitory forefinger. "I wouldn't drink any more of that tonight if I were you. We need to get a particularly early start in the morning. Which reminds me—if you don't mind, will you please excuse me?"

I stood quickly, thrust my plate inside the mess tent, and went on to my own, which was pitched deliberately at some distance from the others. Undaunted by snakes and hyenas the woman had appeared in it the night before, wearing a diaphanous negligee over some very skimpy underthings; it had taken her three-quarters of an hour to become discouraged enough to leave.

Sex has always been for me a necessary adolescent agony to be taken neat and uncomplicated like good whiskey, and this would have been anything but uncomplicated. Patrick Roberts sat on the edge of the cot with one boot on and holding the other in his hand; a brandy snifter rested on top of the foot locker beside him. He looked up as I came in and showed me his frank boyish smile. "Plenty to talk about tonight at the captain's table, what?"

"Don't get me started, Pat. That elephant-cropping job looks better every day. Where in the hell is that bottle? You haven't killed it already, have you?"

"Here you are, *bwana*. Can't handle much of the stuff myself. Whose idea were those damn bongo drums?"

"The woman bought the tape in a supermarket in Dallas. She said it would help her to enjoy an authentic African experience."

"What in bloody hell did she think Africa was? A grade-B movie?"

"I don't care what she thought, or thinks."

Patrick Roberts took a drink of the brandy. "It gives me the creeps, a little."

"Just ignore it. It's only noise."

"I can hardly hear myself think with that bloody racket going on. Well—cheers."

"Cheers."

We drank. Finally Patrick said, "Do you have any aviation oil in camp? Wouldn't hurt to add a quart or so in the morning."

"Sure. Ask Mtule to find it for you before we start out. It's going to be an early one, by the way, on account of we need to be on the other side of the forest by first light."

"You going to try for rhino?"

"You bet."

The pilot poured himself more brandy and rubbed absentmindedly between his bare toes. He asked, with exaggerated carelessness, "Do you have any messages for me to carry back to Chipata?"

16

"Maybe."

Patrick Roberts said, "Of course, it isn't any of my business, but—"

"My kid brother—age twenty-nine—killed a man a couple of days ago. Or tried to."

"Crikey!" Patrick let his breath out with a whistling sound. "A pub fight I suppose. Or was it about a girl?"

"Clare—my sister—didn't say. She was the one who sent the telegram." Hemingway said that it was what you leave out that counts, not what you put in.

He leaned forward on the cot holding the brandy snifter between his knees. "Look here, Houston," he said finally, "don't you worry about a thing now. I'll take care of it all in town tomorrow. Oakley came in with that Milanese outfit day before yesterday. They can send him out to finish the trip for you and I'll book a seat on the Pan Am out of Pretoria to New York."

"I'm not going, Pat."

The pilot set the snifter on his bare knee and stared. "What do you mean—not going?"

"I might send a telegram. Or Flowers-by-Wire."

Patrick Roberts said, "But that's unnatural!"

I got the Beretta from the tent corner and removed the bolt. I swabbed the action and the barrel with solvent and applied a light coat of oil to the gun while Patrick stared morosely at the ground. Like most Irishmen, he tended to elevate all matters of consanguinity to the level of religion. I asked him, "Has Mtule been in to clean the rest of the guns?"

"No," Patrick said. "I don't know. I don't think so." He did not look up. "Those damn drums have got me to where I can hardly think anymore." He decanted what remained of the brandy into the glasses, tossed the dead man under the cot, and worked his bare toes fretfully in the dust. "Damnit, Houston, you really *must* go home and look after this business, you know. We'll cover for you one hundred percent here." He swung his thick legs onto the blanket and sat hugging his knees to his chin like a Hindu squatted before the village temple.

"There isn't a thing I could do," I told him, "if I did go home."

"Why not?" Patrick Roberts asked. "Why couldn't you do anything?"

I was going to try to explain for him, and changed my mind. It was something I had never been able to explain to anyone: how I had been forced to fight free of them like a man struggling clear of a shipwreck; how, even today, separated from them by ten years and twelve thousand miles, I did not feel myself to be entirely immune, like a recovered malaria patient in whom the infection continues to circulate, waiting its chance to erupt again in spasms of fever-and-ague. It was why, when I thought of Fontenelle and Skull Creek, I felt like the "cured" explorer contemplating a return to the fever swamps of the Upper Nile. I had learned to live with this knowledge as a man learns to live with the fact that he is not handsome or clever or that he has a weak heart or that he suffers from incurable impotency, but I had made a promise to myself ten years ago: never to allow them and the past they inhabited to get hold of me again. "Have you ever read Faulkner?" I asked Patrick.

"Who's that?"

"He was a famous literary neurotic they made me read in college," I said, and went quickly out of the tent and across camp with the rifle on my arm, watching where the light of the dying fire shelved into darkness like the yellow bottom of a lake.

Ganeko and Ndumiso were loading boxes of food onto the truck and Mtule sat by the fire with a cleaning rod and a bottle of solvent, replying patiently and monosyllabically to the queries of a Texan who had had one nightcap more than was good for him. I switched on my pocket torch and circled into the darkness behind the latrines and then the hyena cried sharply again. This time it sounded almost underfoot.

There were rustling noises in the tents, followed by the long rip of nylon zippers, and in the dim openings heads began to show.

"Where in the hell *is* that sonofabitch?"

"Sounded almost like he was sitting on the crapper."

"He must be after my lion carcass, the bastard."

They stood closely together, a shadowy knot in the thin inconstant light. Then one shadow, smaller and slighter than the others, detached itself and came flitting toward me across the grass. It was the woman, wearing slippers and a housecoat over the negligee. I dropped the beam of the torch as she approached and her hand fell on my arm again, very cool and dry and nervous. "What a terrible sound," Mrs. Rayburn said in a whisper. "Where is it? You *are* going to shoot it, aren't you?"

I resisted the temptation to shake free of the hand; under the circumstances, to do so seemed not quite of the old school.

"Please do, Mr. Walker," she insisted. "I hate mad things; they're so unreliable. Do you think he's after Billy's lion?"

I looked toward the tents where the Texans stood conversing, arms folded sternly on the monogrammed fronts of their dressing robes. Mtule had laid aside the rifle he had been cleaning and had begun to move toward his own tent, going for his gun I supposed. Suddenly I saw it: a pair of yellow eyes advancing stealthily toward the shoal of light. I shook the woman off, raised the barrel, and swung out the telescopic sight. Then I stepped forward, moving cautiously, breasting the dark with the rifle at shoulder level.

Shining with yellow mockery the eyes did not flinch, gauging my approach. I counted fifteen paces and dropped, snapping off the safety as I crouched on one knee. Now I could see the rest of him—the flattened, elongate shape against the paler dark of the grass.

Behind me to the right Mtule stood in grass to his waist with the forestock of the rifle resting in the crook of one arm. I could not tell whether he had seen the hyena or not. The creature stirred forward suddenly, giving me a glimpse of the rufous hide, mottled and mangy, and the ears pressed flat against the bald-looking dog's skull. I put the sights behind the left shoulder a couple of inches below the spine. I had already begun the trigger squeeze when two things occurred simultaneously.

The first was that suddenly the hyena wasn't there at all. The second was that the woman laid her hand on my shoulder. I shrugged it off violently and swung the muzzle of the rifle toward the deeper shadows where the hyena stood grinning and lolling its tongue as I fired two rounds in succession. Then it was really gone and I stood gripping the rifle by the hot barrel and glaring at her while she stared reproachfully, modestly bunching the lapels of her housecoat in her hand. "You missed it," Mrs. Rayburn said unnecessarily. In the dark it was impossible to tell if she was smirking or not. "What if the filthy creature comes back and claws his way into my tent?"

I nearly explained to her that of all the scenarios I might have invented for the remainder of the evening hers was the most satisfactory. Instead I stood mute in grass to my waist, feeling the metal sear my palm. "If you're feeling more up to it you can cash in that rain check tonight," the Rayburn woman said.

"In my book, nobody gets a second chance. Including me."

"Be careful," she said, "or I'll voodoo you. That's how people get what they want over here, isn't it?"

I drove her like a prize filly ahead of me back to camp, wondering why she had seemed in such a hurry to see that hyena shot. It could have been fear of course, but she hadn't acted scared. Maybe, I thought, it had been simply an expression of that ruthless instinctive putting-away impulse that members of a kind—women especially—so often feel for each other. So far as it occurred to me to think or care what the future held in store for Mr. Jake Rayburn of 27293 Meadowlark Drive, Dallas, Texas, I hoped he would at least be spared symptoms of anything resembling hyenalike behavior.

———

The ground fell and heeled sharply away—to the left first, then to the right—beneath the fixed unsliding trucks, tents, bushes, and trees. Then the airplane righted itself and the country opened out below in a yellow-and-green expanse of bush and plain, copses of the flat-crowned acacia trees threaded by game trails, and herds of running kudu towing long parachutes of yellow dust. Climbing higher it began to buck against a stiff wind and I could see the long irregular line of the mountains, hazy and blue in their tropical cover, and the cloud-dappled plain sliding beneath us in a slow brown wash. Patrick Roberts's expression as he checked his instruments was stoical but I observed small waves of humor breaking through, presumably at my expense. If he wanted to believe that his victory had been achieved at the level of sentiment, that was fine with me. Actually, it was the highly practical thought of Skull Creek Ranches being lost through an incompetent and catastrophically expensive legal battle that had finally made up my mind for me. A patrimony is like a father, you only have one each of them.

The bucking worsened as we approached the mountains. My stomach felt like a shallow well into which somebody was tossing little green apples and I thought how absurd it would be now if we dropped through an air pocket and cracked up. Since that day when my father took off in the little blue-and-white Maule and disappeared forever, flying has come closer than anything to making me know and understand fear. I looked over at Patrick again, but the pilot was gazing through the side window at the tawny bosom of Africa, his savage beloved mistress. Patrick Roberts had lost his heart with the first kiss fifteen years ago and been a gone goose ever since. I, by comparison, had lived ten years in Africa, appreciatively but without surrendering to its spell, holding fast to the single sufficient lesson I had carried with me from boyhood: namely, the absolute necessity to invest nothing of yourself in any place (or, for that matter, any person) beyond mere money.

The mountain peaks vanished under billows of cloud like

white water over boulders in a racing river on which the plane bumped softly. I worked my shoulders into the padded seat, rested my head on the window, and watched the bright infrequent sun burst in sprays through the twilight. I was distinctly aware of Pat grinning at me out of the side of his face and then I was truly aloft at last, the airplane bearing me swiftly, surely, and entirely without sensations of distress toward home.

its because women dont ever want just the one thing but the
opposite one too that i could tell the minute i come in for supper she
had gone ahead and sent that telegram
    draining water off of the boiled vegetables her face wet and
red and when finally she did look at me it was like she had two
faces a blurred one over a sharper and harder one like you were
looking at her through an unfocused camera so i knew then and
when she was done with the beans at the sink i washed my hands
and dried them on the roller towel and got down the whiskey from
the cupboard and poured me a toddy all the time pretending i
hadnt noticed anything looking through the shoppers and cata-
logues at the kitchen table drinking toddy and watching her move
about the kitchen snatching her hair back from the food with a
look on her face like she was undressing and felt somebody watch-
ing and when i caught her eye finally she widened her face at me
vague and innocentlike and said what like she thought i wanted to

23

ask her a question because shed been trying to get him back for ten years and i should have known there was no way she was going to pass up a chance like this one so after all hed be coming home in a couple of days now bragging around about the elephants and lions hed killed and about how brave he is and only him and me knowing the truth about that until he got bored finally with them acting like he was the messiah at the second coming and took the next plane back to africa

if only i knew what she knows i know maybe id know exactly what to do then i made another toddy while she took the roast from the oven and felt better now watching the stiffness go out of her shoulders and neck and that look of being caught without her clothes on going away until suddenly she smiled at me and i smiled back when we both of us heard the old man come grumbling from his study like a sick bear coming out of its den and ma sighing herself downstairs after worrying all day about the homeless the unwed mothers and the battered wives and i knew all i was going to hear for the next hour was quit acting like a stubborn jackass now and oh wont you please just talk to a lawyer for my sake if not for your own while she fidgeted and gave me little nervous glances across the table like she was wondering could she really trust me to handle everything right or not because wanting not just the one thing but the other also makes you scared of everything and when everything scares you like my family has always been scared the only thing you can think about is how to reach out and get control of everything and everyone else too

they will tell you how complicated life is and not to be what they call simplistic about it but when you look at it for yourself you see how they are wrong because what they mean by complicated is what was never important to begin with while the few simple and important things are what nobody pays any attention to or maybe has never even heard of anymore like courage loyalty and honor or even just decency so that if you were a writer and wanted to write a book you would find there isnt anything left to make a book out of *just like if you wanted to do something that would make someone want to write a book about it there wouldnt be anybody that would care*

life is the simplest thing in the world really there isnt anything simpler than life or anyway there shouldnt be

———————
—————

With the single exception of her weight, Jenny Richardson's greatest concern in nearly two years of marriage had been what she always thought about as her morals.

One afternoon a week she put on her hot-pink Western-cut shirt and a pair of jeans and, leaving Bret with the babysitter, drove into town after lunch in the secondhand compact sedan Chuck had bought for her. In Fontenelle, if it were not her week to visit the probation officer, she went first to the Recreation Center where she paddled conscientiously up and down the swimming lanes for half an hour and afterward worked out on the exercise machines in the weight room. Although Dr. Smith regularly recorded her weight without comment she felt disgustingly healthy; at times she seemed to herself to be the only flesh-and-blood person in a world of shades, for whom the wearing of that flesh she had been accused of having deprived others of was a shameful privilege. She would stretch out in the damp swimsuit on the padded bench and lift weights attached to her arms and legs, sweating profusely and growing very hot in the face in the fervor of penitential devotion, and when she was through purge herself in the steamer first and then in the sauna bath. This regimen, she had found, helped to control her eating, though it had no effect at all on her other appetites. Finally, after anxiously weighing, she would blow-dry the heavy fall of the rich mahogany hair that, unpinned, fell below her buttocks now, make up, and dress.

Downtown she would have her hair trimmed by the stylist or her back pummeled by the chiropractor, an enormous man with a red pig's face, the girth of a djin, and hands like hams who called her "girlie" and whose thick blunt fingers occasionally expressed a roving disposition. She would shop lightly, then go for a drink at the Bare Garden where her friend Bette worked bar in the afternoon, and after two drinks drive carefully out of town past the motels, the freightyard, and the cemetery. The probation officer never mentioned the Collins women but talked to her instead about Life Adjustment, Goals Implementation, and the importance of a Positive Self-Image, but once after leaving him she had gone into the Catholic church where the funeral mass had been said and tried to pray. The painted wooden figure of Christ Crucified above the polished silver chalices and the horrible waxen lilies had seemed to her superfluous and artificial, and she had been too nervous to be able to think of anything to say. As a child she had disliked the portrait of Joseph Smith in the First Ward Meeting Hall in Mosiah, Utah, but he at least Jenny felt had looked like a real human being. When she thought of her trial she remembered something like a three-ring circus with the feminist defense lawyer from Denver—she had been a thickset woman wearing a tailored suit, with cropped grizzled hair and the set-jawed expression of a physical-education teacher—acting as ringmaster.

In the somnolence of four o'clock the Bare Garden had the packed-up appearance of a closed theater on Monday afternoon. Rickety blinds with missing slats were let down behind the dirty plate-glass window in which a hand-lettered sign read GO-GO GIRLS NITELY. Inside Bette leaned indolently on the end of the bar, smoking a cigarette fixed in a plastic holder while she watched a game show on the television. Her dyed hair had been teased into fluffy eruptions around her pale face, and she had on black sateen slacks that somebody was going to have to pull off her like a riding boot and a black vest with silver sequins above which her fat white boobs peeked prodigiously. Bette was a believer in satanic inspiration and heavy metal as well as a worshiper of celebrity of any kind, including that of acquitted murderesses turned homemakers. She regarded Jenny, who was one year her senior, with a kind of awe. She said, "Hi there, girl! I been waiting on you since one o'clock. Want to go to a party at the lake tonight?"

"I can't, tonight. I promised Chuck I'd be home by six. He has some meeting he has to be at at seven." She hadn't been to a party without him in two years, but with Bette she felt it almost as a duty to maintain a pretense of sophisticated independence. She dug in her purse for the package of stale cigarettes she had bought weeks before, and lit one.

Bette jangled her bracelets imperiously and blew smoke at the ceiling. "Oh, come on. You're a poop! Don't be his sweet little wifey, Jenny."

"It isn't that. I think Bret's coming down with strep." Bret was not coming down with anything, but Bette's idea of her as a swinger was hard to repudiate. In the presence of Bette she felt like an interesting person, even a glamorous one.

"Well of course, if the poor little squirt's sick. . . ." Bette stubbed her cigarette and squinted at the television, where a woman with a figure like two boulders piled and wearing an obvious brass-colored wig had just won two million dollars on *Wheel of Fortune*. "God, I hope *I* never get married!" she exclaimed, as if marriage were a misfortune that struck more or less at random, like a fatal disease. Bette had a three-year-old daughter whose father, an unemployed oilfield hand, had hung around for several months after the child was born in case anything further were expected of him. Upon learning that nothing was, he had returned to wherever he had come from in the Southwest. "You want Black Velvet," she asked, "or a beer?"

"Not beer. Chuck says I'm too fat."

"You don't look fat to me." Bette scooped ice into a glass and poured a double shot of whiskey over. "Why don't you tell him to go chase himself?"

"Because I can't take any more argument. That's why."

Bette placed a cocktail napkin in front of her and set the drink on it. "Things not going so good with you guys again?"

"Oh, it's just . . . you know . . . I don't know." There wasn't any way to explain it except that after almost two years of marriage you found yourself seeing through the man you had once congratulated yourself on seeing into. In her worst moods marriage seemed to her a good deal like prison, the difference being that in prison she had been conscious of a strange buoyant freedom she had experienced neither before nor since and that contrasted painfully with the torpor and depression which weighed upon her now like excess flesh.

"Chuck's how old now?"

"Forty-one."

Bette lit another cigarette and nodded wisely. "It's probably just male menopause. You know."

"But lately he's been acting more like eighty-one—a real onery eighty-one."

"You think he's maybe like fooling around?"

"I don't think so. Sometimes, I wish he was."

Bette nodded again, vaguely this time, and looked back to the television where the huge woman had been replaced by a little skinny man in his fifties who stood commandingly by the Wheel of Fortune with the assurance of a ship's commander on his bridge. He had on a powder-blue leisure suit, a shirt that was open at the neck with the collar points spread over the lapels of the coat, and a red toupee; the studio makeup made his face look painted and brittle, like a mask. Jenny tasted her whiskey and put the glass down thoughtfully. The little man vanished from the screen and was replaced by a famous actor who talked confidingly on the dangers of drugs. "I bet he gets a gram for doing that," Bette remarked. "Speaking of which, I know where I can get some great stuff cheap, if you're interested."

"I can't do that anymore. It gets in the milk."

"Oh pooh. You're getting to be an old lady in a hurry, you know that? How come you're still nursing, anyway? The mutt's already almost two, isn't he?"

"One and a half."

The little man stepped down from the Wheel of Fortune with strands of red wig in his eyes and an expression of helpless disappointment on his face; he looked as if he were going to cry. He was succeeded by another man with shiny black hair, black conniving eyes in a small rocklike face, and the thin white hands of a cardsharp. "Some creeps have all the luck," Bette complained. "If only I had a million bucks I could get away from this dump and move to California." She stubbed the cigarette resentfully and went to turn off the television. When she came back she gave Jenny four quarters and said, "Put some songs on the box, will you?" She added slyly, "Guess who was in here last night?"

She didn't have to guess but it was thrilling to be told. "Who?"

"Jack Walker, you airhead! Who else would I be telling you about?"

The name was a cool finger tracing her spine. Although they had had only a single awkward encounter some weeks ago, she believed him to be secretly in love with her. She daydreamed about him, brooding over the wild black hair and beard, the furious dark face, the sad, penetrating eyes. Several times, catching sight of his old pickup battered and colorless under the perennial grime, she had followed in her car at a discreet distance, then parked outside whatever building he had disappeared into and waited for him to come out. She was entirely aware of behaving like a complete idiot but she went on doing it anyway. She felt as silly to herself as a junior high brat but it was still the best feeling she thought she had had in years. Each time she caught sight of his truck the day seemed reborn in mystery, the world trembled in anticipation. Each time, she was conscious of an upwelling of the spiritual as well as the animal life in her, and yet she felt weak also and a little faint. He was twenty-nine years old, seven years older than herself. Now they said he had killed a man—or tried to. "How did he look?" she asked; it was hard speaking in a casual tone and at the same time loudly enough to be heard above the jukebox.

"He seemed fairly sober, for once. I guess he figures he don't need any more DWIs on top of everything else."

"What difference would a DWI make after . . . *that?*"

"Not too much I guess," Bette agreed. She added irrelevantly, "My great-grandfather saw Billy the Kid blow the sheriff of Lincoln, New Mexico, away."

Bette bought her a second drink on the house and then it was five o'clock with the after-work customers coming in and time to go. Jenny put down fifty cents and waved at Bette, who was at the other end of the bar putting a daiquiri through the blender as she flirted with a heavy-set man in coveralls old enough to be her father. Outside she paused for a moment on the sidewalk, shading her eyes with her hand against the falling sun for the car. In the middle of the block a tall well-built man with thick but well-groomed black hair was folding himself into a foreign-made sedan that was much too small for him. Breathless and weak-kneed, she watched the little car back away from the curb and cruise down to the traffic light, where it stopped and signaled a right-hand turn. But enough like him to be his brother she thought, as her breath came more quietly and she felt around in her bag for the keys. Home was the last place on earth she felt like going right now. It was also the only place there was for her to go.

Leaving town she braked sharply for an oncoming patrol car and accelerated again, lifting her chin to catch the dry hot wind that instantly vaporized the droplets of moisture on her throat and temples and whipped her clean unpinned hair. The cemetery on its rise of greensward loomed at the curve and she depressed the pedal firmly until the needle climbed from thirty to forty-five and passed it on a rush of air and with averted eyes, defying the plainly posted limit.

The waitress was a tallowy blonde with muddy eyes, a mottled complexion, and a figure like a candlestump whose age I put at around twenty-five although she looked ten years older. Several times while she poured coffee she gave me a sly look out of the side of her face as if she were trying to place me, but I wouldn't have known her from Eve. I'd been gone too long already to recognize the young ones.

Except for the waitress and a well-dressed girl eating a sandwich in a booth at the back of the place I was alone in the café, where I had stopped to evacuate the 3.2 beer I had drunk on the drive up from Salt Lake City and fortify myself with cups of strong black coffee. The fatigue of the long and crowded flight, jet lag, and a twelve-hour layover in New York had not set me up for a family reunion; I felt jaded, irritable, and depressed. On the plane from Pretoria I had drunk too many gin and tonics watching the lunatic movies they showed all the way across the Atlantic and arrived with a hangover at Kennedy Airport, where my luggage—including an autographed first-printing copy of the 1938 edition of *The Short Stories of Ernest Hemingway*—had been stolen from the baggage carousel. After filling out the loss report I had caught a taxi into Manhattan for dinner. The driver, a Jamaican wearing a loud floral-patterned shirt, had taken a wrong exit and got us lost in a neighborhood of the borough of Queens where the faces were shiny black and chickens, which the Jamaican explained were raised for voodoo rituals, flocked like pigeons in the streets. I ate dinner in a French restaurant in the East Fifties, paid a bill that would have balanced the trade deficit of several African nations, and made a halfhearted attempt at getting drunk again in a determinedly chic bar on Third Avenue where I bought a couple of Tom Collinses for an attractive and elegantly turned-out young lady who showed me the hundred-dollar bill she carried tucked into the lining of her little shoe; after the second drink, she tried very prettily and tactfully to learn whether I had been tested recently for a well-publicized infectious disease of the blood. I had not spent time in New York since the late sixties when I lived East during the four years I attended the University of Virginia at Charlottesville, where the Old Man had sent me after taking out a mortgage on the North Section in order to pay the tuition. I had regarded the city then as a prime candidate for thermonuclear reform and twenty-odd years hadn't improved it any; the opposite, in fact. They had built more of the slab-sided high-rise towers of the kind resembling the bar graphs in an urban inflation report, and hardly anybody spoke English anymore. The cab drivers had on—besides the Jamaican shirts—Afghan turbans and Indian saris and knew even less about getting around town than I did. There were fewer newspapers, I noticed, and the ones that remained were illiterate tabloids created by rich and ignorant aliens for consumption by poor and illiterate ones. You could buy sex for about the price of two subway tokens and cocaine was as easily available as condoms. On Central Park South the squat overdressed moguls of the broadcasting, advertising, and real-estate industries, barking from the dim interiors of electronically-equipped limousines like small liners, were brassier and more offensive than ever though not as arrogant as the queers, who wore their shirts unbuttoned to their navels and whom everybody kowtowed to as though they were mandarins. In the capital city of the Land of the Free—even of the Free World itself—you had a sense of the sheer anarchic willfulness superimposed upon the mania for total collective control that has always characterized cosmopolitan culture for me. Oppressed by intimations that were relieved only by the thought that it was after all none of my concern I flagged a cab back to the airport, where I bought a handful of magazines, fumbled my way aboard the plane, and fell asleep while we were still on the runway. When I awoke we were over Omaha, and I sat watching the rich checkered real estate of what was less than a century and a half ago the Long Grass Plains lifting gently into the velvet emptiness of the sandhill country of western Nebraska, from which the Rocky Mountains burst abruptly. I read part of an article about the interchangeability of modern rural and urban life, one of those cleverly simplistic exercises by so-called intellectuals who wouldn't recognize reality if you could take a Ph.D. in it, then stuffed the magazine into the seat pocket and sat back to endure the Mormon banker beside me who drank milk with his lunch and bragged that I wasn't going to recognize Salt Lake City. When I claimed my car from the airport rental agency and drove downtown to buy underwear, shirts, and a change of pants at one of the posh new department stores on South Main Street, I discovered that he had been entirely right about that.

The girl came again with the coffeepot, refilled my cup, and went back to the kitchen where she had a radio set loud, pausing on the way to take the empty plate from the well-dressed girl who was reading the *Fontenelle Fortune* propped against the napkin dispenser. The café was full of blue soft light sealed away from the glare of afternoon by its wide plate-glass window facing the square where the dozen massive old cottonwood trees foamed slowly in the hot wind. A pickup truck ran in and hung its front end over the curb; two men jumped from it and crossed the sidewalk holding their heads down and their elbows out like big awkward birds trying to get up. They came through the door on a flap of dead air, mounted the counter stools from behind, and sat on them with a loose marsupial stride, keeping their backs to me. The waitress shuffled out of the kitchen and moved behind the counter, holding three hairpins in her teeth and reaching behind herself to put back the tallowy strands. The bigger of the two men said, "Hi Crystal. How's it goin?"

"Hi Tom, hi Al. Not too bad. What have you guys been up to, today?"

"Not too much."

"Been keepin outa trouble, huh?"

"Oh I guess. Just another one of them days, you know."

"What can I do for you guys today?"

"Gimme a Bud and a Slim Jim here."

"Make that two of em, Crystal."

"You bet, Al."

Fascinated in spite of myself I sat listening, watching them. Tom and Al Studds had been captain and co-captain respectively of the high school football team before Tom got caught with a bottle in his motel room the night before the Homecoming game senior year and lost his football scholarship from the state university. He had roughnecked for a local drilling outfit for several years after that and finally went into business with his brother as part owner of a small seismograph company. In his glory days as school football hero Tom had chased my sister pretty hard until she gave him the bum's rush. I hadn't seen either one of them for a dozen years at least.

Crystal brought the beers and set a bottle of tomato juice between them on the bar. Tom Studds poured a long shot of tomato until the beer creamed pink over the top of the glass and handed the bottle to his brother. The girl, holding her chin in her hand, watched them as if they had just discovered the formula for penicillin. "Anyone want to roll me for the jukebox?" she asked finally.

"Why not?" Tom Studds said.

She got the leather cup and rolled the dice on the counter-top. Then she gathered them in one hand and dropped them back in the cup and passed it to Tom and he rolled. All three craned on their elbows to look, and the girl went to the register for change which she gave to Tom, but he brushed it aside with the back of his hand. "Tell you the truth, I'm kind of enjoying the peace and quiet. I don't get much of it at work, not to mention what I get at home."

The girl swept up the coins, punched the register, and dropped them into the tray. She took away the empty glasses and came back with two full ones. She complained, "What's the matter with you guys today? You're as much fun as a cold shower this afternoon."

"I dunno," Tom Studds said. "Job's gettin in the way of my life, and I'm sicker'n hell of both of them."

"What's *your* excuse?" she asked Al.

"Who, me? I ain't had to have no excuse for nothin, since I was eighteen years old and pinched the English teacher on the butt, senior trip to L.A."

I stared at the bottom of the empty cup, swamped by a sudden depression. They had been retelling that story—Al Studds and the English teacher—during the four years I had spent at U.V.A. and the two with the U.S. Army on patrol in the Vietnamese jungle; during the five I had knocked about on the West Coast, up in the Alaskan wilderness, and in the Australian bush; and the ten more I had worked in South Africa facing charging Cape buffalo and wounded leopards. For twenty-one years they had relished its wit, originality, and humor—until now this trivial and inane anecdote brought down the hurrying hand in a rush, bearing with it the realization that the strategy was, finally, a failure and that time had not been suspended by violent perpetual action energetically engaged in on the far side of the world. Listening to their conversation I was made aware, brutally and without warning, of the first premonition of middle age.

The girl drew a rolled-up newspaper from behind the register and spread it open on the counter. "You guys seen this week's paper yet?"

"Not really," Tom Studds told her, revolving the sheet to face himself. "Anymore the only time I see a newspaper is elk season, out in the woods with my pants down around my ankles." He shoved the paper at his brother and took a drink of beer and tomato juice.

"Christ, *I* don't want the damn thing," Al protested, shoving it back.

The girl rolled up the paper and put it away again. "What you guys doing over the Fourth?" she asked them.

"I dunno," Tom said. "Take the old lady campin up the Fork, pro'ly. That way she can't complain I didn't do nothin with her all year. I ain't thought about it much though."

"Me neither," Al agreed.

They unwrapped the jerky and chewed in silence, while the girl twisted her finger into her pale unclean-looking hair. Finally Tom Stubbs said, "What you folks make of this Walker thing?"

I thought the girl gave me a quick sidelook then. I started to ask her for more coffee and changed my mind.

Al said, "Hell, it don't surprise me any. Me and Todd Bailey and them was playing cards in camp one night when he bit the head off of a goddamn mouse, I ain't a-shittin you. It come up on the table and run across to where he was at and he grabbed it and chomped down on the sonofabitch. We all of us decided it was time to go to bed, then."

"Remember the time he held up that train years ago out at Greasewood Junction?"

"Hell, they's all of em queerer than a three-dollar bill."

"They say the old lady was hell on wheels when she was young."

"Not the girl though. She's pro'ly haired up and healed over by now."

"No wonder the old man just flew off one day and never come back."

The girl was wiggling like a snake trying to climb out of its skin. At the back of the café the dressy girl continued to stir her coffee and read her paper. She had taken a silver pen or pencil from her pocketbook and laid it beside the cup and saucer.

"I kind of did always like the Old Man though," Al Studds said.

"That treehuggin sonofabitch! He'd of put ever one of us workin guys out of business, if they'd of given him the chance."

"You guys ready for another one?" the girl begged. This time there was no mistaking the helpless look she sent me over their heads. I sat motionless watching them, like a hunter behind a blind.

"Why not?"

"Couldn't hurt."

The girl, her face a study, took the dirty glasses away.

Tom said, "They say he was wound tighter'n a tick when he done it."

"Hell, he's *always* wound."

"I hear his granddad's trying to get another mortgage to pay off them lawyer's bills."

"Is that right? Glenn Wilcox over to the courthouse told Ed Callas at the supermarket they can't find any lawyer wants to take the case."

"Hey, I don't buy that. Most lawyers'd represent the guy that run over their own grandmother if they figured they was any money in it."

I decided that I'd heard enough then. I stood from the table and walked up quickly behind them.

The Studds brothers had the hard-used look of men who abuse their bodies the way they would a new truck, driving it hard at work and off in the assurance that it was under warranty for the first half of its actuarial life and fully insured for the second. Tom's belly bulged in the candy-striped cowboy shirt and Al, by removing his cap to scratch his scalp, exhibited a bald spot the size of a silver dollar. Two heads pivoted on rounded shoulders at my approach; the eyelids flapped and the mouths fell open like a dropped doll's. Deliberately I removed my wallet, withdrew a five-dollar bill, and laid it on the counter between them. I told the girl, "That's for the coffee, plus a couple more beers to keep these old women talking. With gossips like them around, Fontenelle doesn't need any newspaper."

I stood on the pavement breathless with anger as I looked along the line of parked trucks for the little yellow Toyota the rental company had given me, remembering Captain Uncle Jo's remark when he went to live with the Indians about white people being too damn mean. An ancient dilapidated hearse painted in psychedelic colors and driven by a freak who sat bent over the wheel as if he were carrying the vehicle on his back drove slowly past to the stoplight. A woman's voice behind me said, "Mr. Walker?" It was the well-dressed girl from the café. I stared at her, too distracted to wonder who she was and how she had happened to recognize me. After what seemed like a full half-minute I remembered to nod.

"I thought you must be," she said. "Would you please be so kind to give your brother *this?* Thank you!" Then she went back inside the café.

The envelope was cheap drugstore stationery, without address or return address; just the name MR. JACK WALKER printed large in a round feminine hand. I held it against the light and squinted at it. The message appeared to have been written on a small sheet of thin-lined paper too small for the envelope—a guest check probably, begged from the waitress—and folded over, making it impossible to decipher the words. I slipped the envelope into the pocket of the safari jacket and started across the square toward the offices of the *Fontenelle Fortune* which my sister had subscribed to me for for years, until failing finally to renew three Christmases ago.

The *Fortune* was edited behind a wide glass front as clear and relucent as a stock pond in August, in high-ceilinged wainscoted rooms anciently painted the color of a bad hangover and smelling of copy fluid and stale cigar smoke. It was a little past five; two girls sweeping bits of strip-in into wastepaper baskets barely glanced at me as I lifted a fresh paper from the pile behind the door, put down a quarter on it, and ducked outside again where I stood contemplating the boiling cottonwoods before snapping the newspaper flat in my hand. The headline announced the current recipients of the Chamber of Commerce's Man and Woman of the Year Awards, and I read it over three times before allowing my eyes to wander across the rest of the page. Then, very deliberately, I refolded the paper and deposited it in a concrete receptacle stenciled PITCH IN on one side and KEEP FONTENELLE CLEAN on the other.

There was one thing anyhow, I thought as I walked back to the car, to be said for the American small town: They might still be talking about you when news of the Second Coming and the Last Judgment was as stale as Cheops's Tomb, but they would never, under any circumstances, set it up in cold, black print.

The little Jap pinched like a tight shoe but already I felt better with Fontenelle—that pathetic self-designated "city," owned and operated by a big-bellied aristocracy of good old boys priding themselves on their pioneer heritage and up-to-date Chamber of Commerce ideals—behind me. It had seemed, if anything, diminished in its physical aspect, the blank spaces between the buildings downtown having widened and spread until each structure was like an isolated berg in a gray flat plain. On the other hand there did seem to be more people around, including the lounging Mexicans and what looked to be Guatemalans or Hondurans gathered on the sidewalks with their ghetto blasters, seeming not to speak as they leaned with crossed arms against the building fronts, snapping cigarette butts into the street and staring from under sloping dark brows at the passing women and girls. On the high plains north of town though a man could still see forever—or anyway as far as it was in him to see. That at least was not changed since the time of Jim Bridger who, blind and moribund, had rocked out his last days on the west-facing porch of a Kansas City rooming house, telling everyone who would listen, "I wish I was back there among the mountains again—you can see so much farther in that country." Ten miles south of the Walker Cutoff I came to the old fellow's Kilroy, the letters JB carved into an outcrop of sandstone and protected now by a fence from passing tourists who stop to gawk, urinate, take pictures, and leave trash. As a child I had been haunted by the dark upright figure of my putative ancestor slipping on horseback from peak to peak at the back of my mind, a figure that has now faded and died along with childhood itself. Sometime in the late 1850s—according to family legend—a burly black-haired man with a heavy beard turned up in Salt Lake City (a raw unrefined Zion in those days) where he introduced himself around as John Walker, son of Joseph Walker by the explorer's Shoshoni wife. The claim, while unlikely, could not be disproved out of hand, since Captain Walker was known to have married an Indian who, along with their child, vanished from sight and from history after July 1846, when they were last seen in Walker's teepee at Fort Bridger; presumably they had died of disease the following winter. This Walker, who after what proved to be a (fortunately) short-lived conversion to the Church of Jesus Christ of Latter-day Saints had moved up to the southwestern corner of Wyoming Territory where he continued to work as a butcher before getting a start in the cattle-ranching business, was my great-grandfather: a fact that is as indisputable as the previous link is tenuous. History is the most virulent poison in the world, even if it amounts to no more finally than so many scraps and odd bits of paper—plus hearsay.

The plain spread away like the bottom of an ancient sea from which the water had been cataclysmically drained, covered now by a felt of pale fine grass. On three sides the mountains rose hazy blue and sharp with snow gleaming on the peaks, and directly above them a line of flat-bottomed clouds stood in vaporous approximation of the granite silhouettes below. The sheepherders with their primitive wood-and-tin wagons looked older than time against the middle distance, where the abstract silver masts of a large construction project rose from behind the mesa. Hound-colored antelope browsed through waves of purple sagebrush and the sickle shapes of hawks soared above the draws and hollows; I watched one of them as it glided remotely, black against the sky until it banked to display the gray overside of its wings almost invisible now against the blue, peering for prey. Then, without having had sufficient time to prepare myself, I was there suddenly; staring at the Walker Cutoff which for some miles coincides with a section of the Oregon Trail as it winds like a red serpent up the valley toward the cleft in the dark wall of the mountains. I turned onto the road, wearing my Easter Island Stone Face expression and squinting hard against the westering sun.

At the second turn I came on the old Sno-Cat parked on a bench above the creek with one tread gone and the left headlight out. At the fifth I could make out the corrals, outbuildings, and abandoned windmill, the parked horse and stock trailers, and the Old House to the right of the screen of fir and aspen. They were already in the first cutting. The meadows were dotted with the oblong evenly spaced bales and a gentle breeze easing down the valley carried the sweetness of curing grasses. It was all as familiar to me as if I had left home only that morning and at the same time unfamiliar too, as though in my absence some subtle change had taken place, some elusive quality been added or subtracted. Then at the final bend I saw the New House—built by my grandfather in 1935 at a short distance from the old one which my great-grandfather had made of cottonwood logs when the family moved down from the Homestead around the turn of the century and which was inhabited now by Pablo and the seasonal hands—behind the trees. Still the largest and most impressive structure within a radius of at least a hundred miles, it looked strangely diminished and insignificant now: a two-story building, timbered below and gabled in white clapboard above, surrounded by a low rail fence festooned with hundreds of bleaching antlers—that pinprick in space through which thirty-nine years ago I had entered time and which, no matter how old I might live to be or how many houses of my own I might acquire, I would always have to work hard not to think of as home. I drove over the cattleguard, gunning the engine to keep the little tires from catching in the spaces between the rails, across the two low bridges between clumps of willow where slow whiteface cattle grazed a carpet of soft yellow grass, and onto the bench on the far side of the creek. I parked the Jap on the turnaround and sat behind the wheel surveying both houses and the skirted-in trailer where my brother lived with the wary suspicion of a police detective making a stakeout. A dog that was part coyote and part Blue Heeler raised itself to a standing position on the stoop in front of the log house where it had been resting and pointed its nose at the car; it was joined by another that came bounding stiff-leggedly from the barns. The two dogs stood side by side together with their muzzles raised and their tails pointed straight back, watching me. A horse and rider moved out from behind the tractor shed and I watched them approach at a trot across the turnaround. I rolled down the window, put my head through it, and looked up at my sister, who sat holding the reins loosely in her lap. "Hello there," Clarice said.

"Hello, Clare."

Her expression was that of a person attempting to penetrate a disguise at an international costume ball. She asked, "Is that really you?"

"Have I changed that much in three years?" I squeezed out of the Jap and she—in a single lithe movement, like a snake dropping from a tree—dismounted. "Thank goodness," she said, after another swift appraising look, "it was just that silly car."

She had on blue jeans that had worked harder than anything Calvin Klein ever thought of and a dusty black Western shirt against which her long, unnaturally pale hair lay like cornsilk. Tall for a woman and as slender as I remembered her, small-breasted and narrow-hipped, and with a handsome strong-boned face in which the high cheekbones and straight long nose were prominent, she looked more than ever like a white Indian. Her gray eyes were cool within the shadow of the battered, discolored straw hat and had the pointedly ironic expression she had developed at puberty, along with the breast buds and pubic patch. "You haven't changed at all," I said.

"I'm happy with myself the way I am. Why should I change?"

"It happens to some people."

"We're not 'some people,' " Clarice said firmly and shortened her hold on the sorrel mare, which was trying to crop an isolated patch of grass. Her right eye was circled by a livid bruise that must have been quite a shiner only a few days ago. "What did you do to your eye?" I asked.

"I really do appreciate your coming right away," she said.

"What did you expect me to do? Send Flowers-by-Wire?"

"It's been awful. As you can imagine."

"How are they taking it?"

"He's furious, of course. She's been taking Valium and worrying about The Homeless. The Homeless are the latest thing in America, in case you haven't been keeping up."

"He's furious with *him?*"

"Of course, not with Jack—with Ameroil. He wants to sue the company for two and a half million for criminal trespass, plus assault and battery. He's been calling all over the state trying to generate enough pressure to make Bull Humbel drop the whole thing."

"How can he drop it? He has a job to do. And where does Ameroil fit into this?"

"That's who this Joad—the man Jack hurt—works for."

"How badly did he hurt him?"

"At first they thought he wouldn't live twenty-four hours but he's alive still, in a coma with head injuries. Grandy talked with the hospital after dinner today."

"Where is he now? In jail I suppose."

"He's in town buying parts for the tractor. Grandy got the bond money from the Stockgrowers' Association. Judge Thurlow set bail at ten thousand dollars, under the circumstances."

"What *are* the circumstances, Clare? You didn't explain a damn thing in that telegram."

"I didn't think it would be helpful trying to put the whole thing into a cable. I decided the best thing was to wait and explain it to you when you got here."

I imagined my grandfather conversing in a low voice on the phone, reeling in some former associate—attorney, state legislator, U.S. attorney, or local lawman—flapping on the end of the line with the Old Man's IOU snagged like a fishhook in the corner of his mouth. "I guess he figures he has to try," I said, "but to be honest, I don't see what he hopes to accomplish. It sounds to me like you all got the job done this time."

"What do you mean, 'you all'?" she flared. "And don't you think you ought to wait to hear how it happened before you start jumping at conclusions?"

As a child she had frequently looked exactly like that, usually when she was trying to make up her mind to bite or not; in her face there was the same bloody resolve, transposed from the little girl of ten to the mature but well-preserved spinster of thirty-seven whose single desperate ambition, so far as I had ever been able to tell, was the immolation of adult life on the altar of childhood lost. "Oh, come off it, Clare," I said in an affable voice, "and tell me what actually happened, now."

I watched the fury fade in her eyes, wishing I knew for certain whether my sister was really dangerous or not. "All right," she said finally, reining the mare around, "come on with me to the barn and I'll tell you all about it while I put up Princess."

I followed as she led the way across the pale dirt, hard as concrete, to the stables. The sorrel put her back feet down hard, pivoting the hock outward as if she meant to change her direction with that one leg, and I noticed that she still wore the leather pad on the off-front hoof my grandfather had shod her with years before. Clarice snubbed her to the post, unsnapped the breast-plate, and loosened the billet, while the horse lazily switched flies with her tail. Every couple of seconds she had to pause to toss back a strand of hair from her face, while darker circles appeared on the black shirt below her armpits. She got the saddle off and I stepped forward to take it, but she shook her head impatiently as she lifted it by the saddlebow and went past me to the tackroom, her body bent outward against the weight. I waited before following her through the narrow door with its low frame that caused me to duck as I passed under the lintel.

Inside it was cool and dark with a smell of urine, lime, and sweated leather. The sky in the vertical seams of the walls gleamed like the frame of a gigantic brass bedstead and under the flooring fecund rodents scurried about their nests of cornhusks and straw. Clarice dropped the saddle, turned, and flung her arms suddenly around my neck. "It's really wonderful having you home again," she said in a whisper.

I stepped back from her in the darkness and reached to take the arms away. "A week from now you won't be able to wait for me to leave for Africa again."

Her lips brushed my mouth and settled, light as a butterfly, on my cheek. "That's a lie," my sister said, still whispering. "And you know it, Sam."

She let go of me and picked up the saddle and we went on together to the tackroom, where she set it with the blanket on the wooden brace and I settled myself in the swivel chair at the rolltop desk where my father had worked in a clutter of tobacco tins, fly-tying materials, and gun-dog magazines. Clarice took a lancet, a bottle of gentian violet, and a bag of cotton swabs from the medical cabinet and rested one thigh on the low frigidaire. She said, "The first thing is, he refuses absolutely to talk to a lawyer."

"Is he crazy, or what?" I leaned back in the chair and swung my boots up on the desk, not expecting an answer. I had intended it wholly as a rhetorical question.

"He says he can't afford one and we can't afford one, and that a public defender is worse than no lawyer. He says it's a simple case of trespass and self-defense and he doesn't want any help from shyster lawyers and busybodies, as he calls them."

"He kills a man for no reason at all and he calls it *simple?*"

"Damnit, Houston—I'm telling you what he *said!* Anyway, Joad isn't dead, and how do *you* know it wasn't for a reason? You haven't heard one word about what happened, yet!"

I yawned, checked my watch, and looked at the ceiling, trying not to be ostentatious about it. Clarice worked according to certain self-dramatizing instincts for revealing truth slowly and in carefully timed charges like a besieged Indian-fighter rationing ammunition. The last bullet, you always felt, was for herself.

"He's a landsman," she began in a resentful tone, "working for Ameroil on that gas plant they're building—"

"Is that what I saw out there in the Basin this afternoon? Cranes and exhaust stacks and so on?"

"That's right—that terrible mess. They have over a thousand men working out there, mostly drug addicts and wetbacks. I wrote to you about it, and you've probably seen the articles in the *Fortune*. You still get the *Fortune*, don't you?"

"Sure."

I went on staring at the whitewashed fly-specked ceiling while she explained how the Ameroil people had tried for months to persuade the Old Man to sell or lease them right-of-way along sixteen hundred feet of the Walker Cutoff allowing them to run a pipeline from the western gas fields to the new plant and how of course he had refused even to consider the idea, which came as a shock to them since they were accustomed to ranchers grabbing off the highest price they could get for their land and moving to Palm Springs or Phoenix to spend their golden years in the company of disgraced politicians, burnt-out entertainers, and paramedics with oxygen tanks. Finally they were desperate; their geologists had confirmed that the Cutoff where it crossed the North Section was the only practical route for the line to follow and the gas field was expected to be a major producer. They sent their attorneys to protest to the chairwarmers at the National Forest Service headquarters in Fontenelle and filed suit in U.S. District Court claiming that the government owned an easement that constituted right-of-way along part of the Cutoff. Their action made the Old Man livid. He phoned the company's home office in Houston and threatened to have any surveyor, engineer, or other employee caught using the road arrested on criminal trespass charges and sent his grandson to put up a warning sign at the Walker property line. He also ordered my brother, who was mending fence and trapping in the vicinity, to be alert for Ameroil vehicles crossing the line. On the third day after the sign was up a landsman for the company named Frank Joad—the same man who had first approached my grandfather about right-of-way—tried to go through with a load of survey equipment and was challenged by Jack Walker. Joad, my sister said, had assaulted him—with his fists first, then with a revolver—and my brother had knocked the gun from his hand with a cowboy boot which he then used to beat him over the head with. That final detail would have been more than enough to make up my mind for me, if it hadn't been made up already: Grace under pressure had never been Jack Walker's strong suit. When she was through I asked, "I suppose he was drunk when it happened, wasn't he?"

"Well, he wasn't drunk when he called the sheriff, twenty minutes later. He drove straight to the Lone Pine and reported the accident. And this man Joad started it, remember."

"That's his story, of course."

She bridled again, and the look of the lioness gleamed in her eyes. "Would you prefer *his* story then? For God's sake, Houston, it's your own flesh and blood we're talking about. How can you be so callous—so downright cold-blooded about it all?"

"I flew home, didn't I? Twelve thousand miles, eighteen hundred dollars round trip, not to mention God knows how many work days missed in peak season."

"Yes," Clarice acknowledged, "you *did* come home, and I'm very grateful. To be perfectly honest with you, I wasn't absolutely counting on it."

I swung my feet down from the desk, got out of the chair, and followed her out of the barn to the corrals, where the sorrel mare still waited at the post. "What's the matter with Princess?" I asked.

"It's the gelding," she explained. "Grandy and I cut him yesterday morning. I need to check him to see if he's draining all right. Would you hold his head for a minute please while I look?"

I gripped the nervous animal by the halter and watched her as she probed the scrotal cavity for pus. It's marvelous, this strange and monstrous capacity of women—even a cripple like my sister—in certain things. When I heard the distant growl of a truck engine I looked away to the Cutoff where it came up from the creek. "That must be him now."

Holding the bloody lancet in one hand and the purpled swab in the other, she faced me from between the enormous thighs. "It can't be Jack, that isn't his engine." She ducked beneath the belly, made a final application of the gentian violet, and emerged again. "Let's go see who it is. Shall we?"

I let go of the halter, feeling suddenly tired and a bit queasy. "I guess maybe we'd better," I agreed.

Like master and mistress we stood together beneath the antlered crosspole watching the pickup truck drive slowly across the turnaround and stop near the little Jap. It was an old abused-looking Ford riding high on the chassis like an off-loaded tramp steamer, its blue paint sunfaded and stonebruised, its side panels dribbled with tar. The figure in the passenger seat sat slumped with its head against the driver's shoulder and its hat knocked forward over its face; the driver was a wide-shouldered man with wings of black hair falling from under the curled battered hat that kept the upper part of his face invisible. "It's Jack!" Clarice cried, gripping my arm with sharp sudden fingers.

I stared at the dark face, which vanished suddenly inside a blue cloud of tobacco smoke, and then at my sister's pale one.

"No!" she exclaimed, digging with her fingernails and shaking the arm in angry impatience. "Not him—the *other* one!"

The driver climbed out slowly, touched his hat to Clarice, and went around the front of the truck and opened the passenger door. He reached inside and gently shook the occupant, who disappeared promptly from sight below the window. "Oh, my God," my sister breathed in a tragic voice. I took my arm back from her and began walking toward the pickup.

My brother, Jack Clemson Walker III, sagged in the big man's arms like a depleted grain sack, his feet turned in at an infantile angle and his hands dangling apishly around his knees. His head lolled suddenly, rejecting the hat which dropped like a dead bird into the dust, exposing a shock of black thorny curls above a pale forehead. His eyelids rode up and down over his bloodshot eyes and low animal sounds escaped like bubbles from his slack mouth. "Grab onto his legs," the man said, "and we'll get him inside to bed."

"Hurry," Clarice urged, "before Mother gets up from her nap and sees him like this. I can't believe he went out and got drunk today of all days. He's entered in the bull-riding section tomorrow."

Between us we half-dragged, half-carried the sprawling deadweight figure across the yard, up the steps of the little porch, and through the narrow entry into the foetid interior of the trailer with its rank animal smell. Glossy pelts hung from lines stretched beneath the ceiling; others, neatly bound in bales, were stacked along the walls in the bedroom. We stretched him on the bed with a pillow under his head, and then the three of us stood solemnly by his feet as if he were already a corpse. Lying there on top of the filthy blanket my brother had the mangy unclean look of a dead coyote; the teeth showed as yellow points between the pink wet lips. "Where did you find him?" Clarice asked the big man. "He told me he was going into town for tractor parts."

"Three miles north of Grass Creek, making beautiful S turns down the grade. When I waved him over he thought I was a cop and offered to fight me. I got him into my truck and drove his into the willows where the Highway Patrol wouldn't notice it, and when I got back he was out cold on the seat." He took a set of keys on a bear's-tooth charm from his pocket and gave them to Clarice.

She nodded to thank him and passed them to me. I recalled the owner of that tooth: a mean old boar, big enough to have left claw marks like lightning scars twelve feet up the trunk of a pine tree a quarter-mile from elk camp. Together we had tracked him to his den on a thickly timbered sidehill where the dark form moved with massive flowing grace against the white of the forest floor. I saw the morning sun in the tops of the pines and smelled the sharp scent of green needles and the rank one of wet gray logs and over it all the drenching pervasive musk of bear. Clarice said, "Honestly, Chuck, I can't thank you enough. If the Highway Patrol had picked him up—oh, excuse me," she interrupted herself. "Chuck, this is my brother Houston, home from shooting elephants in Darkest Africa. Houston, this is Chuck Richardson, who bought the old Willard ranch at Black Butte."

We shook hands tentatively across the prone unconscious figure on the bed, while Chuck Richardson puffed stolidly at his cheroot. Abruptly my brother rolled onto his left side, gagged, and brought up a gout of yellow bile onto the pillow. His eyes remained clenched shut and I heard myself saying, "Just when you think you've got to where Jack Daniel can't lick you again, he lands a hard one right in your gut."

"When he no longer connects with you is when you're really in trouble." Richardson removed the hat to slick down a wave of the glossy blue-black hair. He ran a tarry finger around the inside of the sweatband, replaced the hat on his head, and looked soberly from one to the other of us. "I've always liked your brother," he said. "Possibly because he reminds me a little of someone I used to know rather well. When he wakes up, tell him to give me a call or come out to the house sometime, if he feels like talking."

He touched his hat to Clarice and walked back to the truck. We stood side by side with our elbows touching and watched it disappear rapidly down the road at the apex of a drifting funnel of scarlet dust. I said, "He's some kind of dude now, isn't he?"

"Well, he isn't your ordinary everyday Wyoming horse

breeder, but I like him. Jack and he are both in Search and Rescue. He used to be a fancy lawyer back East somewhere before he moved out here. He worked with Hal Pearce several years ago in a murder case involving a bunch of druggies and ended up shooting one of them and marrying the other. His name is mud with the Lions Club and Chamber of Commerce types. I think that's probably the reason I like him."

"An ambulance chaser, I see. That's what he meant about talking then. I wondered."

The figure on the bed gave a choked groan and I looked down again at my whiskey-riddled brother, a sodden ruin at the age of twenty-nine. "Oh hell," I said. "Why couldn't I have just sent flowers instead?"

The obvious single effect of an oil import tax," the Old Man said, laying aside the newspaper and starting to refill his pipe from the tobacco jar at his elbow, "is to encourage Americans to tear up their country looking for oil before the A-rabs tear up theirs. It ought to be the other way around."

At eighty-five my grandfather, John Clemson Walker, Jr., resembled daguerreotypes of Old John Brown of Osawatomie, although he had already outlived that more notorious fanatic by a quarter-century. He still slept, my sister reported, not over six hours a night, split wood every morning for the house fires, and rode ten or twelve hours at a stretch, when necessary, with Pablo. A born rancher whose only ambition had been never to surrender an acre of the large tract he had inherited from his father, he had seemed an unlikely choice when the Wyoming Stockgrowers' Association drafted him in the early fifties, first as its candidate for governor and later as its nominee for lieutenant governor after a hack lawyer for the oil and gas lobby beat him out for top place

on the ticket. To nobody's surprise but his own, he won and
moved to Cheyenne, complaining every mile of the trip and
leaving my father to manage the ranch alone. I was a boy of ten at
the time, but I continue to retain apparently indelible memories
of conventions, barbecues, Chamber of Commerce luncheons,
testimonial dinners, fraternal-order jamborees, pink teas, and
cocktail parties, not to mention of the politicoes themselves: big-
bellied lobbyists for the extractive-industrial companies wearing
bolo ties and new-looking Stetsons and elk teeth on their watch
fobs and key chains; small-town lawyers with storefront diplomas
and the talent, competence, and character of an L.A. private
investigator instead of the Lincolns and William Jennings Bry-
anses they considered themselves the modern equivalents of; and
social workers and schoolmarms of both sexes, bored by the
prospect of manipulating juveniles for the rest of their working
lives and salivating at the chance to dragoon the solvent and
independent portion of the state's adult population into compli-
ance with their theories and notions. As a sheep and cattle man
in the old style, descended from a legendary frontier hero, my
grandfather despised these citified upstarts and johnny-come-
latelies and at first he had refused to have any more to do with
them than he could help. In fact, what saved his candidacy was
the fact that the Democratic Party officials hadn't wanted him for
a politician at all. They wanted him for the ideal figurehead he
was and looked: a Grand Old Man (though not so old then, only in
his fifties but fierce-looking and already grizzled) to embody the
state's pioneer past and to stand beside the announcer with his
hat over his heart at the rodeo in Cheyenne in July—while the
real politicians applied themselves to the business of selling out
the state to Texas oilmen. San Francisco money men, and Salt
Lake City developers. Why he failed to see through the charade
is a mystery, but he never did. Instead, he went on working
himself more and more deeply and enthusiastically into the role,
until eventually "the Old Man" was almost as much a state
institution as Old Faithful, the Oregon Trail, and Devil's Tower—

until the moment when, his opposition to industrial development and "progress" in general having become a political liability, the politicians dumped him in the middle of his third convention. Out of office he was out of politics too, though he refused to accept the fact and continued to devote two and three hours a day to correspondence, sending letters, notes, and telegrams to people around the state and in Washington, advising them on some subjects and insulting them on others.

After taking care of my brother I had carried the gun case and the paper bags from the Salt Lake department store upstairs to the bedroom that was, after twenty-one years, still "mine." It was a big airy corner room with two tall windows, one facing south across the creek to the low sagebrush hills, the other west toward the gapped yellow ridge where the creek cut through and the black timbered mountains behind it. The yellow-oak bureau with its framed mirror and the matching oak rocker were in their customary place, and so was the brass bed. So were the book-shelves against the wall. They had left the old paper, which was white with a pattern of red Indians fighting blue cowboys on it; below the molding where the walls made a right angle a long water stain the color of dried blood had developed and blotted out a pair of the combatants. I kicked off the desert boots, lay down on the bed, and drowsed with my eyes shut and my hands folded on my chest for nearly an hour until I woke myself with my own snoring. Then I sat up, stripped to my shorts, and went down the hall to the bathroom, where I showered and shaved with a rusty razor I found on top of the medicine cabinet. Finally, I put on the new shirt and new khaki slacks I had bought and, after some inward preparation, went downstairs to confront the family where they sat in the parlor having drinks and reading the newspapers. For less than three thousand dollars they could have installed a satellite dish and bought a television set, but for them it would have been the equivalent of putting Muzak in Windsor Castle. And my grandfather would probably have had a heart attack just watching the anchorpersons on the evening news. "I don't want the goddamn sonsabitches in my living room," he said.

He sat in a hard straightbacked chair with his lean denim legs crossed at the knees and a tall glass of whiskey poured straight in his hand; the sections of several newspapers sprawled in disgrace at his feet. The other hand held his pipe as if it were a gesture, in a posture of quiet and remote disdain that was repeated by the arched brows and lifted chin. He rose from the chair in a single economical movement as I entered; while my mother, laying aside the crossword she had been working and setting her manhattan on it, turned in her chair with both arms extended and her mouth arranged in a *moue* to accept a kiss. She was a large big-boned woman with pepper-and-salt hair pulled back in a kind of bun, a wide flushed face with wide cheekbones and driving blue eyes, and bony elbows, wearing a skirt fastened just below her bosom and a flower-patterned blouse on which a pair of tortoiseshell eyeglasses on a silver chain rested. We kissed and I shook hands with the Old Man, who said only "Welcome home, Sam," before getting me a whiskey. Clarice gave me a look that said "You behave yourself" and took her drink away to the kitchen with her. I settled myself in a large understuffed armchair that was worn through to the wood on the arms and that still smelled of dog after twenty-five years, hoisted an ankle onto my knee, and stared through the amber liquid at it. "Well," I said, feeling already the chill of that frozen self-consciousness I have always felt in the presence of my family and that comes directly from the knowledge that I am seeing them for what they actually are, nothing about them concealed or mysterious, while for them I am—will always be—a romantic enigma, essentially an artificial man.

"You look wonderful, Sam," my mother said. "How do you keep your Hollywood figure?"

"The way I live, it isn't hard."

"You've never said anything about my Hollywood figure," the Old Man said. "And I'm over twice his age, too."

"Your father always stayed nice and trim," my mother said. "It's in the Walker genes I guess. I wish it was in mine."

"You're looking in pretty good shape yourself, Ma."

She sipped her manhattan, set the glass down as though it was a lead statuette, and shook her head. "If it wasn't for Valium I'd be in as many pieces right now as a dropped mirror."

"I told her she was crazy to mix Valium and bourbon," the Old Man said. "Of course, she wouldn't listen to me. "

"I married into a family of crazy skinny people," my mother said. "How do you suppose I kept my sanity all these years except by learning to be crazy myself?"

"You," the Old Man said in his quiet sardonic voice. "You're crazy like a fox, Grace. You don't fool me any. Never have."

"If you have to be crazy," I said, "that's the only way to be it."

The Old Man knocked the dottle of his pipe out in his hand and stared at it consideringly before depositing it in the ceramic tray on the table beside him. "Your brother now," he said, "he's *plumb* crazy."

"So I've been hearing."

"You heard right then." He repacked the bowl, tamped the tobacco down with a yellowed finger end, and thrust the bit between his teeth. "Wyoming is still Wyoming, Sam, even if you can't plug a man in the belly anymore and get away with it. There isn't a jury in this state would convict him for what he did if he had a sharp lawyer behind him. You tell him when he gets up from his nap out there. I'm through wasting breath on him, myself."

"I know he'll listen to you, Sam," my mother said, taking up the glass again. "You and he were so close when you were children." She hiccuped twice and, laying a hand on her bosom, closed her eyes. "Do you want me to call for the ambulance?" the Old Man asked.

I said, "Another manhattan would be a lot quicker," but they didn't seem to have heard me. My grandfather struck a wooden kitchen match on the side of the box and sucked the pennant of yellow flame down into the bowl. Blue smoke rose in a twisting double helix that came apart in the air and spread against the ceiling. "He's crazy," he said. "The last issue of my own flesh and blood. I'm glad his father didn't live to see it happen."

My mother put the empty glass down unsteadily on the corner of the table and hiccuped again. "I'm sure he'll listen to Sam now," she said. "They were as close as twins almost when they were boys." She laid her head back on the antimacassar and began to cry. "I've always known there couldn't be a God," she said. "If there were, He would have given me peace of mind."

My sister, wearing an apron tied about her middle, stood in the door of the parlor to say that supper was ready. I unclenched my stiffened fingers, picked up the empty whiskey glass, and followed them out of the room.

———————

I sat toying with my fork and the good food I wasn't hungry for and fixed my eyes on the elk head on the opposite wall, while Clarice continued her expert needling of my mother. "All this time and money wasted," she said. "It's ridiculous, Mother. This isn't New York City or Los Angeles. There are no Homeless—so called— in Wyoming."

"Certainly we have homeless people in Wyoming. Martha Adams says they come by the shelter every day looking for something to eat and a warm place to sleep. It's a national crisis, Clare—not just a problem they have in the big cities."

"Martha Adams is a meddling, sentimental old fool. What she calls 'the homeless' are just plain, old-fashioned, everyday hobos—people who spend their lives bumming around the country and loving it."

"Martha is not sentimental, and she certainly isn't old. She's only two and a half years older than I am!"

"We are all The Homeless," I said, "and thank God for it." I winked at the elk, whose glass eyes held a dusty expression of unamusement; probably he had heard this conversation, or variations on it, a hundred times. We had tried packing him out on a green saddle horse that had never smelled fresh-killed game before. Pablo had led the horse over to the field-dressed carcass with the gut pile beside it and dipped his right hand into the body cavity and smeared the still-warm blood over its nose and inside the nostrils. He tied it to a tree, cinched the off hind leg against the belly, and tied the two front quarters across the saddle skirts while the horse rolled its eyes and the nerve ends twitched in ripples beneath the hide. When he had the meat secured Pablo let the leg down and my father untied the horse and worked it in an expanding circle around him until it seemed used to the load. Then he gave the lead to Pablo, who started carefully down the trail with the horse. Afterward Pablo told how when they reached a steep place the horse had started to trot, making the quarters slap against its flanks. We saw it rear and try to bolt over Pablo who made a swan dive across two logs, and the three of us stood watching as it took off at a gallop with the saddlebags, the empty rifle scabbard, and the two quarterings of elk flapping from its shoulders like stubby vestigial wings through thickets of dwarf aspen onto the steep treeless hillside where it disappeared abruptly sideways in a cloud of pink dust shot with flashes of orange ribbon. My father handed Pablo his rifle and told him to climb down and shoot the horse, but when we had worked out a way on the sidehill we saw it on all fours in the creek with the saddle under its belly and the meat hanging in the mud. Later, Pablo and my father had brought the head with its seven-point rack down on another horse. "She's a frustrated old witch is what she is," my sister said. She gave me a broad wink, which I did not acknowledge, across the table. "I bet she doesn't let some of those guys sleep there for nothing."

"What a terrible thing to say about Martha. You don't know what you're talking about, Clare."

"And she's a hypocrite too—'What have you done for Jesus today?' and so forth. What has *she* ever done for Jesus, except to prove that His religion is for a lot of sentimental old idiots wanting to run other people's lives for them?"

"Some people need to feel they have something they can believe in, something they can go to for comfort. What difference does it make to you what her beliefs are? It's a fact of life in this day and age that some people *have* to have their lives taken care of for them by other people."

"It doesn't make any difference. I just hate hypocrisy, that's all. Especially when it's based on a false ideal."

"Martha is not a hypocrite. Sometimes I wonder how seriously she honestly does take her religion, but after all it's the good she does that counts, not any justification for it, and Martha Adams has always been a very committed person. She has a wonderful reputation in this town among caring people."

"Oh, my God." My sister groaned, rolled her eyes, and gave me a long conspiratorial look. "Why couldn't you have just stuck to sculpture, Mother?"

"You shouldn't sneer," my mother told her, "at people who take an interest in the welfare of other people. If this were a truly caring society it wouldn't be as necessary, but— When I visited the Soviet Union with Women's Onward March for Peace and saw how even the least privileged there have warm overcoats and good shoes—"

I said, "Can it about the Soviet Union, Ma. We've all heard a hundred times about the people's paradise they showed you there."

The Old Man poured coffee into his saucer and drank noisily. "Don't waste your breath arguing, Sam. Haven't you learned, at almost forty, that all women are biologically determined socialists?"

"*I'm* not a socialist!" Clarice cried. "I'm not a Christian either."

I concentrated this time on the oil portrait of my father

63

hanging over the sideboard beside the Old Man's. The dark eyes seemed to pursue me with their searching, single-minded melancholy that seemed an invitation, even a challenge, to something. Like a city bus passenger seated between two lunatics I carefully avoided looking at either woman.

"Poor Jack," my mother said. "He must be completely exhausted. He's hardly had a wink of sleep since it happened."

"Exhausted hell," the Old Man said. "He'll discover, in the next couple of weeks, that Jack Daniel's no substitute for a sharp lawyer."

"Why," she exclaimed, "he hasn't had a drink in days! He promised me faithfully that he wouldn't."

The Old Man grunted contemptuously as he got out his pipe. Unable to bear it any longer, I pushed back my chair and stood up from the table. "Excuse me," I told them. "I'll be back in a couple of minutes."

I had forgotten about the letter until, squirming in agony against the chair back, I heard the soft crackle of the envelope in my pocket and decided to deliver it immediately. In silence unbroken except for the squeak of a floorboard and the light chitter of silverware and old china I went around the end of the table, through the darkened hall, and onto the porch where mosquitoes funneled beneath the ceiling light. The sky behind the black silhouette of the mountains had a shine on it like a theater curtain about to rise as I crossed the lawn beyond the screen of trees and broke through into the turnaround, where the dogs saw me from the trailer. I moved cautiously forward and spoke to them in a reassuring voice that was almost a whisper as they got to their feet and stood watching, keeping their tails up and their muzzles raised, as I approached; for no particular reason, I was anxious to be my own announcer tonight. The tails began to quiver as I came closer and finally to wag, and as I passed the dogs they stretched out again on their bellies in the cooling grass and laid their noses between their paws. I went around behind the trailer and climbed the three rotten steps to the little porch where I jabbed the electric bell decisively, took a step back, and waited. When after almost a minute nothing had happened, no sound within, I rang again. My hand was still on the bell when the door opened inward suddenly and my brother stood before me, naked except for briefs and socks. In the half-light his body was like a piece of well-articulated statuary, the eyes as blank as a statue's or those of a man regarding himself in a mirror. He looked haggard, pale—and completely sober. I said, "A girl in town this afternoon gave me this to give to you: ash-blonde, well dressed, fairly pretty, with a Southwestern accent. I didn't know her from Eve but she had no trouble telling who I was, apparently." I took the letter from my pocket as I was speaking and, when I was through, handed it to him.

"I appreciate it," my brother said. He did not look at the envelope.

"My pleasure."

"How was your trip?" The voice sounded mechanical, conveying no interest, emotionless.

"The bastards stole my suitcase in New York City."

"Them goddamn druggies is everwhere anymore."

"I'll say. Those folks live in a jungle, back East."

A light that might have been the prelude to a smile showed in his eyes but passed without disturbing the composure of the lips that were just discernible in the black pelt of his beard. Through the door I could see the empty bottles, the roasting pans piled in the sink, the saddles, the guns, and the traps along the wall. A silence, in which I felt increasingly awkward, followed. "I appreciate it," my brother repeated finally.

"My pleasure, as I said. Should I tell Ma you'll be over to eat in a few minutes?"

He shook his head. "I got part of a deer roast I need to finish. Better eat here tonight."

"She was expecting you. I'll tell her, though."

"Thanks," he said, and shut the door.

I walked back across the turnaround, through the bright

65

cold circle the arc light threw and into the massed blackness of
the trees, feeling the old shame again like a cold finger. It had
been the most shameless—the *only* shameless—incident in my
entire life, as I have always been ready and willing to admit to
myself. But it was my shame and mine alone, which I had not
involved him in and which he did not share since he had been a
minor at the time, not treated seriously by the law which had
decided finally to treat the episode as a prank. Why then did he
rise before me always like a ghost, or a carved statue above my
own tomb? Why, after so many years, was he unable simply to lay
it aside and let by-gones be by-gones? God knows he had enough
problems of his own now to worry about—at last.

When I reentered the dining room Clarice and my mother
were still arguing about Martha Adams while the Old Man sucked
at his pipe with the abstracted serenity of the quietly mad. "You
just had a collect phone call from somebody in New York City,"
my sister said as I took my place again at the table.

"Some crank, probably. I don't know anyone in New York."

"It was a woman speaking very bad English, I could hardly
understand a word she said. She said she was in a hurry but that
she'd call back."

I thought of the Hemingway and, feeling suddenly better
than I had for at least forty-eight hours, reached the bottle from
the center of the table and poured a full glass of the dry red wine.
"It must be somebody from the airport calling to say they found
my suitcase," I said, and tossed off the wine at a single draft.

A watchful householder and family man, he prowled on bare feet from front door to back, checking bolts and chains but leaving the windows partly raised behind the screens to thresh the heavy darkness. Under the black sheen of the sky the forms of buttes and mesas stood gently articulated; demons, he knew, lurked among the night's sinister projections, but lately he (forty-one years old last December) had been assuming a proclivity on their part for younger—and more innocent—opponents than himself. He turned from the window and stumbled against a toy tricycle that sent him careening in the direction of a shape that materialized as his great-grandmother Pinckney's graceful and ineffably fragile Chippendale table. His momentum miraculously arrested, the table undamaged, he stood bent on one foot holding his toe and exclaimed *Damn!* under his breath through clenched teeth, as though to consign to the infernal regions all tottering eighteen-month-old blobbets and the mothers who had borne them. The sustained clank of air in the pipes and the harsh sound of evacuating drains reminded him that this particular mother was now in her second ablutionary hour behind the closed—and locked—bathroom door.

Fuming, yet inwardly gratified by this reprieve from the nuisance of toothbrushing, he went on to the bedroom where he undressed quickly, tossed back the light summer blanket, and lay down under the top sheet. Their room, as usual, was a shambles, smeared and festooned with scraps and banners of bright female habiliments. Why, he wondered, was a bachelor's stash of soiled laundry or sloping pile of unwashed plates considered an emblem of moral anarchy, while a woman's chaos was regarded as an aspect of virtuous domestic life? This one was even worse than the first one had been, in matters of tidiness as well as in her taste for intolerable music, the loathsome music-dramas of Strauss and Wagner having been replaced in his life by the screeching inanities of Springsteen and Osbourne. Well, he reminded himself, you make your bed and then you lie in it—until the bedsores come, if need be. Maybe before marrying a twenty-one-year-old wife he should have heeded the sour prophecies of the thirty-seven-year-old one he was leaving. Across the hall the plash of water ceased abruptly, and then the bathroom door opened and he saw her standing in it, surrounded like a minor devil by clouds of steam and naked except for the towel she clutched with pointless modesty about her middle and the other turbaned around her head. Fat drops of water slid down her long brown legs and fell from the ends of her fingers to the floor near her pink bare feet. "I didn't know you'd gone to bed already," Jenny called.

"I'm just lying here, waiting for you to finish up in there. Did you know you're dripping water all over the floor?"

"I came to get my hairbrush. I'm going right back again."

"The last time you were going right back the phone rang and the tub went over. Remember?"

"I'm *going*. Chuck! Don't be a pain, all right?"

"It's eleven-thirty already. Aren't you coming to bed soon?"

"Not till I finish my bath and dry my hair."

"You've been finishing for almost two hours now. You're going to burn out the pump if you don't quit running water."

Clenching the towel more tightly around her, she made wide eyes at him in irritation. "I had to wash my hair in the sink first. Talking to that creepy probation officer made me feel yucky all over." Jenny reached the hairbrush from the bureau, thrust the handle piratically between her teeth, and confronted him grimly across the threshold. Never take a bone from a dog, nor a lady from her bath.

"Okay," he said, "but try and hurry it up now, Jen, will you please?"

She padded back to the bathroom on soft wet pugs and Richardson, taking up a hunting magazine from the pile beside him, began to read. He had worked his way through one story and into the next, having to read each sentence over two and three times, before he dropped the magazine on the floor among her pink-and-white underthings. He clasped his hands behind his head, lay back on the pillow, and shut his eyes, trying not to think. Thinking led always to a perception of obligations, very occasionally imaginary ones. Instead he allowed the drowsiness to raise and lower him gently as though his body were a raft on undulant water. He was aware of a dark figure making its way in a crouching position along the bank, through the brush beside the river. From the water's edge it appeared to beckon him, with neither command nor importunity in the gesture, its face indistinct beneath the black circle of its hat. He opened his eyes suddenly and saw his wife standing before the mirror brushing back falls of mahogany hair which, released from the hot comb, spread in a fan between her naked shoulder blades. Of Attic shape and long-legged, supple as a discus thrower, her rounded arms streaming like olive branches, she appealed to him through his irritation as a creature forever young, youth being not a temporal condition of her existence but its nature. Of course, she was no more the maiden on the Grecian urn than he was the fair

69

youth with his pipe: If any couple had ever succeeded more passionately than they in winning toward the goal he could not think who that might be. "You look gorgeous," he told her. "Come along to bed, now."

"Just a *minute*, Chuck! I'm almost done."

She went on combing while in the mirror he watched her face relax into the concentrated, faintly smug expression of a pretty girl of twenty-two succumbing to the image of her own charms. That expression as he watched grew steadily more distant, as if, preoccupied by some new thought, she were ceasing to see herself. "Jack Walker's brother's in town, isn't he?" Jenny asked finally.

His hand leaped like a fish on the sheet. "As a matter of fact, he is. How did you know?"

"I saw him downtown this afternoon on the square."

"How did you know who it was? You can't have ever seen him before in your life."

"I didn't have to," she explained. "They're like identical twins almost, except for their ages."

She dropped the still-hot instrument on the delicate finish of the Louis Quinze armoire (an inheritance from another dead grandmother) and reached behind herself to smooth the heavy mane with her hand. Then she came around the end of the bed, perched beside him on the mattress, and yawned with the pink elasticity of a pleased cat while she rubbed his leg with a plump bare knee. "Maybe the kid's going to let us have some sleep tonight. He hasn't even turned over since I gave him the Nyquil at ten."

"Hmmm."

"I think his ear felt better today, too."

"Hmmm." He thought: So she's been hanging out on the square again.

"How did *you* know?" Jenny demanded.

"Know what?"

"That his brother was in town."

70

"I was on my way home to relieve the baby-sitter when I saw him ahead of me doing ski turns down the highway. I pulled him over and got him into the truck and drove him out to Skull Creek when Carletta said she could watch the kid another hour. His brother had just arrived from Africa when I got there. He struck me as the type of humorless guy that could get mean in a big hurry, but when I brought Jack in he looked like a fellow that had just seen his own ghost."

Jenny said, "*I* think he's a hunk," and smirked.

Good God he thought. Why is it that when women talk about men they exhibit all the innate delicacy of a diabetic fat woman in menopause? "You'll be a hunk yourself if you don't quit hanging around downtown drinking beer."

But she only smiled at him as, lifting the corner of the sheet between two fingers, she swung those remarkable legs into bed beside him and drew the cover over her breasts. Sullen with offended male vanity, he rolled away and lay with his back to her, still trying not to think. "So that's how come you were late getting home," Jenny said. "Why didn't you tell me, Chuck?"

He shrugged his shoulders under the sheet and went on lying there, not thinking.

"Chuck," she said after a while.

"What?"

"I've been thinking."

"I've been asleep."

"You have not."

They lay silently apart from one another on opposite sides of the bed for what seemed to him like several minutes before Jenny said, "Chuck," again.

"What."

"I want you to do me a favor."

"What is it."

"I want you to talk to Jack Walker."

Talk to Jack Walker, he thought. Good God in Heaven.

"Chuck."

71

"I'm listening."

"What do you think?"

"I don't know."

"He knows you. You've been in Search and Rescue with him for years."

He rolled onto his back suddenly and lay with one arm across his face, like a soldier fallen in battle.

"I know," Jenny said sympathetically. "The last thing in the world you need is another me."

He rolled again, threw his arms about her, and drew her hard against him. "No," Richardson said, "the last thing I need in the world is another *me*."

C ome in," the Old Man called from behind his study door, so I did.

He was working at the big mahogany desk set against the wall between the two tall north-facing windows with the battered old manual typewriter drawn up beside him on its wheeled table and the also old and very fat Blue Heeler asleep at his feet. The top of the desk was covered with papers and books, ceramic pencil holders and ashtrays, and a row of pipes resting upright on the sides of their charred bowls in the walnut rack. Above the desk a large signed and expensively framed photograph of the former lieutenant governor taking the oath of office hung beside a camera portrait of my paternal grandmother, who had died in her late fifties of no apparent cause beyond the strain and fatigue of having been married to John Clemson Walker for thirty-five years. Around the room were photographs of more politicians, prize-winning pigs and sheep, and slaughtered game animals, U.S. Geological Survey maps, and ancient calendars with faded picture-postcard scenes on them; in the corners rust-pitted shotguns, unstrung snowshoes, and fishing rods tilted against the discolored plaster. There were a couple of overstuffed armchairs and a dropleaf table with an old-fashioned oil lamp with a china base and sloping piles of yellowed magazines on it, and tall bookcases built of varnished pine planks and filled with reference books and texts, volumes of Western history and memoirs— *My Life on the Plains* by General George Armstrong Custer, *On the Border with Crook* by Captain John G. Bourke, Washington Irving's *Adventures of Captain Bonneville, U.S.A.,* which had been among my favorites as a boy—and Department of Agriculture and Forest Service reports. My grandfather had on a Western-style shirt dyed a Garibaldi red and a silver-and-turquoise bolo tie, clean but faded-out blue jeans, a tooled leather belt with a silver buckle on which were engraved an elk's head and the inscription WYOMING IS WHAT AMERICA WAS, and a pair of well-polished lizard-skin dress boots. "We haven't got a lot of time," he said impatiently, putting up the pocket watch he wore suspended on a piece of rawhide string, "but you might as well sit down, anyway."

He gestured as he spoke toward one of the armchairs upholstered in ancient, sunfaded green plush pitted with burns and spotted with crumbs of dry tobacco, but I already had a leg over the old bronc saddle that rested on a blanket spread across a sawhorse near the bookcases. The leather was worn shiny black with use and age; the mohair cinch had been many times replaced and the stirrups and leathers were almost new. As a boy I had won several firsts and seconds in the saddle-bronc division in that saddle before graduating to bulls. The Old Man rolled the chair about to face me directly as I sat mounted and stretched one arm on the desk, while crooking the other to allow the hand to rest upon his thigh in an attitude that suggested a cavalry captain dictating orders to an adjutant. "I didn't want to discuss it last night in front of the women," he said, "but we have one hell of a mess on our hands here. The way the situation's going they're going to send him up for life—or worse, if he refuses to cooperate."

"I haven't the slightest doubt of it, myself."

"That boy hasn't drawn a sober breath since he left jail. If I'd known he was going to behave like this, I'd have seen to it that he stayed there. He's got an open-and-shut case, where all he has to do is walk out and look the jury in the eye. Wyoming is a state where the people still look after their own."

I thrust my boots into the stirrups and sat with my arms folded, looking down at my grandfather. Against the depthless blue of the Fourth of July, Old Glory kicked feebly on a fitful breeze. That was the way it had worked out the time he stuck the shotgun barrels into the ribs of the man from the Bureau of Land Management, so that was of course the way he saw it working now. "Frontier justice has been gone a long time, you know. We've had law and order out here for over a hundred years."

He lunged in the chair, snatched a letter blade from the desk, and parried it like a stiletto. The wheels nudged the Blue Heeler sharply, causing it to growl and snap at the air before settling down again with its muzzle between its paws. "What in hell's the difference if the fellow that ties the noose has got a law degree or not?"

"Maybe none. In that case, what are you worried about, then?"

The Old Man slapped the blade against his pant leg. He stabbed the palm of his hand with it. "There's something about all this that don't add up, Sam."

"Doesn't add up how?"

He glared at me. "If I knew I wouldn't be discussing it with you, would I?"

"You might."

"Nothing about the way he's acting makes any sense. Get him away from the women this weekend and have a talk with him. It might be he'll listen to you. You and your brother were two peas in a pod when you were younger."

"I can try."

He looked suddenly comforted—almost pathetic. "Do that then. He needs someone to make him take a serious look at the situation. I've been too busy getting a haycrop in, not to mention dealing with those scoundrels at the bank."

I said carefully, "What's the trouble at the bank?"

"Your sister didn't mention it?"

"No."

"They're getting ready to foreclose on the North Section for the timber value. My operating expenses were almost sixty thousand dollars in excess of profits last year, and I had to take out a second loan and put the land up for collateral. I haven't paid them a cent for six months now and they're getting pretty onery— starting to lean on me hard now. That's why I agreed to write a goddamn book."

"*You're* writing a *book?*"

"Your sister didn't tell you about it?"

"Nope."

He looked disappointed. "The folks at the oral history department at the university wrote me last year, wanted to know if they could interview me about politics in Wyoming in the fifties. I told them that politics is the curse of history and history is the curse of man, and hung up."

I said, trying to keep a straight face, "That sounds like Marxism to me."

"*What did you say?*"

"That's what Karl Marx wrote: History is the curse of mankind, not to be removed until after the revolution and the withering away of the state."

76

He quit toying with the letter blade and glared at me again. "Marxism? What does what I just said have to do with Marxism? Marxism is a bunch of goddamn politicians trying to get control of the world. Didn't they bother teaching you anything at the University of Virginia? Christ knows they charged me plenty for it."

"I'm sorry. But that isn't what Marxism is about—theoretically, anyway. But it was a mistake to tell the university no. You could have taken an enormous tax write-off on those tapes."

He stared at me pityingly. "Do I look like a fool to you? After this business with the bank came up I called them back and asked would they be interested in publishing my memoirs in addition to interviewing me. So they sent me another letter, this time from a professor in the history department, wanting to know how soon could I get the book written. They're afraid I'm going to die before it's finished of course, but I told them to relax, I'm a young man yet. That history professor drove over here in April: only forty-five years old and heart-attack material if I've ever seen it, fat and soft-looking like an old woman, looked like he never did a hard day's work in his life. I asked him if he wanted to walk up and look at the Homestead, and you know what he said to me—a kid of forty-five? 'Better not,' he said, 'I'm getting to be too old for that sort of thing.'" The Old Man snorted contemptuously and struck the pile of typescript with the back of his hand. Then he got out the watch again. "Almost eleven o'clock already. Better ride herd on the women now, if we're going to make it up there in time for the barbecue."

He got out of the chair in a single movement, with the suppleness of a man yet in his prime. "I'm glad you were able to get back, Sam. You have a talk with him, find out what's going on here, convince him he has to talk to a lawyer. I'll do what I can to make the goddamn politicians let go of him. If I play my hand right, when the governor says jump, Bull Humbel will be asking how high on the way up."

The brisk tap of women's heels descending broke out on the stairs, not quite covering the murmurous duet of *How do I look* and *Does my scarf look tied straight* as I swung out of the saddle feeling sore and wrung-out as a dude dismounting from a runaway horse.

The flag was carried by a lean tall rider in yellow chaps and a white straw hat mounted on a long-maned high-stepping palomino gelding and followed by a cowboy astride a big Appaloosa and carrying the Buffalo Flag. As the final notes of the national anthem, played unresoundingly by a trumpeter borrowed from the Fontenelle High School Band, quavered and died I looked sideways at my sister, whose wind-whipped hair was in her face but whose eyes had a soft and churchly attentiveness. In the announcer's box above the chutes the Old Man's new Stetson was a white oval on his red shirt front as he prayed (my grandfather, who believed privately that churchgoing was for scoundrels, pacifists, and women) *We thank you God for the bounty you have seen fit to bestow upon us in the past and for that which you may bestow upon us in the future. On this Glorious Fourth, celebrating the freedom of Americans from foreign domination and despotism at home, we pray that we and our animals may not suffer serious injury and that, at the conclusion of this Sixty-second*

Annual Rodeo celebration, we may return to our separate homes in safety while I stood pummeling my hat with my hands and wishing I was at a Bantu calabash party instead. "I wish they wouldn't begin always by mentioning injuries!" my mother murmured; to which I responded with a look of polite incomprehension before gazing away toward the granite mountains on the horizon and the line of clouds above them like another country.

I was thinking that when you have arrived at a certain stage in life you discover not only that you don't care to fake it anymore but that you couldn't fake it even if you wanted to. For me, all of this had been over and done with fifteen years ago, while for my family in general and my sister in particular, there never would be anything else. We sat together in the crowded stands with our elbows touching, drinking beer, while Clarice yelled and stamped her boots on the sagging wooden plank and occasionally snatched off her hat to wave it at the contestants. She kept pinching my arm and attempting to solicit enthusiasm with brightly encouraging glances while I sat, bored almost to tears, filling myself with beer. At last she cried, *"Come on!"* and seized me by the hand, pulling me onto my feet. "Don't be such a bear, Houston," my sister said. "Let's go get us a hot dog, and some more beer."

"Clare!" my mother called after us. "Don't you two be gone long, now. The bull riding is next after the saddle broncs."

I gave her a mildly supercilious stare, thinking—as I had thought so many times—that it is the certainty of where they have come from, not the uncertainty of where they are going, that drives men mad. "Don't worry about it, Ma. We'll be back in a couple of minutes."

"Would you like us to bring you a hot dog, Mother?" Clarice asked.

"Oh no, Clarice, thank you, I couldn't eat a bite. I'm so nervous always, you know, before he rides."

I said again, "Don't worry, Ma—I promise we'll be back with you to see him ride."

We picked our way down among the beer drinkers and fried-chicken eaters and walked on toward the refreshment stand. Men turned to stare at us—at her—as we passed. Clarice said, "For heaven's sake, Houston. Why do you have to be so cruel to Mother always?"

"How do you mean, cruel? All I said was, look—don't worry about it."

"It isn't what you say, it's how you say it. You know what I'm talking about as well as I do."

I gave two dollar bills to a little skinny man wearing a shapeless, colorless hat with three bullet holes through the crown of it and handed her one of the dripping cans. "It's all such a bloody act, Clare. The old bitch is tougher than boot leather, but she comes on like the princess finding the pea under the mattress."

"Well, you could at least try to be just a little bit patient with her, couldn't you, Houston, while you're here? She hasn't had any sleep to speak of for a week, worrying about him."

"She should be worried about him."

"I didn't mean . . . that. I meant about the bull ride."

"I knew what you meant."

"Well, why did you have to go and bring up the other then? Today's the Fourth of July and I want to enjoy myself and just—*forget!*"

"I'm sorry," I said. "I'll shut up now and try not to spoil the fun."

The bulls stood patiently crowded on planted hoofs, ruminant and lazy. Flies crawled on the glossy humps and in the folds of the pendulant dewlaps. The slow bovine eyes conveyed a depthless peace and the horns were worn and blunted, apparently no more lethal than the head of an old walking stick. Clarice put her hand through the fence and touched a wet black nose; a deep interior rumble passed through the enormous bulk like a diesel engine turning over. "Nice bull," Clarice told it. "Good bull. I wonder which one Jack drew?"

"None of them, yet. They don't draw until just before the event."

The bull dropped a sleepy eyelid at her, and lifted it again.

"This is a good bull," my sister said. "I want him to draw this bull."

She took my arm and we walked on past the pens. I felt the light tension of her fingers through the shirtsleeve and smelled the clean fresh odor of her sunwarmed flesh. Beyond the long aluminum stock trucks reeking of ammonia were the horse trailers where pretty girls in tight blue jeans and bright blouses curried the shiny well-conditioned animals while the families sat in lawn chairs eating cold ham and potato salad. From the entrance gate a line of vehicles crawled in a slow cloud of yellow dust toward the stands. "Look at all the tourists in their dinky little cars," Clarice said contemptuously. "California, Illinois. Until about ten years ago, this was strictly a local rodeo."

"What's the difference, Clare? They're just ordinary Americans like us, out seeing the good old U.S.A."

She let go my arm suddenly and glared at me. "They are not 'just like us'! This is our country, not theirs! They're invaders." She stepped away from me so briskly that I had to hurry to keep up with her as we retraced our steps back to the stands. She went with her chin up and her elbows out until, as we approached the chutes, she stopped and pointed. "There's Jack!" she exclaimed.

"Where?"

"Over there." She got behind me and laid her arm across my shoulder. "Up there on the fence in the red-and-white chaps. I thought for sure you'd recognize those chaps." They had been a present from my father on my fourteenth birthday and I had worn them, gloriously, for ten years after that. My sister laid a finger lightly against my cheek. "We'd better get back now," she said, "before Mother is upset."

On the way I stopped to use the jakes. They were two pits dug in the ground with a bunker of whitewashed cinder block built over them, divided in two and with an open entrance at either end, one marked COWBOYS and the other COWGIRLS. Inside the air was thick with bluebottles and the stench of raw sewage. A cowboy wearing a black silk scarf knotted at the throat and a dusty black hat with a sugarloaf crown and a row of toothpicks stuck behind the ribbon stood above the farthest hole. I moved up beside him and had started to unzipper myself when the cowboy said in a low voice, "Just put your hand over here, pardner, and take it."

I wet myself getting back inside my pants. "You filthy pervert!" I began. Then I saw that he was holding out a package, wrapped in brown paper and tied with string.

The cowboy's eyes were a cold gray with sharp black centers that retracted suddenly like the point of a mechanical pencil. He muttered, "Sorry, wrong party," tugged at the brim of his hat as if to draw it over his face, and went out quickly. "What's the matter with you?" my sister asked when she saw me. "You look as if you'd seen a ghost in there." High in the stands a woman was on her feet, staring about herself under a floppy straw hat. "Nothing," I said. "We need to get back now and take care of Mother."

The last saddle-bronc rider was in the chute. I watched without seeing them as they came bucking across the sand, the cowboy stroking the roan shoulders with his spurs and holding his left hand above his head; it was not until they were nearly to the fence that I was aware of something going wrong. The outriders were alongside now but they were not close enough to bring the rider off. The inside one spurred his horse and leaned for him but the roan was against the rail now, squeezing him out, and when it bucked again the cowboy hit the fence with a dull sickening crack. He lay on his back in the heavy yellow sand while the men came swarming over and then his hands and feet beat the ground in a rapid convulsive tattoo. They tore his shirt open and removed his boots and I thought, watching the ragged repeating flash of his wedding ring in the sun, the spinal column's gone. Even if he lives, that's one item he won't be needing anymore. The cowboys on the rail were yelling and waving their

hats at the orange-and-blue-painted ambulance that appeared to
hesitate, as if to decide whether it could still be of use or not,
before responding at last with a lurch and making its way slug-
gishly across the arena, past the clowns who were doing something humorous with two chairs and a tripod camera under a
stream of hectic jokes from the announcer. The medics got a neck
brace on him and lifted him onto the gurney and slipped the
metal sides in place, and when they had him inside the ambulance someone went back for his boots and placed them with him
in the vehicle. Then they shut the doors and the ambulance drove
slowly back across the sand with the blank sky glaring in the
small rear windows. "The poor young man," my mother said. "Is
he going to be all right do you think, Sam?"

"Of course he is, Mother," Clarice reassured her quickly;
but I said, "His spine was crushed. I think he was dead before
they even got him in the ambulance."

My brother came out of the chute riding a bull called Satan's
Dream. I didn't see much of the ride because of my sister
jumping up and down almost in my lap and squealing and my
mother clawing at my arm like a bear, the two of them going on
long after the outriders closed on the bull to drive him toward the
catchpen while the announcer shouted *He's on the ground now
where he can hear you, ladies and gentlemen, so let's give him a
big hand—a big hand, ladies and gentlemen, he deserves it!
Eight seconds on one of the rankest bulls you'll ever see—a real
mother-in-law bull, ladies and gentlemen, a spinning sonofagun,
and Jack Walker's going to score high on this one! An outstanding
ride, ladies and gentlemen, by Fontenelle champion Jack Walker,
grandson of Clem Walker—a local rancher, here with us this
afternoon, and a former lieutenant governor of the great state of
Wyoming!*

Around us heads were turning to nod and grin (it was like a
bad dream really: They had to be aware *In the news this morning:
An Ameroil employee remains in stable but critical condition at
South Bridger County Hospital this Fourth of July where he is*

THE HOMESTEAD

being treated for severe head injuries. Frank Joad was injured just one week ago in an argument with a local man over) as I almost shoved the women down from step to step, forcing a path between the bobbing admiring faces. Finally we were on the ground, Clarice striding ahead and my mother following at a more sedate pace wearing her public expression of gracious receptivity. We had passed the stock pens and were nearly to the chutes when my brother appeared suddenly out of a thick cloud of sulfur-colored dust, walking slowly and a little painfully but with a face like one of those old-fashioned lanterns from which the light shows raggedly from all the little punched-out holes.

I watched her note curling up black in the flame, except for the orange spots and the handwriting coming through spidery and white like a photographic negative, and dropped it down inside the stove. She was the best woman I ever knew, but I could not take money from her even if she owed me anything and even if she hadn't been married to who she was married to so that taking money from her for a lawyer was almost like taking money from him, and dirty money at that *they say the only kind of bird dont flys a jailbird but maybe its the only kind they dont torture to death either i aint afraid of going to jail if thats the way its got to be all right maybe i dont look like much of a hero but who in hell does he think he is looking at me with that kind of shocked and pitying expression like i was some roughneck that had just had his face burned off in a gas explosion and didnt know it yet maybe i am going to be a murderer finally but i know right from wrong still and whats right is to protect whats closest to you even when theyre wrong too since nobody in this world today has a monopoly on right or wrong not the folks that believe in the heart or those that follow the mind only and both kinds wanting to control not just the other one but themselves too and everything else that happens to get in the way*

shes trying get me under her thumb too of course but i aint going to be a pushover for nobody including my sister if only i knew what she knows i know i could tell her not to worry then that there has to be a way to get clear of this thing without anyone having to stand up and tell what he knows in a court of law or anyplace and if she cant trust me now to do the right thing shell have to suffer for it then because you dont have to be a hero to be brave like my brother the lionkiller thinks who believes that bravery is something alone and above and without unconnected to past or present man or woman like life itself as he sees it

the night she was dressing for the prom and i cried begging her not to go grabbing at her dress as she sat putting makeup on in front of the mirror with the top of it coming off of her shoulders where she hadnt zipped it all the way up in back powdering her face and laughing at me until at last she got out the scissors and cut off a piece of hair at the back where it wouldnt show and gave it to me saying there now youre my own true sweetheart no matter who takes me to the prom kissing me hard on the mouth and putting me outside of the room so that for a little while anyway i felt better going slowly downstairs and out into the yard to wait for the red pickup with the silver stallion on the front of the hood watching from behind the barn as tom studds drove onto the turnaround and pointing the cap pistol at him as he come out of the house with her on his arm wearing a blue candyass tuxedo with frills down the front of it like she really was a queen and them driving away together side by side in the red truck and that was twentytwo years ago now even if it seems only like the week before last and even if she aint really my sister anymore since even though you need time to live in like a fish needs water still in the end it is time that kills you and ruins everything else

I lay drifting gently between waking and sleeping, watching time flow in bright colorless ripples across the ceiling into a corner of the room where it pooled and thickened in a dark compound heavy with the collective odors of childhood: woodsmoke and furniture polish, mildewed carpet and the dry rot of old plaster, the urine funk of generations of my father's bird dogs, and a half-century's accumulation of cooking grease in which the fry of bananas predominated until, in a moment of lucidity, I recognized it as a present smell connected with the muffled footfalls in the kitchen below. Home for me has always been a stink as well as a place.

Except for the sculptor's block belonging to my mother, her collection of art books, and a pervasive fragrance of mothballs and lavender, the room was preserved exactly as I had left it more than a decade ago. It was authentically the Sam Houston Walker Room, lacking only the red velvet cordon and the little sign, neatly lettered with my name and the date of my birth and of my death, on the golden-oak stand in the doorway. The books of my boyhood filled the bookcase shelves: Hemingway and Kipling and London and Crane—above all, perhaps, Joseph Conrad; the Civil War and Western history volumes, some of them still in their brittle long-faded jackets, others mended along their spines with heavy tape; my shooting and hunting books; and the nearly complete files of *Outdoor Life* and *Field & Stream* from 1955 to 1965. Above these a gallery of inexpensively but carefully framed photographs hung: of Snake, the fine quarter horse I had broke and trained and who had ripped his belly open on a pine snag in the mountains and had to be shot there along the trail after I had taken the saddle and packs off; of myself with my first buck deer, a four-point taken with the new Browning .270 rifle my father gave me on my fifteenth birthday, and with the six-point bull elk I had patiently bugled in, yard by yard, until the great lust-blackened face was tossing just in front of my own and I released the arrow in panic under a full eighty pounds of pressure without even knowing it. My black-powder musket hung with its powderhorn and bullet pouch above the door, and behind the relucent glass front of the oak display cabinet my collection of rocks, fossils, birds' nests, and arrowheads appeared undisturbed. They weren't, though. The evening before I had unfastened the doors and withdrawn one specimen and then another until finally I had taken out and looked over the entire collection. Each item had been removed, carefully dusted, and exactly replaced within the past several days.

Lying in my boyhood bed with my hands crossed on my chest and the top sheet drawn up like a shroud against the morning chill, I thought how the self that I had been the day before yesterday, let alone the boy of twenty-five years ago, was as dead as the old man of sixty years from now. And if they are dead, I asked myself, what of these appurtenances and possessions that had never had a life to begin with? The man whom they call Jesus Christ is supposed to have said, Let the dead bury the dead—a maxim that the American Indian in his superior wisdom amended to, Let the living bury the dead *together with their possessions.* This worship of the past, I thought, this stifling sentimentalism and nostalgia, accomplishes nothing but the castration of the present moment, which consists of pure Action and is therefore the only reality we know or have. As for the future, which of course is imaginary, the sole way of forfending it is—I admit— the one my family has chosen: to defy time by refusing to advance in it. Which is why it is ironic that they should have made a hero of Captain Uncle Jo who, as a *real* man of action, understood and accepted the inevitable consequences of human activity; putting aside, when he retired to California, his beads, deerskins, and moccasins, and fitting himself out in the high-collared shirt and black silk-lapeled suit required by the conventions of the civilization he had prepared the way across the Rocky Mountains for—without, perhaps, being particularly happy about that, but also, probably, without worrying too much about it.

The sickening odor of banana fritters grew stronger and the neurotic tap-tap of my mother's heels back and forth across the kitchen louder and more frenetic, but plumbing sounds from inside the wall told me that my sister was not through using the bathroom yet. Outdoors behind the woodshed sharp cracking sounds alternated in rhythm with grunts and cropped profanity as the Old Man attacked the morning's wood supply with his ax and wedge. I closed my eyes and for a moment I was a boy again, fighting for the privilege of sleep; fending off the inevitable summons to chores, breakfast, school. The banana fritters sizzled in the pan and my father's voice—quiet, soft, courteous; a bit remote and full of the habitual resigned melancholy that characterized him in my memory—was just audible downstairs, although the words themselves were indistinguishable. I lay on my back on the raft Clarice and I had built at Lake Adeline and watched my father fly overhead in the blue-and-white Maule across the red ragged mountains into oblivion. Then I was no longer on the raft, seeing sunspots behind my closed eyelids and feeling the heat of the summer sun on my belly; I was in closeted stifling darkness touching with my fingertips the cold rounded human heads and hard torsos limbs hands and feet in the thick camphor-lavender-mothball smell among the hanging ghostly garments trying to scream and no sound coming backing out quickly patting along the wall for the right door this time whispering crying ma ma your mother is in new oar lines full of water where me and cissy almost never—

The cold floor slapped the soles of my bare feet and I stood swaying giddily, trying to balance against the blackout waves of sleep before grabbing my shirt and pants from the chairback. The bar of sunlight had slipped diagonally across the wall and rested now across the photo portrait of my father, wearing his Army lieutenant's uniform like a hero's sash. The face was that of an insistent ghost staring in through a windowpane on a dark night; a rugged, handsome, saturnine face that had filled me with an unassailable conviction of well-being and security before I grew old enough to recognize in that withdrawn impassivity the stigma of the hopelessly reconciled, the gratefully defeated—defeated, moreover, by nothing, since no man ever lived a more quiet and uneventful life. You were not strong enough for her, I addressed the portrait silently. You were almost a coward, I told it, despite that Purple Heart they gave you. But not quite. You were really just a disappointment and an enigma—a riddle mooted finally by an unknown but timely mechanical failure.

When the gush of water and the clank of air in the pipes finally stopped and stayed that way for five minutes I took my kit bag and a towel and went into the bathroom, where I sponged my face, shaved, and brushed my teeth. She had left it as severely neat as a Marine officer's w.c., none of the usual female mess of spilled face powder, grains of mascara in the sink and strands of hair behind the taps, damp face towels on the toilet tank, and pools of water beside the tub. I inspected my face carefully in the glass, searching for missed bristles, but found nothing. I was spotlessly, hopelessly, clean and decent, prepared to descend among them and do what needed to be done, face what needed to be faced—including the god-awful banana fritters, which I had lost a taste for around the time I developed an appetite for less innocent pleasures but which my mother had insisted on serving me as a treat on every one of my visits home since I became a freshman at the university, an incredible twenty-one years ago now.

Good morning, Sam," my mother said, coming over with the coffeepot to peck my cheek. "Were you comfortable last night? I meant to ask Clarice to help me change that old mattress—we bought that bed for you at Sears Roebuck when you were ten years old!—but I've been so busy with the Women's Center—we had a girl in the other night whose husband had beaten her black and blue with a frozen elk salami—I was so exhausted I never—you *will* forgive me, dear, won't you?"

I took my cheek away and went on to the table, which had been laid for five people. My sister was at the stove turning strips of bacon in the pan with a fork and my grandfather stood bent over an ironware bowl in the dry sink, splashing water into his face and snorting. Outside the windows the morning was a chill dusky blue but inside it was warm and yellow, heavy with the smell of pig meat and eggs frying. I asked, "Has anybody called the hospital this morning?"

"It isn't even seven o'clock yet, Sam!" my mother cried, but the Old Man lifted his face from the roller towel above the dry sink and shook his head impatiently. He blew his nose on his fingers and dipped them into the bowl and dried them carefully on the towel before he said, "I was planning on giving them a call as soon as I'm done eating."

"I thought I'd better ask before he comes in."

The Old Man swiveled a cold blue eye at me over his shoulder. He said, "Your brother is a grown man. What he needs is a swift kick in the butt, not a lot of damn mollycoddling. You had a chance to talk this thing over with him yet?"

"Not yet."

He took his place at the head of the table and spread the place setting with his strong brown hands. "I left a message with Hal Pearce's secretary in Jackson last week to give me a call as soon as he gets back, but he must be down in Arizona still, working for the goddamn wetbacks."

"You mean you've got a quarter of a million dollars or so to lay out for this business?"

The Old Man gave me a warning look that I interpreted to mean "Not in front of the women." He said, "Hal's a millionaire several times over, Sam. He handles a few big cases a year just for the money and works for charity—so called—the rest of the time. If he can justify wasting a month representing some rag-head organization, why the hell shouldn't he be willing to do the same for my grandson?"

I drank coffee and thought about the enormous sum of money involved, of the bankers demanding to be paid, of the second mortgage, of the probability of losing the North Section. To them it meant mainly the Homestead, sheer sentimentalism; to me it meant the timber stand, so many board feet at so many cents per board foot. Clarice brought the filled plates and my mother went around the table with the coffeepot, refilling cups. They untied their aprons finally and sat down, while the Old Man speared a piece of bacon and tasted it. "Goddamnit, Grace, I told you if you served me any more of that Utah pig I'd throw it out the window. The damn stuff tastes like it was blessed by a Mormon bishop. If you can't get good bacon in town, then for Christ's sake give Palmer's in Rock Springs a call and tell them to send up a side." She looked put out, and I smiled to myself as I took up my fork. My father had needed to get drunk in order to cope with my mother; he would start drinking before dinner and by ten or so have a good head of steam up. At least once a month Clare and I would waken in the middle of the night to hear their voices rising and falling, mingling like opposing gusts of an angry wind through the house.

As always there was enough food on the Walker breakfast table to feed one of the smaller African nations for a week. Besides the pancakes, the banana fritters, and the home-cured Utah bacon, there were antelope sausage and half a sugar-glazed ham, two kinds of eggs, sourdough biscuits and buttered toast, fruit preserves, and a small dried-apple pie. My mother and sister picked at their food, but the Old Man ate with silent concentration and the ravenous appetite of a ranch hand of thirty. The fifth place setting remained empty. When we were through eating, my mother brought over the pot again and poured fresh coffee, removed the plates, and put up the uneaten food. She brought my grandfather's smoking things in the heavy ceramic tray and the Old Man thumbed tobacco into the charred bowl of his pipe and fired it with a wooden safety match, sucking and blowing like Poseidon. When he had the pipe burning evenly he said, behind the pall of blue smoke, "You don't seem to care for Hal Pearce then. Do you have anyone else in mind?"

"You mean, a lawyer?"

"Hell yes I mean a lawyer. Lawyers are what we're talking about, ain't it?"

"What about Tom Fuller then?" I said, to irk him.

It was like mentioning the name of Robert E. Lee to old John Brown, but my grandfather never moved a muscle or pulled a breath while the ladder of smoke ascended evenly, without a break, toward the ceiling, and I thought that here was one of those occasions where a notoriously short temper misfires for no apparent reason other than that, like many other volatile substances, it is often unpredictable in its reaction. Discreetly I searched the Old Man's face for some spark of the old fire rekindling itself—the grim fury that had projected those shotgun barrels under the shoulder blades of the BLM man and later generated enough antifederal feeling in Bridger County to knock County Attorney Tom Fuller into a cocked hat. But there was no spark, and I was ready to conclude that the Old Man, know it or not, really *was* an old man at last, when he removed the pipe from his mouth and stared at me with a face that looked as if it had been carved in the side of Mount Rushmore; making me understand that what had been missing in that expression was not anger but simple human regard—as well as that, in the same instant, I had ceased to exist as a human being for John Clemson Walker. At the sink, my sister had turned to glare at me with an expression that said plainly *That wasn't funny and don't you think for a moment that it was* when suddenly, and for no reason at all, I thought of Candy Fuller dressed as a witch for Halloween, holding a glass of whiskey in her hand and grinning at me with her blue-painted face. A little less help from all of them and I'd be a married man today with a potbelly and three or four kids, practicing law in Cheyenne and keeping an eye peeled for the main chance in the gubernatorial lineup every quadrennium. My grandfather replaced the pipe in his mouth, got up from the table, and left the kitchen without saying another word as the telephone rang on an imperative note in a room in which the temperature was low enough to hang beef in. My sister answered it on the third ring, frowned, then held the receiver toward me. "Yes?" I said into it.

"Is this Mr. Samuel Walker speaking?"

"Yes it is."

"Mr. Walker, I have a collect call for you from Nilsa Martinez in New York City, will you accept the charges?"

"From who?"

"Nilsa Martinez in New York."

"I don't know anyone in New York."

The operator spoke briefly with the party at the other end. I heard a low indistinct jabber in which I was unable to make out the words. "She says she found your book," the woman interposed.

"I'll take the call," I said.

Nilsa Martinez spoke in a slow, hesitating voice. "Allo, thees eez Nilsa. I have your book."

"What book?" I asked cautiously.

"Eez a book of storeez, my boyfriend he find zem in a hallway. Ve-ry valuable book, zee man tell my friend."

"What man?"

"Zee man at zee . . . bookstore. My boyfriend he show it to heem. Ve-ry, ve-ry valuable, thees man say."

"Did he find the suitcase too?"

"My friend he find only zee book. In a hallway. On zee Upper West Side."

I said, "I appreciate your calling, Miss Martinez. How did you know where to reach me?"

"Eez name and address written in zee book. I try calling you zee other night."

"If it isn't too much trouble, you could send it by registered mail to the same address. I'll send you a money order, of course, to cover the expense."

She hesitated again, as if I had confused her. "Will zay give me money?" she asked at last.

"The post office won't, of course. I'll be happy to send you something extra for your time and trouble."

"Oke," Nilsa Martinez said. She still sounded confused. "When I have zee time, I send zee book to you."

"If you could get it off to me tomorrow morning I'd really appreciate it."

"Oke," she said again, and paused. "How you going to send me zee money?" she asked.

"Tell me where you want it sent and I'll buy a money order this afternoon."

I signaled to Clarice for paper and pencil and wrote down the address the woman gave me. It was for a hotel someplace in the East Thirties. In the background I could hear another and older woman's voice saying something in Spanish, as if Nilsa Martinez were being prompted. I said, "All right, Miss Martinez. You send the book out by registered mail first thing in the morning; I'll get the money order off in the afternoon mail. And thanks so much for taking the trouble. I appreciate it.

"That was some woman calling from New York to say she found my Hemingway," I told my sister after I hung up, but she went on standing with her back to me at the sink and made no reply beyond a slight shrug of her shoulders.

I ignored her, finishing my coffee in a leisurely way, and then went upstairs, whistling, for the Beretta and a box of shells. I put the safari jacket and the desert boots away in the closet with my mother's old clothes and the half-formed and misformed busts, torsos, hands, and feet she had produced thirty-some years ago when she was studying sculpting with the artist from Jackson Hole, a blond good-looking man whose name I no longer remembered. The rifle in its hardside travel case lay under the bed. I unpacked it, removed the action, and coated the trigger assembly with a light coat of lubricant. I replaced the bolt, picked up the shells, and went downstairs again and out through the kitchen, where Clarice and my mother were drying dishes.

On the turnaround, squeezed between the big high-riding pickup trucks, the Jap looked smaller and more foreign than ever. I took four bottles from among the empties on the floor, carried them into the meadow, and I fixed them in the top of a tall sage bush. I paced off a hundred yards and stretched on my belly on the hard uneven ground, facing the bush and the dark line of the forest beyond. On a good morning I can place six 280-grain bullets through the necks of a half-dozen bottles, and today felt like a good morning; everything blue sky and early white sun, the hills the color of pink champagne and the aspens turning over slowly like a well-cast fly line on an easy wind. I settled against the clay, breathing in the acrid smell of bentonite and the resinous one of sage, and when I touched off the first shot the report split the peaceful Western morning with a clean supersonic wedge, releasing a little of that chambered violence that life at home in the bosom of my family has always produced in me.

The envelope was dog-eared and soiled and smelled faintly of cooking grease. Below the Fontenelle postmark, superimposed on the crookedly pasted stamp of yesterday's date, the address had been typed inexpertly on an antique machine with fouled keys, matching the single brief line across the sheet of cheap notepaper within: "To Who it may Consern—Ask Jenny Peterson were she goes with Jack walker After the Probaton Ofiser. (Signed) Old One Eye." Each time he sat back on his heels to dip the brush into the tar bucket, the letter crackled ominously in the seat pocket of his jeans where he had tucked it.

He was as usual thoroughly tarred; the atmosphere around him was distorted by heat waves and the poisonous fumes. Business this summer was good owing to the Ameroil construction; he had not been really clean since before Memorial Day. Dragging the deadweight of the buckets after him he had backed across one roof after another, laying dark sweeps of shiny tar under a buoyant glaring sun. From eight in the morning he worked in a limbo of heat and the dry wind, scarcely aware of the rough unfinished pine boards under his hands, the dull boom of the empty shell beneath his boots, and the awkward foreshortened shapes of the workmen walking about on the ground below him; until at four in the afternoon he descended finally with sore shoulders, stiffened knee hinges, and a head that felt as if it held the sun itself inside it. The life of a roofing-and-siding engineer, Richardson reflected, was bearable only when compared with the life of a practicing attorney-at-law.

A train passed along the grade below the embankment, causing the half-built structure on which he was perched to rattle like a flimsy bedframe and adding the acrid fume of diesel smoke to the piney one of tar. The Union Pacific Railroad contributed negatively to the working environment, but this one was a low-rent job to start with; conceivably, he thought, the railroad felt the same way about the Doll House, which the new annex was expanding by a third of the original capacity. Everything booms in a boom, he thought: that's progress. Since May the girls had been working as hard as he and he had tried to accommodate them, making as little uproar as possible as he worked on the roof he was covering to be over their heads. Now they lay slumbering away the hot desultory afternoon, refreshing their energies for work; only in the window that stared from under the gable where the annex joined the main building had the shade not been pulled. Stroke by stroke he backed slowly toward it, dragging the bucket behind him. *Ask Jenny Peterson were she goes with Jack walker After the Probaton Ofiser.*

The creak of arching rails and the rumble of heavy trucks died away as the train disappeared like a serpent around a curve. Once again the brush went *slap-slap slap-slap* laying down the tar and suddenly Richardson was aware of another sound, the rhythmic groan of exhausted bedsprings. He glanced over his shoulder at the window and saw that it was open about a foot at the bottom, where a few inches of gray muslin fluttered on the stiff breeze. Richardson looked quickly away and went on spreading tar and backing up to the window; any decent girl, he thought, would have got up, shut it, and pulled the shade before now. *Ask Jenny Peterson were she goes.* It was nearly quitting time; below him the workmen were walking about gathering their tools and throwing them back into the pickup trucks.

He kept smearing and backing, smearing and backing toward the window, from which the sounds of love flowed quite distinctly to him now. His discomfort deepened into resentment; they were both of them behaving in an extremely inconsiderate way toward the hired labor. Richardson, as he went, was acutely aware of the absurd spectacle of his own blue backside—which he could see with as much clarity as if he were watching a home movie of himself—advancing upon them. He had covered thoroughly up to the ridgepole; all that remained for him was to paint his way back to the window and down the jointure of roof and sidewall to the ladder. His heels were against the sill now. On all fours, with his rump almost pressing the pane like a large blue nose, excruciatingly exposed, he plunged the brush deep into the bucket, turned suddenly, and began applying a heavy coat of tar to the lower part of the glass. It went on pleasingly like black butter, scored strongly with brushmarks. Behind the window the sounds ceased abruptly and then the window went up and the girl stuck her face so close to his that he could have kissed her without moving his head. She had a pale underbred face framed by fluffy pulled-out curls and smeared heavily with lipstick; her gray tubular breasts touched the sill and her pale blue eyes had a bored look. She said in a dry, weary voice, "Give a girl a break, can't you, good-looking? He said he'd pay me double to let you watch." Behind her Richardson saw a man who appeared to be in his seventies sitting up in the bed grinning at him. His scrawny chest was smeared with sparse white hairs and his small chinless face was prickly with a weak gray stubble, but his yellow eyes gleamed with the triumph of a man who has successfully assaulted his Matterhorn. Richardson said in a formal voice, "I beg your pardon." He lifted the bucket by its wire handle and backed away from the window and down the slope of the roof to the ladder, which he descended.

Below the workmen were already gone; the blue pickup stood lonely among the stacks of two-by-fours, the sand and gravel piles, sacks of concrete, and sections of wallboard. Richardson went over to it and set the tar bucket and the brushes in the bed. Then he went on to the main building, where he waited in the Gay Nineties reception room until a dark Spanish-looking girl with bedroom eyes and wide hips appeared and said, "I'm sorry, we've only got one girl available before six and she's with a client now."

Richardson told her, "I'm the roof-and-siding engineer. You need to call the ambulance immediately. An elderly party appears to have just had a heart attack upstairs." The girl clapped a hand to her mouth and vanished, and Chuck Richardson, after stopping at the drive-in liquor store for a bottle of gin, drove home. They were taking the ambulance out just as he passed the Volunteer Fire Department barn.

In the cramped, primitive kitchen Jenny, wearing shorts and a halter top, was spoon-feeding Bret his supper. Richardson, as he passed behind her, maliciously poked her bare midriff, anticipating the leap of elbow followed directly by misdelivery of the payload. "*Chuck!*" she squealed, stamping her bare foot as he knelt reverently as if before an obi at the pinewood drawers under the dry sink. "How often do I have to ask you *not to disturb the baby when I'm feeding him?*"

"If he's willing to let a little joke distract him from his supper, he can't have been very hungry to start with." He felt her eyes on his back as he brought up the vermouth and stood it in the sink with the gin bottle still in its paper sack. She asked, in a grudging voice, "How did your day go?"

"Not too well, actually. For a voyeur, it was pretty disappointing in fact."

"This isn't going to be a martini night, is it?"

"You eat cookies for lunch, I drink martinis for supper. Personally, I'll take drunk over fat any day."

"I don't eat them for lunch very often. And I'm not fat, anyway."

"I don't drink martinis that often, and I'm not a drunk, either."

She sighed tragically. "Take your damn bottles outside then, and let me finish giving the kid his supper in peace. *Please,* Chuck?"

"I'm going, just hold your horses." He got down a glass and the ice bucket, and placed the glass inside it with the ice cubes. He found a tray and put the bottles and the bucket and the silver jigger on it. The jigger was for appearances, like a Gideon Bible in a guilty motel room.

"Did you call Jack Walker today?" she asked.

"No. I didn't."

"I was hoping maybe you had."

"I'm thinking about it. I haven't made up my mind yet."

"What is it you always say about that?"

" 'There is grief in indecision.' "

"Yes."

"Well?"

"I told you: I'm thinking about it."

Like an overceremonious footman, he carried the tray stiffly into the yard and set the tray on the cedarwood table with its joined benches. He took the chilled glass from the bucket, dropped two cubes of ice into it, and poured the gin over them; finally he added one carefully measured drop of vermouth. Making a martini was a beautiful and precise ritual, like casting a dry fly to a trout or picking up a girl.

Richardson sat cross-legged with the drink on the grass, removed his boots and socks, and worked his cramped and sweating toes toward the cool roots. The slow stamp of hooves drifted over from the corrals and somewhere the call of a meadowlark dropped like a handful of gold coins between the silver plink of the ice. Evening was seeping like water in the basins, valleys, and hollows, down the sad runneled faces of the mesas, and through the angled cuts of the washes; spreading its soft blue shadow across the plains where the forms of living creatures appeared as if by spontaneous generation, the whiteface cattle blocky and awkward in the foreground and beyond the paler and more delicate shapes of antelope glimmering like holding trout in quiet shallows. At the back of his mind a glow was already beginning to spread where the gin had got into it.

Three hundred yards out a buck antelope stood alert at the center of a circle of yellow grass in a wash of lavender sagebrush. It was a fine buck, big-barreled, with strongly curved horns and a heavy mask, and he watched it while he finished the martini. In a few years he would be teaching Bret to hunt a buck like that with a black-powder musket: how to pick his way over ground that looked at first sight to be of an open flatness equal to that of a boardroom table, under the almost supernaturally acute vision of the dark mooncreature eyes; lower than a snake on his belly across an acre or two of shale-point and prickly pear until he reached that bush, rock, or ridge of clay with the wind hard in his face, staring at the quarry twenty-five yards away; the sharp goat's face pointed at him beneath the eighteen-inch height of horn and every muscle of the hound-colored body tensed to run while he lined up his sights and called the shot. And afterward: how to field-dress the carcass, not cutting into the paunch or bladder, and how to bleed it, and where to find the water to cool the meat with. At evening they would build a fire of sagebrush together and cut fresh meat to roast on the coals, he feeling it new all over again because he had someone to share it with now, along with the whiskey they would drink after they had set the coffeepot among the hot ashes and squatted on their heels above the fast-cooling ground to watch the autumn moon float free of the prairie swells, while coyotes nattered and the coffee began to boil. Supposing, that is, that he still had a son. *Ask Jenny Peterson were she goes with Jack walker After the Probaton Ofiser.*

109

From the open window behind him the terrible music volleyed against the evening stillness; tight-lipped, he set the empty glass on the grass and sprinted toward it. "GODDAMNIT JENNY! TURN THAT CRAP DOWN OR SHUT THE GODDAMN WINDOW!" The frame dropped abruptly and he returned, panting and heavy-footed, across the grass to the picnic table, where he mixed another cocktail.

Between the sun and the western mountains a thunderhead, angular and gray, had risen like an old man sitting up in bed. Richardson stirred the fresh drink with his finger and watched it, warily. This one tasted distinctly less ambrosial than the first one had; a bad sign. What kind of man, he wondered, spends his time writing ugly notes to women's husbands? He could see the room; upstairs of some bar probably, dingy and square with stained wallpaper and falling plaster, unmade cot bed and dirty dishes piled near the hotplate, a pawnshop TV set on a broken-backed kitchen chair.

The light winked out suddenly in the cocktail glass and he looked back to the sky, where the old man by lifting himself higher on his hands in the bed had just succeeded in smothering the sun. A sharp small wind sprang up, printing patches of dust and straw on the air, and fell back without diverting a flight of swallows as they swooped and darted against the opaque light. In the prickling of his flesh he felt the thrill of anticipatory awe that storms always produced in him—having learned, from experience, that anything at all could come out of a storm. The wind gusted again, stronger this time and colder; cutting at his face like a saber and raising a line of dust devils that went whirling past him on all sides like a cavalry charge.

His first marriage had taught him—among other things— that he was no natural husband; his second that he was no natural father either. He thought: The hell with women, the hell with Fontenelle, the hell with all of them. He had tried—honestly and sincerely tried—to put solid rock beneath his feet, and it hadn't worked. It was as though, for all his so-called hard-won peace, what he inwardly craved, and perhaps required, was a dispensation that would return him to his old ways, just as she apparently had returned to hers: to the violent divisions, irreconcilable opposites, unregenerate prejudices, perversities, and antagonisms—in sum to the huge and healthy sadness of the old and unreformed Chuck Richardson, the cat who walked by himself, pissing, fighting, and bedding where and whenever it pleased him.

The first cold drop lanced against his temple, and he looked up to see the gray ragged line of the rain sweep forward toward him up the slope, the bright pennants of lightning, the wheeling birds like scraps of paper. Then he snatched up his boots and raced to the house. In the lean-to he used for an office he sought for several seconds among the pile of papers on the desk before going on to the kitchen where Jenny, drugged with sound, stood with her arms plunged in soapy water and holding a ginger snap between her teeth. "WHERE IS THE PHONE BOOK?"

"WHAT?"

"I SAID: WHAT DID YOU DO WITH MY FUCKING TELEPHONE BOOK? I'VE TOLD YOU A THOUSAND TIMES IF I'VE TOLD YOU ONCE NOT TO TAKE IT OFF MY DESK!"

Her jaws worked deliberately against the cookie as she considered. "I THINK IT'S ON THE LAUNDRY HAMPER IN THE BATH-ROOM!"

He gave her a killing look as he stalked past her out of the kitchen. As he had expected the directory was not on the hamper; on an impulse he continued through to the bedroom where, after a brief but furious search, he discovered it on the floor of the closet amid piles of her clothes. He extracted it grimly and returned to the office, threw himself into the broken swivel chair, and sat with the book open on his lap at the letter W, trying once again to think.

Presently he dropped the book facedown on the desk, took a small brass key from his pocket, and unlocked the lower-right drawer from which he lifted a heavy file bound in blue cardboard.

111

The newspaper cuttings were yellowed between the shiny white magazine ones, which appeared as resistant to time as they had once seemed to him to be to reality. The *Time* photograph in particular had struck him as incredible: the haggard zombie face (she had been twenty-five or thirty pounds thinner) framed by the terrible stiff hair, the empty eyes fastened on the manacled wrists with the flat unexpression of an exhausted animal taken from a trap. He did not flatter himself that he could have succeeded in convincing a jury against Hal Pearce's smoldering rhetoric: Lacking the victimological sophistication of the feminist lawyer he had finally imported from Denver, as well as the preponderance of females she had managed to pass onto the jury, Jennifer Grace Petersen would today almost certainly be enjoying a thirty-year stay in the Women's House of Correction at Lusk, Wyoming. The fact that she had rather obviously been with child during her trial had probably helped as well.

He replaced the clippings in the file and returned everything to the drawer, which he carefully locked once more. Outside the rain had ceased. Mists stalked the hills like bound remorseful ghosts, and the ice bucket on the picnic table overflowed with hailstones. What a bore it all is, he thought: justice and women, women and love. But I'm going to get to the bottom of this.

He heard from the kitchen the rattle of pans, the soft pad of bare feet as she fixed their own supper: perhaps it was out of consideration that she had turned off the radio. Washed, powdered, and lightly swaddled; full of mother's milk and processed apricots, Bret—his son the antelope hunter—slept peaceably in the room beyond, his fat limbs jerking as he belched contentedly through moist lips. The sun, as if confused by the darkness of the storm, seemed to be attempting a second ascension, sparkling in the ends of the grass blades, riding the sweep of the telephone line, and caressing the contours of the handsome green-glass bottle on the cedarwood table. It came to him suddenly, the reason for this unexpected lifting of the weight that had lain all day upon his shoulders: No day could be accounted entirely unlucky that contained two cocktail hours.

Without troubling to pull on his boots he walked out across the chill soaked grass and retrieved the bottles and the bucket. Back at his desk, he poured a handful of hailstones into the glass and added the gin and the vermouth. He resettled himself in the chair, reached for the telephone book, and ran a finger down the W column until he came to the name he was looking for. Then, after circling both the name and the number with a stub of broad pencil, he lifted the receiver and, in a series of swift stabbing motions, dialed the Walker ranch.

How did you make out in town today?" the Old Man asked as I climbed the porch steps and took a chair with himself, Pablo, and the quart bottle of whiskey. In the twilight I was unable to see my grandfather's expression as he sat in the willow-back rocking chair with one hand trailing above the whiskey glass and the other cradling the bowl of his pipe, but I believed that I could discern from his voice that he had decided to accept the Tom Fuller episode of that morning as a joke in poor taste, best forgotten.

"Not too well, actually."

"Bull Humbel wouldn't listen to reason, I suppose?"

"He doesn't even know there is such a thing."

"That ungrateful sonofabitch," my grandfather said. "I told you, didn't I? You should have listened to me and saved yourself the trouble—and the time."

"I had a discussion with the sheriff also."

"Jake Buckley? That Mormon hypocrite? What did you want to waste your breath on him for?"

He sat growling to himself and for a while the three of us were silent as the storm thrust itself above the line of the mountains like a great stone face—the God of Anger. Low crashing sounds descended distantly from it and a small cold wind sprang up. Along the buck-and-pole fence coming up from the creek a figure moved with a hunter's stealth, a rifle pressed under its arm. "Looking for coyotes," Pablo said. "Them sonsabitches has been all over this country the last couple years, Sam. Dirty slinking varmints getting bolder, more onery ever day."

I watched distastefully the dark crooked shape as it moved up and disappeared around the end of the barn. I had spent the day talking myself hoarse in behalf of a cause that was showing itself to be more hopeless than even I had supposed. Bull Humbel had had on the same suit—lime-green polyester with yoked shoulders and imitation-horn buttons—he had worn at my last meeting with him three years ago, the jacket fastened over a belly that bulged in exactly that degree of rotundity fashionable with Lions Club, Rotary, and Chamber of Commerce lunchers. Bull Humbel had been born middle-aged and lived a middle-aged life, and now he was no longer middle-aged and resented the fact, as if he had calculated that by forfeiting youth he was securing immunity to age and was only now discovering that he had been tricked in the bargain. The truth was that he did not deserve the distinction ordinarily due a man of his years, having long ago sacrificed, through excessive caution and the habit of maintaining forward motion by seizing lines thrown out to him by bigger, swifter, and more aggressive men, whatever chance for intellectual ripeness and professional seniority he might once have possessed. Holding his jowled and liver-spotted face inclined at a self-important angle, he had sat behind his desk clutching a university mug in one fat hand and a closed pair of Ben Franklins in the other as he droned on through an expression of provincial

respectability and in the semijocular tone of a loan officer sum-
marizing near-usurious terms; explaining the constitutional con-
cept of the equality of all men before the law, the importance of a
decent regard for community mores, the necessity of avoiding the
appearance of evil, and the nonnegotiable value of an honest
reputation. The old fart, I thought as I listened to him: as if he
himself hadn't offended a hundred times against all of them,
either in the spirit or the letter, these past thirty years, and as if
I—of all people—didn't know that he had. After my interview
with Bull Humbel I had gone to the sheriff's office, where the
Mormon Hickok had received me warily, drinking a diet Pepsi
and eating home-made chocolates from a box. Big-bellied and
-buttocked, the hem of his religious garment ridging the denim
on his broad thigh, Sheriff Buckley had discoursed gravely and
portentously while the scanner on the desk between us squawked
and barked and a succession of deputies came and went without
knock or apology to whisper in the chief's ear and glance with
frank cop suspicion at the civilian intruder. "So what I'm sayin to
you," the sheriff had concluded more or less affably as he extended a meaty paw toward the chocolate box, "what I'm sayin to
you, Mr. Walker (if you get my meanin) is (and this is strickly
between me and you, understand) that if the justice of the peace
was everthin he ought to be (though of course me and you knows
he ain't a whole horse anymore) and if your granddaddy didn't
just happen to be who he is (and me and you knows what kind of a
difference *that* makes), your brother would be enjoyin the com-
forts of home in my nice comfy jail right this very minute, ten
thousand bucks or no ten thousand bucks (which would of been,
by the way, more like a hundred thousand), and you can bet on
it." My next call—which I was resolved not to mention at
home—was to the bank, where the loan officer was a stranger
who had moved up to Wyoming from El Paso eighteen months
before. He was dressed to suggest a rancher in his going-to-town
clothes but instead of the rancher's leanness he had the wide
womanish hips and sagging belly of a money man and the coarse

thick face of the heavy drinker. His thinning steel-gray hair was combed back straight and wet over a mottled scalp, and gray bristles sprouted from his nose and ears like little puffs of smoke. He rose heavily from his padded executive chair to offer me a fishy hand and then sat back at once, looking politely unenthusiastic while he listened to my inspiring and wholly fictitious assessment of the economic future of Skull Creek Ranches; the name of Walker, apparently, failed to command attention in Fontenelle as it once had done. When I finished speaking the loan officer's protuberant eyes had a faraway softness, as if he had had a vision of 640 acres of prime lodgepole pine already reduced to so many square feet of lumber. On my way out of town I had made my final stop at the radio station, where I offered the manager and owner one thousand dollars cash between them not to broadcast those medical bulletins, and they had both got on their high horse to give me the party line about the responsibility of the media to a free society and the sanctity of the airwaves as a public trust; again, it had been worth a try. There are no laws that I know of against trying to bribe journalists, but that doesn't prevent them from assuming a prissy attitude when approached, like an Old Dominion debutante offered ready money at her coming-out party.

The cloud mass had spread as it moved out above the mountains so that it no longer resembled a head but had instead the sinister diffuse shape of a water stain. "The folks out at the plant site are going to get the hell beat out of them again," the Old Man remarked in a satisfied voice. "Last week a hailstorm took their power out for four hours and a couple of their big cranes were hit by lightning. By God," he added, "if that pigheaded brother of yours had the sense of a jackrabbit, I'd hire the best lawyer in the country and sue Ameroil for twenty million bucks. I could operate this ranch for twenty years and not make a penny with the money we'd have coming from those sonsabitches."

"That boy is a fine boy," Pablo told him. "Don't you say nothing bad, Clem, about that boy. He's only doing what he thinks in his mind the good Lord's telling him to do." Pablo had worked for my grandfather for twenty-five years since he moved down from Montana, where he had herded sheep for a good quarter-century before that. He was half Basque, half Mexican: a wiry small man with a dark pointed face that might have been carved from a stick of mahogany and the nose, mouth, and chin of a twelfth-century gargoyle. His hair—which he cut himself, using sheep shears and a bit of mirror—was parted Indian-fashion at the center of his scalp and fell in a long ducktail over the collar of his frayed shirt. His thin lips failed to cover the sharp points of his twisted yellow teeth, and his eyes were like bright talismanic stones. Pablo's beliefs were orthodox Catholic but the enthusiasm with which he expressed them was Southern Protestant. Except for the few times a year when he drove into town and got drunk, he was a conscientious worker and a faithful employee. Pablo spent the summer herding sheep on the North Section, with a day or so off now and then when my grandfather sent up one of the seasonal hands to relieve him.

"So you've always said," the Old Man told him. "I suppose the reason is all the years he spent as a boy tagging around listening to you?" He gave Pablo a sharp look then and held his hand out for the bottle. "Give it to me now," he said. "You've had more than enough to drink of that already." He set the whiskey on the floor by his own chair and refilled his pipe, while I sat listening to the low conspiratorial voices of the women in the lighted kitchen and watched the dense tumulus of the storm propel itself through the diamond clarity of atmosphere. Every few seconds it glowed and flashed with interior light and then the thunder rolled in like a dark wave, carrying the acrid odor of rain mixing with dust and the pungent one of wetted sagebrush, while my grandfather drew on his pipe with the fierceness of an aged field commander directing the action from a remote eminence. "Hal Pearce called me finally this afternoon," he said. "He got back from Texas yesterday."

"What did he have to say?"

118

The Old Man's voice was bitter. "He said he was too busy this summer—doesn't have the time to take on another important case."

"You don't say."

Once more we were silent, contemplating the storm as it assaulted the Basin of the Green River with full fury. I reached the bottle from beside my grandfather's chair and poured myself a couple of fingers of the whiskey. I did not look at Pablo as I did so and set the bottle by the rocker again when I had finished. "It riles me, goddamnit," the Old Man said suddenly, "how a fellow like Pearce can find the time to run all the way down to Texas to defend a lot of foreigners that are busy trying to steal this country from the ones that settled it and made it, and then come back up here and let my grandson hang. And with all he owes me politically too."

I said in a mild voice, trusting to the darkness to hide the smirk that I felt on my face like honey, "There's always that fellow what-his-name. Chuck Richardson, isn't it?"

The Old Man cleared his throat with a sound that was like a stifled roar, but he said nothing. The storm was dragging itself away to the east now where night rose in the Basin like a dark progressive sea, and suddenly the telephone shrilled across the scrape of crickets and the purl and suck of the creek. It was interrupted at the third ring and presently we heard my mother's nervous uncompromising steps approaching the screen door. It's Nilsa Martinez, I thought: She wasn't able to send the package. "Sam, it's for your brother," my mother said. "Would you mind walking over to the trailer, please, and tell him he has a phone call waiting?"

I unfolded myself slowly out of the chair and without bothering to reply dropped off the porch holding the whiskey glass in my hand. I went over the lawn under the trees and across the turnaround to the trailer, where the kitchen light was on. I wasn't thinking of my brother but of the girl, Nilsa Martinez, whose boyfriend of course was the culprit, attempting to extract a return from this last item of his theft. Welfare bums, drug addicts, thieves—in some African societies even today, human parasites like these are casually yet summarily executed without scruple. My boots knocked on the wooden steps and my fist sounded unnecessarily loud on the flimsy door, which opened after a moment to reveal my brother holding a hunting rifle in one hand and a cleaning rod in the other. I said, "Ma asked me to tell you you have a phone call waiting at the house." With the light behind him I couldn't be certain, but even in the darkness I thought I saw his eyes fixed greedily on the glass.

"I'll be over," he said and shut the door, and I turned and had begun making my way back among the shadows when suddenly it came to me, the explanation my mind had been groping toward since I finished tearing that telegram into bits that evening out there on the African veldt that seemed already so gravely, so peculiarly distant. "*Drugs,*" I said aloud, at a complete halt. Then, with the stealth of a man who carries a valuable object on his person and is in fear of being violently apprehended with it, I went on rapidly through darkness, under a faintly luminous sky, to the house.

The cup rose jerkily from below the table and I used both hands to guide it safely onto the top. The powdered dairy substitute gave the coffee an unpleasant chemical flavor, but real milk had not seemed worth the wait. Through the partly drawn blinds I watched the men with their lunch pails form a queue at the corner of Central and South Front streets, waiting for the buses to carry them to the construction site. They stood in bent or disconnected attitudes, patient and unresponsive as cattle, but even these imported drudges were ahead—at twelve dollars an hour—of the ranchers who had endured here all their lives and who now faced, most of them, the choice of going bankrupt before or after shooting themselves.

It was twenty minutes past eight in the morning and I was sitting alone at a table with an unwiped top drinking the weak almost tasteless coffee, listening to Spanish music drifting in from the kitchen, and feeling used as a prostitute's dirty sheets. I had flown twelve thousand miles at great personal expense and inconvenience to be with them and do what I could for them, only to discover that they had, apparently, no use whatsoever for my help, preferring instead to rely on their own preformed and totally unrealistic notions which they were obviously determined to act upon—if "act" was the appropriate word for such pathetic fumblings. Chuck Richardson was a wet wick if I ever saw one, but my brother had deliberately gone and hired him as his attorney for no better reason than he knew him in Search and Rescue. My sense of responsibility was screaming at me to get on back to Africa, but they would expect my presence at the courtroom debacle and afterward at the auto-da-fé. Finally, my Hemingway had never arrived and I had had no reply to the several messages I had left for Nilsa Martinez at her welfare flophouse off lower Fifth Avenue. "I apologize for being late," a voice behind me said, "but there's a saying that no man ever shot an elk after waking up beside his wife."

The strength in the large brown hand felt directly connected to the gas-blue eyes deep-set above high cheekbones beneath a forward brow; the jaws, I noted professionally, were wide and muscled—the jaws of a carnivore. "Most men wouldn't want to, would they?"

"With most men it doesn't make any difference what they want." Richardson took one of the black rootlike cigars from his shirt pocket and thrust it between his strong square teeth like a quid of tobacco. "You're not a married man, are you?"

"Christ no. I have enough problems in my life without being married too."

We grinned at each other through the smoke and I found myself feeling more cordial toward him. I asked, "Should we order now or would you like coffee first?"

"Better go ahead and do it now. They run the slowest sweatshop in the Northern Rockies here."

"I noticed that. Apparently the place has changed hands since I ate here three years ago."

"It was bought a year and a half ago by a Mexican family from Chihuahua. The Mormons converted them down there, got them legalized, and set them up in the restaurant business. I think the Mos got taken, myself. These folks were born Catholic and by God they'll die Catholic, no matter what they tell the brethren in Salt Lake. The food they serve would roast the bowels out of an INS agent—supposing he didn't starve to death while he was waiting—but I figured what the hell, the cooking's good and we want time to talk anyway."

We bent forward across the table on our elbows until our hatbrims touched, holding the menus close against our chests like poker players. "What's yours going to be?" Richardson asked.

"What do you recommend that's safe?"

"Don't worry, this isn't Africa. Usually I have the Spanish omelette with ham and home fries on the side."

"I'll have the eggs *rancheros* and the same."

The coffeepot came wavering up between us and Richardson grabbed it barely in time. "Now we need another cup," he said, addressing an invisible presence.

"*Che?*" a voice from beneath the table croaked.

With his hands the lawyer described a cup in the air and made a pouring gesture. He looked at me quizzically. "*Habla español?*"

"Sorry, just Bantu, Swahili, and Afrikaans. And a little French. You seem to be doing pretty well yourself though."

"That's the end of the line, I'm afraid. I guess when the *reconquista* is finished I'll just have to sit back and order by number."

"You sound like my sister. She thinks we're being invaded by the Mexes—scared to death they're going to turn us into another Third World country up here."

"Your sister is a percipient woman. A few years ago I made a trip to Puerto Vallarta with my first wife. Nothing works in Mexico except the human reproductive organs, and they never take a night off. For six months after I got home I thought about becoming a U.S. Border Patrol agent."

"Hell, I've lived in the Third World so long I've quit noticing the people. They breed up to a certain level and then a plague or a famine comes along and wipes out one-half or three-quarters of the poor bastards. Everything for the best in the best of all possible worlds and so forth."

The requested plate and cup were hoisted up and I looked away, peering through the plate-glass window onto the square. Nowadays the old men did not gather on the steps of the courthouse or the feed-and-lumber store as they had once done to gossip, spit tobacco juice, and smoke; instead they got in their cars and drove very slowly along the streets, squinting at the pedestrians through pale rheumy eyes. The psychedelic hearse I had observed on my first afternoon in Fontenelle went by the restaurant and stopped at a newspaper-vending machine, where the driver climbed out to buy a paper. He was a tall man with a figure like a Chinese noodle, long hair falling to his waist and fastened at the nape with a rubber band, and a black patch over one eye. "It occurred to me you might think I wasn't being exactly aboveboard asking you not to mention to Jack that you were having breakfast with me this morning," Chuck Richardson said.

"Christ, no."

"Purely as a matter of curiosity, what is your grandfather's opinion of me?"

"He thinks you're out to win yourself a lot of notoriety by representing one of the best-known families in the state in what's bound to be a pretty juicy legal case."

"I see." Richardson stared at the bottom of his empty cup. "As far as notoriety goes, I've had so much of that already I honestly think I wouldn't say no to a little quiet trust-and-estate work for a change. Maybe you've heard." He flung around in sudden impatience toward the kitchen. "What in hell's keeping breakfast, anyway?"

I said, "Look. I understand that you're trying to save my brother from an almost impossible legal situation and for no money too, since he himself never had a cent to his name and my grandfather is completely broke, like every other sheep or cattle man in this country. I was just letting you know—since you asked—where you stand with the family. That's all."

"Out of curiosity again: Why do you refer to your brother's as an 'almost impossible' situation?"

"Because it is, isn't it? He *did* beat this Joad to death, for no better reason than the guy refused to turn around in the road."

"You say 'to death'? The last time I listened to the radio— which was about half an hour ago—Frank Joad was still alive and in stable condition in South Bridger County Hospital."

"He won't be, for long."

"This is just a guess," Richardson told him, "but I bet you've been saying that every morning for the past ten days now."

The plates arrived garnished with red and green peppers and savory with bacon grease and butter. I poured coffee and then we spread the napkins on our laps and ate rapidly, in complete silence. When we had finished we sat back and watched while plump brown paws fumbled blindly among the polished plates and the loaded tray, like the carapace of an ancient land tortoise, trundled away to the kitchen. The lawyer said, "Of course I understand that—in one sense at least—it would be simpler for everybody concerned if Joad *did* die. But what I specifically want to discuss with you this morning is this: I think your brother may be trying to protect somebody."

"You think *what?*" I set the cup down on the table and stared at him.

"I believe he may be covering for somebody, no idea yet who or why; perhaps a woman, though. So many things begin—and end—with women, don't they? Does he have a girlfriend that you know of, for instance?"

"None that I ever heard about. He's never been much of a ladies' man. In fact I haven't noticed him to be especially comfortable around women."

"What sane man over the age of fourteen and with an IQ above room temperature is?"

We stared at one another but this time we did not smile. "My suggestion seems to have surprised you," the lawyer said, almost gently.

"I'm not surprised, particularly. I'm wondering why the hell I ever let myself get mixed up in all of this in the first place." My heart was pounding as if I were back home in the tall grass, waiting to be ambushed by a wounded leopard. Whatever else my brother was, he would be nobody's hero—nobody's sacrificial lamb.

Chuck Richardson removed the cigar he had been gumming from between his teeth and examined it with bemused curiosity as though he had discovered it growing there; then he stubbed it absentmindedly in the coffee cup. "Sometimes, when I get going hard on a case, my imagination runs a little haywire, like an old woman trying to figure why the neighbor's wife takes half-hour deliveries from the UPS man between three and three-thirty every afternoon. So let me ask you. Do *you* have any ideas about what he may be up to? Why is he so dead set against settling this business out of court? Why won't he open up even to me—his own attorney?"

The line of men was gone from the corner of Central and South Front; it had been replaced by a group of loiterers who lounged against the wall of the Fontenelle Hotel, taking their hands out of their pockets only to snap the burning ends of cigarettes into the street. They were the Central Americans—Guatemalans, Salvadorans, Hondurans; whatever—I had noticed hanging around ten days before. I said: "My sister has been telling me about the drug business and everything else that's been going on around here since they started work on that gas plant in April. I think he's cut himself a piece of the action, if you want to know the truth."

The lawyer looked at me with something like disbelief. Then he dropped his eyes as if he had been caught staring at the victim of a terrible accident. "I see," he said at last, speaking a little stiffly. "You old Africa hands don't have much left in the way of illusions, do you?"

The creature waddled toward us again between the tables to place a soiled and crumpled guest check in a puddle of spilled coffee. Chuck Richardson watched it go with a bemused expression. "I'd guess a severe case of panpygoptosis, wouldn't you?"

"Panpiggy *what?*"

"Medical lingo for Duck's disease."

"I would have said an obese eight or nine myself." I slapped down the check with one hand and reached for my wallet with the other. "Illusions or no illusions, breakfast's on me."

"Give me that, Houston," Richardson said. "What in hell has become of the once-respected—and once even respectable—legal profession when an attorney isn't allowed to buy his client's brother a three-dollar-and-ninety-five-cent meal?"

"Actually it comes to a tad over that, but the tough part's yours anyway. You get to figure the tip."

"All right then." He counted out five one-dollar bills from his billfold and placed them carefully on the table away from the spilled coffee. Then he glanced at the fat dark-skinned woman who had emerged from the kitchen to take her place behind the register: a huge shapeless figure with a tobacco-colored face completely expressionless except for the wide, ferociously turned-down mouth, wearing a dirty smock dress printed with schematic smiling faces and the legend HAVE A NICE DAY. "Ten percent for the church—if they're lucky; fifty percent for Big Mama over there; and forty percent for Cousin Miguel and his family, but maybe she'll catch a cent or two in trickle-down. Shall we?"

We stood together outside enjoying the stiff blue wind striped yellow by the sun where it lanced between the false fronts of the dingy two- and three-story buildings. Around the square, glass doors flashed and winked with the exuberance of early business and from the freightyards beyond came the sharp odor of diesel exhaust and the high impatient fume of idling locomotives. At the horizon on two sides the highest mountain peaks showed, blue on blue against the sky, veined with silver and white, and I remembered the fine mornings of my young manhood from which the atmosphere of earth seemed to have been stripped like old paint, leaving only the thin sharp desiccated smell of dust and the fragrance of tiny desert flowers. "Interesting, isn't it," Chuck Richardson remarked, "that the place I chose to run to is the place you had to run from?"

I thought of my family—of their crippling neuroses about change and time, their xenophobia, their totally paranoid fear, and their morbidly unhealthy closeness—and shook my head. "It wasn't the place I was running away from," I told him. Then I went stiff all over suddenly like a dog.

Unconscious of my attention, the well-dressed anonymous-letter writer continued across the sidewalk in front of the Fontenelle Hotel, where she had just come out of the café there, and climbed into a little white Ford car that stood parked at the curb. All the leering wogs—and myself—watched her as she drove away.

---

stroke-four *stroke*-five *stroke*-six

She felt the pull of the brush in her hair roots as it drew down through the pale mane with the rhythmic control of a bellows, its whisper echoed lightly by the following pass of her hand.

stroke-seven *stroke*-eight *stroke*-nine

With each stroke she observed her face take on a higher color in the mirror, from which the backing had peeled with age to leave dead spots nearly undetectable now in the twilight cast by the forty-watt bulbs screwed into rose-shaded sconces on the dim papered walls.

stroke-ten *stroke*-eleven *stroke*-twelve

Her slender arms rising from the loose falling sleeves of the peignoir had the whiteness of a priestess's poised for the down-stroke, the fatal arc traced out to the last nuance of motion by her unflinching eyes.

stroke-thirteen *stroke*-fourteen *stroke*-fifteen

Her hair glowed in its whispering ends, lifting away from her face on the static-electrical current. There were times when she regretted almost to the point of shame that strange supernatural blondeness that, by some sort of genetic fluke, had sprung out among a family of black-haired people.

stroke-sixteen *stroke*-seventeen *stroke*-eighteen

My brother, she thought, is an egocentric idiot like all men, and as for the other, he's just a public-defense lawyer, an ambulance-chaser—

The violence of her emotion checked the downsweep of the brush and she paused for several seconds to register the image of her own dramatic scorn before following through with the stroke.

stroke-twenty-five

She set aside the enamel-and-silver-backed brush her mother had brought from New Orleans thirty-eight years ago, before she was born, and, lifting her chin to an elegant point that revealed perfectly the column of her slim white throat, smiled coolly at herself from beneath dropped eyelashes. On the vanity top was an assortment of vials, tubes, and jars above which her hand hovered with the exquisite control of a master painter selecting his colors. Among the containers a few soiled tissues lay crumpled: rogue items in a room where every other object seemed to know its exact place and keep it. As a girl she had fastidiously rejected female disorder—that fecund compost of cosmetics, damp face towels, cotton swabs, deodorants, suppositories, and dirty underthings. By the age of seventeen or eighteen she had long since conceded to other girls—the basketball players and volleyball stars, cheerleaders, and homecoming queens—the flotsam of school pennants and prize ribbons, stuffed bears and hootenanny guitars, animal and movie-star posters, record albums and bridal dolls, along with acne, bad teeth, fat thighs, and redheaded boyfriends in size-thirteen sneakers. The lights in their pink sconces glimmered against the drawn window shades as they stirred softly on the night air, and she leaned closer to the mirror in which her hair clustered around the pale oval of her face as though she were bent over her own reflection in a quiet pool. The real question she reminded herself, making a *moue* for the glass and carefully applying lipstick; the *real* question is just how close he's willing to play it. . . .

She frowned and, setting the applicator aside, laid a fingertip on the delicate skin under her unbruised eye and drew it taut. Then she released the pressure, applied it again, and compared. In the bad light she couldn't be certain, but it appeared to be a new line. She sighed and, with the thrust of pity she always felt at the poignant wear of time upon things, noted also that the sleeve of the peignoir, purchased a decade ago in an elegant shop in Salt Lake City, was starting to unravel. Growing old was more than a trial and an inconvenience; it was an affront to dignity, striking at the very heart of her being. Her wristwatch said seven minutes to ten, he would be here any minute now. *Why* did I ever bring him back? she asked herself, rapping her knuckles sharply on the vanity. Why *did* I? With every hour he spent at Skull Creek she was aware of her control slipping another notch, and now there was this fellow Richardson to worry about. Without knowing why, she felt intuitively that Chuck Richardson was a dangerous man.

Her response to her brother's acquiring a lawyer had been cautious dismay followed almost immediately by something like panic, which in turn had given way to a cold calculating resolve of which she had not known herself to be capable. Of course, it was all *his* influence, but she was not thinking about that now. Now—for the first time—she understood that trusting Jack depended upon his complete awareness of her need: an awareness she had never fully postulated and that she no longer dared to presume. Until Richardson her mind, beguiled by the fathomless complicity they had always shared like the air between them, had stared right through the danger as though it were a phantom rather than a reality. Is it possible, she wondered, that in less than three weeks' time I have managed to convince myself that he really *does* know everything? There was hope now in the thought, as well as dread, and she realized that here was an ambiguity she could not tolerate and that must be resolved immediately— tonight if possible. She jumped up from the table and ran on slippered feet to the window, where she drew aside the shade and stood gazing between the clotted trees to the single light that seemed to reach out to her like a finger across the darkness. At his knock she dropped the shade abruptly, called "Coming!" in a sharp whisper, and applied a final stroke of carmine to her mouth. Then she opened the door, standing aside for him to enter, and closed it softly behind him. "I thought you quit smoking for good twenty years ago," she said. "I wish you wouldn't, in my bedroom."

He took the cigarette from his mouth and stared at it as if he expected it to explain itself. "I was in Wendell's Drugs this afternoon to buy shaving soap and bought a pack, I don't know why. Do you have anything I can put it out in, then?"

"No I don't."

He went over to the window, drew aside the shade, and snapped the butt into the night, where it arced against the blackness for an instant like a shooting star.

"*Houston!*"

"What's the trouble?"

"You go downstairs *right this minute* and pick that up! Grandy would have a *fit* if—!"

"Just hold your horses, Clare. I'll get it in the morning."

"You really are disgusting, do you know that? Where do you think you are—Niggertown, South Africa?"

"As a matter of fact, a lot of those black villages are an improvement on Fontenelle: cleaner, more civilized. The people are less mean too."

"They probably are, it wouldn't surprise me at all. It takes human intelligence to be really mean."

"The folks here sure are human then." He stood grinning at her, looking smug as ever with his white even teeth and patent-leather hair as he rocked provocatively on the balls of his feet; a bit unsteadily, she noticed. She asked, "Can't you think of anything to do in the evenings except drink?"

"Not in this dump I can't."

"Lower your voice," she cried in a whisper, "before you wake up Mother!" The knock at the door came before she finished speaking. "You see?" she hissed, turning her back on him and pleasantly aware of the silken swirl around her bare ankles as she did so. From the dimly lit hall her mother's slept-on face frowned at them.

"What on earth are you two squabbling about at this hour of the night? Your grandfather's exhausted, he's asleep already, and I'm in bed trying to read a Women's Commission report before the new medicine Dr. White gave me makes me sleepy enough to— Can't you both try to be just a *little* more considerate of other people's—?"

"It's okay, Ma," Houston said. "We'll be quiet, now."

"For Heaven's sake, Mother, it isn't *that* late; only a little after ten o'clock." As if, she thought scornfully, she needed absolute peace and quiet to obliterate her mind in.

"Clarice—*please*, don't argue with me tonight. You know how it upsets me. I absolutely have got to get some rest, this terrible thing with Jack is so exhausting, and I have a commission meeting at ten o'clock tomorrow morning. If I need to go into the hospital again the insurance company won't pay for all of it, and where your grandfather is going to find the money to pay this Mr. Livingston I don't know, it's all so unfair, life that is I mean, you'd almost think Somebody was punishing us for something we've done—"

"No one's trying to punish you for anything, Ma," her brother said. "Go on to bed now and don't drink too much of Dr. White's horse medicine, all right?"

She heard the flip-flop of her mother's slippers going back along the runner carpet to the bedroom and the rustle of the door closing at the end of the hall. "Christ," Houston said, "is she zonked tonight."

"Dr. White's the new man at the hospital; he's the biggest quack they've had up there yet. She goes to him because none of the other doctors will write her prescriptions anymore. She's been drinking codeine since before supper."

"Better keep an eye on her. Remember Gay Williams, the math teacher in junior high, who passed out and choked to death on her own puke?"

"And you kept waking me up every night for a week, spitting oatmeal and going gluph-gluph-gluph." She had to smile at him then in spite of herself; for almost the first time since she had watched him climb out of the little car, she felt close to her brother again.

He sat first, then lay, on her great-grandmother's crazy quilt. He said, "God, I'm sleepy already. Can't handle life in the fast lane anymore, I guess. Tell me whatever it was you wanted to tell me and then I think I'll go into town for a little nightlife."

"Take off your boots first if you're going to lie on that quilt." Staring at him sprawled like that on the bed, she felt all her reawakened affection drain from her. "What I have to say to you I can say in thirty seconds, anyway."

"Shoot then."

How could she ever she marveled, contemplating him, have imagined that she could have expected anything—anything at all—from her brother? "I want you to leave now—tomorrow, if you can get a ticket. You're not doing anyone any good here; you're only making everything worse."

He sat up suddenly on the bed. "You want me to go? Back to Africa? Why, for Christ's sake? I only got here last week."

"I told you: You're spoiling everything. As long as you've been home it's been like having a bull in a china shop, smashing things and urinating on the floor."

"What in hell is the matter with you, Clare? You telegraphed for me to come, and I came. Now I'm trying to do the best I know how to do for everybody concerned, and you tell me to go. What is it that you want from me, anyhow?"

"Nothing," she cried passionately. "Absolutely nothing—really. Just get on the plane and go back to Africa and play at being Ernest Hemingway again."

"Now hold your horses a minute," her brother said.

She sat down at the vanity, where she took up the hairbrush and resumed stroking her hair with a shaking hand and tears in her eyes.

"I had a breakfast meeting in town this morning with Chuck Richardson," he said.

The hand in the mirror paused almost imperceptibly before completing the stroke. "You did? Whose idea was that?" It was his own of course, she thought: You can count on my brother to do just exactly the wrong thing at exactly the wrong time.

"It was his."

"What did he want to talk to you about?"

"He thinks Jack may be trying to protect somebody in all this."

"That's ridiculous. Who would he be protecting? Jack doesn't have a friend in the world besides Pablo."

"His idea is it could be a woman."

Her laugh, which felt to her like a cough, almost choked her. "So much for your Mr. Richardson then. It doesn't sound to me as if he's getting off to a very promising start."

"Maybe not. Incidentally, we agreed not to say anything to him about our getting together."

Already her mind, stunned momentarily by the blow, was regaining its alertness. "Do you think that's really being fair with Jack?"

He shrugged and spread his hands. "I've suspected for several days now he's holding out on us."

"About a woman?" Again she felt the harsh laughter rising, but this time it did not reach above the top of her throat.

"Not a woman necessarily. But *something*. Or someone."

All her life she had prided herself on her ruthless yet totally discriminating hate, which she knew how to deploy with surgical precision. Now, staring into the smooth handsome outrageous face, she felt that she had never experienced hatred in her life before. "Do you know," she said quietly, laying down the hair-brush on its back, "do you know what the matter with you is? I've known it for a week now, but I haven't been able to tell you. The trouble with you is, you don't *believe* he's innocent, you don't even *want* to believe—don't ask me why, I don't want to know, I probably will never know. I don't care anymore. You've never cared, ever since you were a boy. You're just incredibly selfish, totally self-centered, always looking out for number one—not thinking about anyone else's feelings, not caring about the family or the ranch or Wyoming or anything at all except what *you* want and what *you're* going to do!"

Her hair had fallen across her shoulders, and over her bosom the peignoir had come loose. She clutched the lapels together with a trembling hand, panting with the exertion of her rage, and glared at him through the hot tears until finally he swung his feet down and stood from the bed. "Well, good night, sis," he said in a calm, even voice as if nothing at all had happened. "Guess I'll run into town for a bit." At the door he paused and looked back at her, his hand already on the knob. "Incidentally, I spoke with the hospital half an hour ago. They say there's been some improvement in the brain waves and that he's responding to stimuli better. Could be Jack's got lucky and he's going to pull through after all."

After he had gone she sat for what seemed to her a long time, holding in her hand the silver-and-enamel brush. Then she threw it down with a clatter and ran to the window, where she pulled back the shade and stared out again at the night. From the marsh below the stock pond peepfrogs chorused like a shrill warning of the blood, but across the yard the square of yellow light was a solid, plain and clear. Gently, she let the shade slip; from the closet she took a light topcoat which she threw around her shoulders, stopping only to fasten the middle button.

A pencil of light underscored her mother's door, but from

the master bedroom where the Old Man slept a staggered sequence of grunts, rattles, and snorts issued unremittingly. She belted the coat more tightly at the waist, snatching her hair back from the high collar, and hurried on, going Indian-fashion on the sides of the thin slippers along the runner carpet, down the stairs, and across the darkened parlor among the druidic shapes of the furniture. From the porch she saw the taillights of the rental car vanish around the final curve, heading toward town.

The arc light made a glassy circle of green, wet with dew, antic with darting moths. She was across it in moments, the slippers light and soundless beneath the frowning windows, the frog chorus urging her to still greater effort as she swept on toward the trailer. Then her foot was on the polished step, her hand gripped the chilly knob, and she was through the door in a rush without having knocked.

Jack Walker sat reading a book in the shabby Barcalounger with his feet up and a bottle of Jack Daniel's and a glass beside him. His grown-out beard was matted and dirty-looking, his eyes were bloodshot, his cheeks drawn and gray. He looked not just tired, she thought, but positively old; for the first time she noticed that, though not yet thirty, he had patches of gray coming at the temples. He looked up from the book as she stood there, his eyes bright, ironic, and unsurprised under the jagged black forelock of his hair. He said

Y eah," the drunk at my elbow was saying, "the sons-abitches got me on the run for sure this time, Sam." He nudged his drink on its paper coaster closer and hung his face, like a red sodden moon, over my left shoulder. "And you know why?" he demanded. "Because me and the old lady has always lived the American Way of Life—that's what for. Because we believe in stimalating the economy and Buying American whenever we can."

I moved my own drink over and ducked away from the face, which exuded heat and fumes like a dirty lantern. I had chosen my position deliberately: From where I sat I could watch not just the bar and the tables around it but the restaurant at the back, which was visible through the serving window as well as through the door. There had been a demure formality amounting almost to elegance about her clothes that suggested to me that she was not the kind of girl to walk into a bar alone. And the Last Chance Saloon was Fontenelle's classiest restaurant, where you could order fettucine instead of beef if you knew to ask for it and where the waitresses understood you when you said Montepulciano, even if they couldn't pronounce it themselves.

"Got a beautiful home," the drunk said. "Got two trucks, a 'eighty-seven Ford three-quarter-ton with the four-sixty engine and a 'eighty-eight Ford Bronco with the fuel-injection three fifty-one. Got four snow machines, three Yamahas an a Skidoo. Got me a VCR with a four-foot screen an three CDs, one in ever bedroom but one. Got a twenny-three-foot boat with a Evinrude one fifty-one on her an a boat trailer. Got four pure-breed quarter horses an a superdeluxe four-horse trailer with a changin room up front. Got a nylon hot-air balloon. Got a outdoor swimpool for the kids takes up the whole back yard almost. Got enough rifles an shotguns to start Worl War Three with. An you know what? Them sonsabitches is trying to take it all away from me." He hiccuped and held a hand up at the barmaid while playing with the other among the pile of bills and change in front of him. "Two more whiskeys here," he told the girl. "The most expensive you got." He jerked his head to indicate me. "Me and him graduated from high school together, I hate to think how many years ago." The face had a blurry familiarity but I had not been able to assign a name to it yet, though a youthful version was vaguely identifiable with the classmate voted Most Likely to Succeed. It was now a quarter to twelve; I had long since given up hope of the girl and devoted myself to serious drinking instead. The barmaid came with the whiskeys and Most Likely to Succeed held his to the light and squinted through it. "To the U.S.A. of A.," he announced. "Land of Freedom an Opportunity!" The jukebox, which had begun to play again, covered his toast almost entirely; I raised my glass in salute and drank politely. I seemed to have forgotten the extent to which the civilized world is addicted to oblivion.

"Want to buy a good electric organ?" Most Likely asked. "Top condition—never been played. I got to sell it on account of I made a down payment on it with this six-hunner-dollar bonus I got and my wife went out the very same day an spent it on one of them rowing-exercise machines she saw advertised on sale. You can have it for two hunner fifty flat if you take over the payments."

I finished the whiskey and told him good night. I was aware as I walked to the car of my feet not falling precisely where they should, and I became involved in a brief but irritating misunderstanding between the doorlock and the key. I backed carefully into the road, made a conscientious stop at the light, and drove painstakingly through town again to pick up the highway going north. Silver moths whirled and danced in the twin shafts of the headlights, as the street unrolled ahead like a worn gray carpet. I speeded up and relaxed in the molded seat, gazing into the swirl of insects in which one shape in particular stood out, pale as the rest but larger and swelling more so: a huge moth's head with grimacing, weirdly human features. It floated up quickly, struck with a soft solid bump, and careened away out of the swath of the lights; the only other sound was the slight squeak of the brakes and the whir of the engine rising above the noise the tires made. In the rearview mirror the street was an empty shadow, broken at intervals by splashes of cold sodium light. If a tree falls in a forest and there is no one to hear it, is there anything to hear at all?

Guided by the blind unthinking instinct that instructs a wounded animal to flee downhill, I pressed the accelerator to the floor and drove on.

---

*close the door before you call every gnat and goddamn
mosquito between here and jackson in*
  *i didnt have to look at her a second time to know what was her
problem but she was just going to have to trust me now to do the right
thing law is like dynamite i told him use the wrong charge or too
much of it and you end up and everyone around you in a billion
pieces and yes he said but the trouble is sometimes you find out you
need more of it than you thought you did i cant make you an absolute
promise maybe you cant i said but i can sure as hell promise you you
wont have a client then never mind he told me theres a saying in the
medical profession that doctors always bury their mistakes but in the
legal business its more often the other way around but anyway i have
me my own lawyer now just like nixon or delorean*
  *she stood there just inside the door with the moths and gnats
diving around her like flies after bad meat saying you are sure hes
the right one arent you dont let houston shove him down your throat
while she twisted the belt of the raincoat in her hands and stared at*

me with those big eyes like a cats you are sure jack arent you and i thought come on now for christs sake you dont have to pretend to me anymore though if you want to pretend thats okay too it dont matter to me one way or the other hes smart all right a rich dude from new york city but he aint any smarter than me and her looking back at me trying to decide did i know or didnt i playing with that damn belt like she dont know whether to take the coat off or keep it on until i said for christs sake take the goddamn thing off or quit messing with it and she took it off then and set with just that robe on like she was doing some kind of hollywood cheesecake

she said houston called the hospital tonight they said hes going to live after all maybe so then of course i knew for sure why because women only love themselves finally and everything else all the things they say and probably even think they love the people animals places things are just something to practice all the little sacrifices on in order finally to make the great big sacrifice that is you

or maybe its that the world is herself or part of herself and thats how she really loves it like a horse looking out across a broad valley to the mountains and not seeing the basin or the river or even the mountains themselves on the other side but just five thousand or so square miles of prime horsepasture anyway youd think she would have known maybe remembered understood and trusted but i tried telling her just the same then setting there like a pinup girl on one of those old curledup cocacola calendars you see in hunting cabins and feedstores and toilets in gas stations how it was me that chose him and not my brother and how i aint paying him for any more than to knock this thing dead in its tracks so it dont get up and walk any farther and to keep me from spending the rest of my life hiring more lawyers to convince more juries that so long as the dead dont lie the living can tell the truth until just when i was thinking whether i had said enough or not and could i quit talking now she jumped up and kissed me hard on the mouth and was gone running back across the grass toward the house holding the coat tight about her like she had stolen something valuable and was looking for a safe place to hide it at

H ello, O.K."

"Chuck Richardson. How you doin?"

"Okay, I guess. You're a tough guy to get ahold of."

"I been in and out. Like usual."

"You must be keeping busy—like everyone else—this summer."

"I don't know. About like usual, I'd say."

"I have a job for you if you want it. Nothing big."

"It might be I could help you out," O.K. Pickett agreed.

His voice was even sadder and more warily laconic than Richardson remembered it. He had a clear vision of the shanty in which Pickett lived beside the railroad tracks in Green River, alone with the egg stove, the cot bed, and the lines of drying half-washed clothes that hung across one of the two rooms, summer and winter. O.K. Pickett was an ex-cowboy turned cop who had been fired from the force after a wrongful death charge had been (unsuccessfully) brought against him, and who made a bare

145

living now working as a private investigator and part-time range detective.

"Have you been following the Walker business up here in Fontenelle?"

"I reckon I might of read a story or two about it."

"Jack Walker is my client now."

"Okay," Pickett said cautiously, and it seemed to Richardson that he could hear the toothpick going in between his upper front teeth.

"Frank Joad lived in Green River for more than a year before Ameroil transferred him up to Fontenelle. I'd like to find out something about his reputation while he was there. Did he have any DWIs or get busted for possession or write any bad checks or try to put the make on the neighbor's teen-age daughter—the usual sort of thing."

"Okay."

There was a long silence in which Richardson imagined the toothpick being drawn out, carefully examined, and replaced between the teeth. Finally O.K. Pickett said, "That all you need?"

"Right now, that's all."

"Okay." The longer silence that ensued suggested that he had put away the remains of the toothpick and was now packing his lower lip with chew. "Wife doing okay?" he asked at last.

"Oh, Jenny's fine." O.K. had done the investigative work on her case prior to the trial two years ago and had—apparently—a warmer regard for her than he seemed to have for most females of honest reputation. "I'll tell her you asked about her."

"Okay," O.K. Pickett said, and hung up.

The phone rang almost immediately and when Richardson picked up the receiver he had the investigator on the line again. "Chuck."

"Yes, O.K."

"When did you say you needed the information by?"

"I didn't say, but something by early next week would be appreciated."

"Okay," Pickett said, and was off.

He replaced the receiver and continued for a while to tilt backward in the swivel chair with his bootheels resting on the corner of the desk. He had in mind as well another job for O.K. Pickett. This one had nothing whatever to do with Frank Joad, but, for the time being at least, it was more a fantasy than a real idea.

I was at the Bare Garden and already on my third drink, which I had been nursing for half an hour while I tried to ignore the male stripper who had just worked himself down to his shorts to the vociferous enthusiasm of the Fontenelle Women's Bowling League. I took another sip of the whiskey and dug out the heavy gold watch and fob from the bottom of my jeans pocket and read the time. I was carrying the watch because the band on the three-thousand-dollar wristwatch I had bought in Paris had snapped as I was mounting a sixteen-hand half-broke gelding belonging to my grandfather and the horse had shied and stepped on it. The pocket watch, my great-grandfather Walker's, had been presented to me on my twenty-first birthday by the Old Man. I had carried it with me to Charlottesville that fall and worn it ostentatiously in the pocket of the riding-pink vest I had purchased, until the fair-complected, cornflower-eyed, golden-haired young lady (a thoroughly modernized descendant of one of the Old Dominion's oldest families) I was in love with that fall condescendingly detached the watch and fob. On my return to Skull Creek after graduation the following June I had bedded it in clean linen handkerchiefs and put it away at the back of the bureau drawer, bought a twelve-dollar Timex to wear on the rodeo circuit, and forgot all about the piece until the French watch got stompled. It had started up at once and kept perfect time, its chief disadvantage being its clumsiness—that Victorian weightiness connoting the bourgeois notion of time as being of supreme importance, every second gatherable as a gold piece. When I placed the watch by the bedside at night the dark, which ought to have had the effect of isolating the loud, almost violent tick, seemed instead to diffuse it mysteriously in space until the creeping gray light revealed both it and the water stain on the wall that I could almost have imagined to have darkened and spread in the two weeks I had been home. I put the watch away, finished the whiskey, and prepared to go; after several nights spent hanging around in bars, I was beginning to lose interest in my brother's mysterious correspondent. Also I had to stay sober enough to drive home safely.

As often happens when I have drunk too much the previous night I had awakened at around four-thirty and lain, with a creaking head and a polluted mouth, as light crept through the room like water into sand, trying to reconstruct the events of the previous evening. I had been driving slowly, it had been more of a nudge than a hit; no screams, and only the empty street in the rearview mirror. Probably, I concluded, the Jap had grazed some dopehead, who had picked himself up afterward and stumbled into a downtown alley where, at this moment, he was waking up on a flophouse pallet, a little sore and bruised but dimly incurious about the night's adventure. I had risen early, dressed, and gone downstairs to examine the Jap. There was a crease, faint but definite, in the right front fender which might well have been there when I drove the car off the rental lot at the Salt Lake airport. Finally, I had switched on the ignition and listened to an early news broadcast, whose featured story concerned a debate in the state legislature over the use of poisoned bait to eliminate predators.

Of far greater concern and annoyance to me was the Martinez woman, who had phoned again—collect as usual—to say that the cost of mailing the package as requested was ten seventy-five, that she was very sorry but she did not have ten seventy-five, and that she would have to have the money first. Her manner was reasonable but I heard again, in the background, the female voice prompting insistently in Spanish. Nilsa Martinez explained that since in order to go to the post office it would be necessary for her to take the morning off from work, she thought it only fair that I should reimburse her for her loss of pay. I had replied ironically that I doubted that my book was worth her morning's wages and that I would need to consider her offer and call her back. Naturally, she didn't have any job. It had occurred to me that if I could only stall the bitch for a couple of weeks more I might have a chance to pay a visit to the East Thirties address on my way through New York and confront Nilsa Martinez and her boyfriend in person.

The ladies of the Bowling League had finished stuffing the front of the stripper's shorts with bills and were lifting him down in triumph from his platform to dress as the professional girl, who had been enjoying a drink at the bar while she observed the proceedings with a cynical stare, remounted to her little stage. The strobe lights on her naked flesh might have been the visible imprint of the cold rapacious eyes of the construction-gang zombies watching her, and I was remembering nostalgically the randy cowboys, liquored sheepherders, and rotten-lunged miners who had patronized the place in my youth when a pair of hands slipped deftly across my eyes and a girl's low voice behind me said, "Sam Walker . . . can you guess who this is?"

I give up," I said, restraining an impulse to tear the hands away. In Africa, you learn quickly to mistrust surprises.

"Just *guess*," the voice insisted. "Think a long, *long* way back—further than you like to think you've been alive."

It came to me all at once then. "All right, *Candy Fuller*. Take those hands away now and let me look for myself."

The blonde hair was as natural as the gilt on a municipal statue and in the corners of the eyes a few light crow's-feet showed. Otherwise she was exactly as I remembered her, minus even perhaps twenty or twenty-five pounds from her palmy days as Prom Queen, Homecoming Queen, Junior Miss, and Most Popular Girl. "You wouldn't win any game-show prizes," Candy said, "but it has been twenty-one years, after all. I recognized you immediately; you've hardly changed a bit."

"Thanks. Neither have you."

"The hell I haven't."

I signaled the bartender, who was a pale alcoholic with a

damp skin and a spine like something sprouting from a cellar floor. "One more of what I'm having and a Crown and Seven for the lady."

She slipped around the barstool and put a hand on my arm. "Not bad. I see you have a little of your memory left, anyway." Her hard lithe body pressed lightly on mine and I was aware of the faint unsettling odor of warm girl. The bartender brought the drinks and palmed the five dollars I gave him. He was sweating profusely, as if he had just completed a marathon. "Don't I even get a kiss," Candy Fuller asked, "after twenty-one years?"

I hadn't realized until I kissed her that she was quite drunk; it had always been difficult to tell with her. For an instant the hard point of her tongue probed my clenched teeth before withdrawing. "I can't believe it," she said. "The last time I saw you I was eighteen years old. It just doesn't seem possible."

"What doesn't seem possible?"

"That I'm thirty-nine goddamn years old. Twenty-one years ago I thought middle-aged people were born that way, like niggers. And now *I'm* middle-aged—I guess. And all it took for it to happen was twenty-one years that felt more like twenty-one months."

"If it makes you feel any better, I'm right up there with you."

"It isn't the same for a man." She raised her glass to drink and I saw with amazement that it was half empty already. She had on false eyelashes and a thick layer of makeup and the lids of her eyes were painted bottle-fly blue. "What have you been doing with yourself?" Candy asked, in a tone which suggested that whatever the answer would be, it couldn't interest her much.

"You mean—for the last twenty-one years?"

She stirred her drink vaguely with the swizzle stick. "You're some kind of hunter in South America or someplace, aren't you?" She might have been asking, You're a bond trader in Salt Lake City, aren't you?

"I've been a professional hunter in Zambia for ten years and part owner of a safari company for five. I worked as an elephant cropper for the Zambian government for eighteen months until one afternoon I came close to getting myself squeezed to jelly between a bull elephant's toes and figured I might be pushing the odds a bit."

"That sounds dangerous." Candy rattled the ice suggestively in her empty glass and put the end of the swizzle stick in her teeth. "Are you going to buy me another drink?"

I showed the bartender two fingers; in reply he lifted his chin weakly above the stainless-steel basin where he stood bent with his thin arms plunged to the elbow in soapsuds. "How about yourself, Candy? What have you been doing to make twenty-one years go by like water?"

She shrugged, as if she found even less interest in her own life than she had in mine. "I have two kids, six and eight. They're staying with their dad in Cheyenne for the summer. Ed and I have been divorced for almost a year now. You remember Ed Chapman, don't you?"

Ed Chapman, the son of a well-to-do local contractor, had been in the class immediately behind me in high school and gone on to attend the university in Laramie. I recalled him with distaste: a bald-headed young man with a puffy face and prominent front teeth who wore penny loafers and carried a battery of ballpoint pens in a plastic holder clipped into his shirt pocket. "Is that so? I hadn't heard. Nobody bothers telling me anything in Africa."

Her thin shoulders lifted ironically under the low-cut blouse of blue velour. "He was afraid what he called my 'partying' would hurt his career; he wants to get elected governor someday. I hated living in Cheyenne, just a bunch of greedy politicians and their boring wives. Here no one pays attention no matter what you do."

"Not to let on about anyhow."

"I heard about your brother," Candy Fuller said suddenly.

"Yeah. Well."

"Is that what you're back here for?"

"Uh-huh."

153

"How long are you going to be around for?"

"As long as there's something for me to do."

"What *is* there for you to do?"

"Not a whole hell of a lot, actually."

She took a butane lighter from her purse and I held it while she lit a cigarette, her small breasts rising sharply under the velour as she inhaled. I had seen them just once, the day she had changed out of her swimsuit on the bank of North Fork, causing two bulldozers grading the highway above the creek to nearly collide. Then I got out the pack of Marlboros I had bought at Wendell's Drugs and lit one before returning the lighter to her. Every afternoon after school, throughout the second half of my junior year and all of my senior one, Candy and I had gone to Wendell's to drink milkshakes and smoke. I tasted my first cigarette through a strawberry milkshake at Wendell's and was a fairly heavy smoker until sophomore year at Virginia, when I quit at the insistence of the progressively minded coed I was trying to impress. I asked, "How's your dad doing these days?"

"He's okay. They made him party chairman a few years ago, and now he says he's thinking about running for governor." The irony in her voice, I felt, came just short of sarcasm. "That's what everybody wants these days, isn't it? To be the one sitting up there in the control seat, pushing all the buttons."

"Tell him hello for me, will you?"

"Of course I will. He always liked you, you know, even with everything. He always said Ed was a phony." She wrinkled her nose and revolved the glass, which was empty again, on the wood. "I guess that was one time I should have listened to the old geezer."

The bartender came along arching his eyebrows suggestively, but I shook my head at him. "Let's have just one more," Candy said, "for old times' sake. Isn't it funny: I feel like we're still buddies, you and me—after twenty-one lousy years. I'll get this round," she added, waving one hand at the bartender while she fished with the other inside her pocketbook. The cigarette

was doing something to my nerves, besides which it tasted awful.
"They say your grandfather hasn't mellowed out any," Candy said
irrelevantly.

"He definitely hasn't."

"Looking back it seems pretty dumb, doesn't it?"

"Can you think of anything that doesn't?"

She considered. "Probably not."

"You know, I was thinking the other day that it feels good to
be almost forty. I wouldn't be twenty again for a million dollars."

"Well *I* certainly would," she said emphatically. "I'd *pay* a
million, if I had it."

The drinks came and she touched her glass to mine.
"Cheers. It's wonderful seeing you again, Sam."

"Thank you. Same here."

"What about," Candy asked, looking at me over the top of
her glass, "your sister?"

"What do you mean, what about her?"

"Well, how is she?"

"Same as ever. She hasn't changed since she was twelve or
thirteen years old."

"She always hated me. Even before everything."

"She still does hate you."

"Did she say something about me?"

"She didn't have to. Clare doesn't change her mind about
anything. Or anybody."

"I always thought," Candy said, "that your sister would have
made the best politician in the family."

"Not Clare. Politics is the art of compromise, which in her
book makes it a species of pornography."

We finished the drinks and I said, "Better be getting home, I
guess. It was great seeing you again though."

She looked disappointed. "You're leaving so early? You're
no fun anymore after all, Sam."

"Sorry about that. It must be my age showing at last."

"Oh *boo*." She leaned closer, her shoulder pressing mine,

and I smelled Crown Royal and perfume, too much of both. "If you're old, then so am I. I'm leaving too."

Behind the glare of the sodium lights a million bright stars bored thinly in from space as we stood facing one another awkwardly outside the Bare Garden. Some of that light, it occurred to me as I looked at them, would have started on its journey to Earth exactly twenty-one years ago.

The high-pitched, nasal-sounding voice that succeeded (almost) in covering the snarl when it tried hard enough (because of wanting something badly enough) had failed to disguise the loathing with which the object of its call inspired it. Although Mayor Edwards was certainly not his own worst enemy, he was unquestionably Caleb North Richardson's most flattering one.

There was always, with Joe Edwards, the problem of how to transact the necessary business without appearing to do it at His Honor's express command: of arriving at City Hall with a professional promptitude which nevertheless fell short of suggesting the fawning alacrity of a courtier attending at a levee. The manner, he had discovered, came easiest if you began by concentrating on the mayor's physique, which approximated the pear shape of Louis-Philippe, and on the loose buck-toothed grin, the baggy blue suits and sweated nylon shirts that marked him as the small-town businessman afflicted by delusions of grandeur he actually was: the trick thereafter being to respond to his elephantine feints of raw aggression with a diffident and calculatedly infuriating languor. When, at eight-thirty in the morning, Jenny had yelled from the yard that Mayor Edwards wanted him on the telephone, his response had been to shout back at her to explain to His Honor that he was too busy to come to the phone now but that he would be happy to return the call when he found time later in the day. Then he had stood leaning against a fencepost with his arm extended along the top rail and watched her scamper back to the house, while he imagined the mayor slamming the receiver into the cradle, tapping furiously with a pencil end on the desktop, and finally barking at the fat-dog secretary to bring him the morning mail. Because he would not place that call again, or even allow the secretary to place it for him; rather than demean himself so greatly he would work himself into a quiet fit of the kind that so often—Richardson reflected patiently—produces a coronary occlusion. So he had waited more than an hour before returning to the house and dialing City Hall, which informed him that Mayor Edwards was in executive session at the moment but that he had a matter of extreme importance to discuss with Mr. Richardson and would he please call back in three-quarters of an hour? Round Two, then, went to the mayor, who was an acknowledged expert in having the last word; and at twenty minutes past one Richardson phoned again and was presently connected with Joe Edwards who explained, vaguely but portentously, that the matter at hand concerned his client, Mr. Jack Walker. They had made an appointment to discuss it at three-thirty that afternoon in the mayor's office.

"That creep," Jenny had said when he told her. "What do you think he wants to talk to you about Jack for?"

"I don't have the faintest idea. If I did, I probably wouldn't go."

"What makes it any of his business anyway?"

"It isn't any of his business."

"Then why," she demanded with impeccable feminine logic as she stared at him over the top of her drawing pad, "are you going at all?"

"Just because. When your mayor asks you to do a thing, you do it."

"*Oh shit!*" Jenny said, getting up from her chair and dropping the pad between them on the table. Her drawings, he had noticed, were becoming increasingly modernistic and bizarre, hinting at buried states of mind he preferred not to speculate upon. This morning, however, she was looking particularly wholesome, dressed in white on which her bare rounded arms showed a healthy brown and her braided hair like a streak of dark fire. "It's not ladylike to use words like that," Richardson told her, but she only wrinkled her nose at him and made a *moue*, causing her to look younger and more innocent still. "What's a lady?" Jenny countered pertly.

" 'A virtuous wife is a crown to her husband, her children rise and call her blessed.' "

She put her chin in her hand and widened her eyes at him in mock surprise. "Are ladies virtuous?"

"In theory. And in poetry."

"What about in life?"

"That depends on how much theory and poetry you've read."

"How about your wife—was she virtuous?"

"You mean Christine? Not very."

"But she was a lady!" Jenny cried triumphantly.

"She was a New Englander," he corrected. "That's always been enough for some folks."

The triumphant expression died in her eyes and was replaced by a speculative look as her thought apparently moved off in another direction. "I guess by now he's starting to be nervous," she said.

"Who is? Jack?"

"No, dummy! The mayor."

"What does that fat sonofabitch have to be nervous about?"

"He doesn't like people poking around in his town."

"I don't give a rat's ass for his town. I'm defending a man who's going to be prosecuted on a first-degree-murder charge."

"You never know, do you? And he doesn't either."

So he was on the outskirts of Fontenelle now: a shabby small desert town which remained, beneath the raucous boosterism and self-affirmative posturing, deeply and inexpungeably ashamed of its incontrovertible virtues, like a virtuously plain woman who, convinced of her latent talents as a seductress, is eager to deny her natural qualities of modesty and fidelity. He drove past the running electric sign in front of the bank (WE BELIEVE IN FONTENELLE BRINGING YOU TOMORROW ONE DAY EARLY) and past the square where another car turned in behind him and followed closely, the staring eye painted on the long bullet nose glaring in the rearview mirror. It was the bizarre-looking vehicle—the ancient repainted ambulance or hearse—he had been noticing around town for the past several weeks. He watched it in the mirror until it turned out abruptly after he had gone several blocks and shortly before he reached the narrow dirt street running between the lumber yard and the railroad tracks where they had set the double-wide trailer that was serving as the temporary City Hall until the new, very large and expensive one they were building to honor the new prosperity was completed. The trailer rested on cement blocks in a grove of tired-looking cottonwood trees with several cars drawn up in front of it, one of which was the mayor's official sedan. Wide and glistening white, it stood out from the others Richardson thought like the village whore at a church wedding.

My God, Candy, that was great! Why didn't we try this twenty years ago?" Pressing against me from ankle to shoulder, her hard emaciated body emitted heat like a warm steampipe.

"You were too young for me then, Sam—mentally, I mean."

"That's absurd. I wasn't any less mature than you were. You wanted to get married, didn't you?"

"*You* know why," she said, after a minute.

"You mean my sister?"

"I mean all of them."

"Look, it wasn't just my folks that were against it."

"Why don't we just not talk about it, Sam, after twenty-one years—okay?"

We lay quiet under the pulled-up sheet, listening to the clatter of tricycles along the sidewalk and the nag of bored young mothers sunning themselves on the steps beneath the open windows where her immaculate white curtains had fluttered softly all morning over our lovemaking. When she took my hand in hers

161

and squeezed it absentmindedly I rolled onto her and kissed her hard on the mouth, tasting stale whiskey and nicotine. But she said, sharply, "I don't want to again," and I rolled away and lay on my side, watching the fat white clouds beyond the swelling curtains while she rose, wrapped herself in a dressing gown of a hard blue color, and sat down to primp at the vanity. I asked her, "Remember driving up to the lake together after the prom?"

"How could I forget? You were absolutely disgusting the whole time."

"How do you mean, disgusting? All I wanted was what you gave me half an hour ago."

"In the back of a pickup truck? The cops would have nailed us before you got your pants on, and you'd have ended up doing twenty-five years for statutory rape."

"It would have been worth it. Right now I'd have only four more to go."

She got up from the table and pulled on the sash ends at her waist. "I'm going in to take a shower now. You can get the coffee started if you're looking for something useful to do."

But I continued to lie there beneath the sheet, basking in the warmth of this long-deferred victory, until I heard the hiss of the shower behind the closed bathroom door. Then I kicked it away and stepped out of the bed, pulled on my clothes, and stalked on bare feet to her little kitchen, feeling lionish. I filled the kettle and set it on the stove to boil and poured freeze-dried coffee, which was the only kind I could find, into two cups. In the refrigerator were a half-dozen eggs, three slices of freezer-burned bacon, half a loaf of store bread, a quart of skim milk and another of orange juice, and two cartons of cigarettes. I found a plastic bowl under the sink, broke all six of the eggs into it, and added a little of the thin grayish milk before putting the bacon on to fry. "Look at you," Candy murmured from the door. "A perfect little house-husband. Am I supposed to be impressed, Sam?" She had on designer jeans this morning that emphasized the startling thinness of her thighs and hips. In broad daylight her makeup was a mask, and her false eyelashes looked as if they had been soldered onto the lids.

"Not really. Blacks and women have been doing it for centuries."

She lit a cigarette and cocked it at a provocative angle from her hip. "Nobody's got any woman's work out of me for a year and nobody's going to get any out of me again, either. I don't even bother cooking for myself if I can help it. They usually feed me up at Al's before I go to work and most of the time I don't get up for breakfast." Since her return to Fontenelle from Cheyenne she had been working five nights a week as cocktail hostess at Al's Supper Club.

"Is that how you stay so skinny, not cooking for yourself?"

"I'm not skinny."

"You're skinny."

"The closer the bone, the sweeter the meat. Right?"

"To a point, yes."

Candy took the juice bottle from the refrigerator and set it on the counter. "Orange juice is the best medicine there is for a hangover. Much better than coffee."

"I don't have a hangover."

"Well I do," she said. "I have a hangover every morning."

I slipped the spatula under the omelettes and turned them easily; the odor made me almost lightheaded with hunger. "Pour yourself coffee if you want it. The eggs will be ready in a couple of seconds. And how about setting the table while we're waiting?"

"The table? Usually I just eat in front of the TV."

"Well, this morning is special, all right?"

"If you say so." Candy shrugged, stubbed the cigarette, and carried a handful of stainless steel and two paper napkins into the dinette. I slid the omelettes onto the plates and ran hot water into the frying pan in the sink. "The last time we ate breakfast together must have been—"

"*Please* don't mention twenty-one years again," she interrupted. "I found three new lines beside my eyes this morning.

163

Would you move *that-way* a moment so I can reach the place mats?"

When she had finished setting the table I proudly carried in the filled plates and poured coffee. I pulled out her chair and held it for her and she slipped into it, remarking, "Thank you," in a diffident voice; when I bent to kiss her she leaned sharply away and pointed with her fork to my place. "Go sit down now," she told me, "and eat your breakfast before it gets cold."

They were excellent omelettes, despite the paucity of ingredients. I ate ravenously and watched her thin brown hand listlessly poke the tines of the fork among golden layers of egg. "How do you like your omelette?" I asked.

"It's okay." The hand put down the fork, strayed to the cigarette pouch beside the plate, then picked up the fork again.

"Occasionally in camp if I'm up early enough I cook breakfast myself. A couple of months ago I took out a German party that had brought with them a couple of quarts of Black Forest mushrooms from Bavaria. They made the best mushroom omelettes you ever tasted, believe me."

Her hand struck at the pouch and snatched a cigarette. I watched her carefully as she reached for the lighter and thumbed the flint, noticing how tired she looked. There were circles under her eyes, her cheeks were wan beneath the makeup and, despite their thinness, slightly flaccid. "Do you have to work tonight?" I asked.

"No, thank God. I'm off now until Thursday."

I pushed my plate away, got out the Marlboros, and lit one. "What do you do with yourself around here when you aren't working?"

"Watch TV. Do the laundry. At night if they have a band at the Bare Garden I go dancing with Tim."

"Tim who?" I asked, too quickly.

"Just some guy I know at the radio station. I think he's probably gay, though he's never said anything to me about it."

"I remember you liking to dance," I said, relaxing. I had a

sudden vision of her at eighteen, a long-maned voluptuous beauty in a pink dress with a white orchid pinned to the bosom, surrounded by beaux in powder-blue tuxedos; and of myself, watching jealously from the sidelines. Dancing, as far as I have always been concerned, is for happy children and trained bears.

"What do you have to do today?" she asked.

"Me? Nothing at all, really."

"Then why don't you spend it with me?"

"That's a thought."

Candy leaned for the channel selector at the end of the coffee table and switched the television on; wavering distorted shapes and intersecting lines of chaos flashed instantly in color on the yawning screen. "You need to forget about your family for a while and just relax," she said. "I bet it's been years since you watched a good American TV show."

He waited on the fresh-carpented steps beneath the candy-striped flag snapping on its pole while Mayor Edwards's secretary glared at him for several seconds through the window before she released the electronic lock that protected the Chief Executive Officer of the City of Fontenelle from political assassins. The secretary was a plump woman of a certain age with thinning hair of no noticeable color and eyeglasses the size of dessert plates on a black nylon cord. She watched suspiciously as Richardson closed the door, put the end of her tongue out, and ran it around her mouth like an elderly obese dog that has retained the protective impulse beyond the loss of courage and stamina to obey it. She said, "The mayor is on the phone right now. Would you care to have a seat while you wait?" Her voice, which sounded simultaneously timid and hostile, had a muffled quality, as if she were unable to decide which tone should be allowed to predominate.

Richardson lowered himself reluctantly into one of the

molded-plastic chairs diabolically favored by government pur-
chasing agents from the local to the federal level, balanced the
scuffed leather portfolio on his knee, and sat gravely regarding
the framed documents and honorary plaques on the wall. He
guessed from the bottle of window cleaner and the rag on the
magazine table that the secretary had been reverently polishing
them before his arrival. On an adjacent wall hung the architect's
idealized drawing in pen and ink of the future City Hall, a self-
consciously modernistic horror of Bauhaus descent modified
considerably by the Mormon ecclesiastical tradition. Small
towns, Richardson reflected, produce two general classes of
ambitious men: one which decamps at the first opportunity for
the big city, and the other which remains to boast of the whole-
someness of small-town life while working beaverishly to urban-
ize it. "The mayor is off the line," the secretary announced
grudgingly. "I'll ask him if he's ready to see you now."

"Is that Richardson out there?" Joe Edwards shouted
around the partition wall. "Tell him to get his ass in here pronto,
Carol."

"The mayor says to go in now," Carol translated primly,
rolling a government form in triplicate into her typewriter and
staring determinedly away as he passed by her desk. Secre-
taries had always had the affinity for Chuck Richardson that
yard dogs have for postmen, or fading wives for pretty secre-
taries.

Mayor Edwards sat in his shirtsleeves in a high-backed
executive chair with a paper cup clutched in his large red hand
and a half-eaten tuna-salad sandwich on a square of waxed paper
at his elbow. His mouth being full of bread and fish, he restricted
his greeting to a nod and a diffident wave of his free hand toward
the plastic chair that had been carefully placed in front of—but
not too close to—the desk. Through the partly open door at the
mayor's back the end of a conference table surrounded by folding chairs was visible, and from somewhere beyond that flowed
the low discreet chitter of electronic keyboards. Richardson

set the portfolio against the chair leg, fixed his gaze on the capacious suitcoat of blue polyester spread largely upon the coatrack, and waited patiently for the loose loud chewing to subside.

Finally the mayor swallowed. Then he drew the back of his hand across his mouth and said, "I had to give a talk at Chamber today and didn't get a chance to eat lunch." He was grinning now, as he always grinned even when talking: a loose, sarcastic, faintly derisive grin in which the lips dropped away from the long yellow horse teeth and the eyes, which were the coldest and least expressive blue Richardson had ever encountered, glittered as though from behind a mask. Somehow, he thought, the most ghastly thing about that grin was the fact that it represented a genuine, though fundamentally dishonest, attempt at being agreeable. "Take your time," Richardson urged him, equally disingenuously. Watching His Honor at table was never an agreeable experience.

Still grinning, Joe Edwards took two paper packets from the desk, tore away the tops, and stirred sugar and powdered milk into his coffee. He paused as if to admire the mixture and then tasted it, the loose elastic lips quivering like those of a horse at water. "The doctor's told me to go easy with the caffeine, but the stuff they make next door's so darn good I can't resist sending Carol out for one more cup."

"If I were you I think I'd go easy anyway."

The mayor's grin widened until he resembled a dog watching a chop about to fall to the floor. He set the cup down again, tore away a sandwich point with his yellow teeth, and recommenced the slow loose chewing, while Richardson studied a blown-up aerial photograph of the town that suggested a sense of distance he found reassuring. When he had looked at it long enough he lifted the portfolio onto his knee, withdrew a handful of papers, and began riffling through them while the chewing continued. "Do you have any objection," he asked at last, "to making this a working lunch? The ladies at the Doll House are sleeping cold until I can finish putting a roof over their heads."

Without ceasing to masticate, the mayor raised his pale, slightly bloodshot eyes. "Anytime you're ready, Richardson."

"I'm ready."

Mayor Edwards replaced the remnants of his lunch on the waxed paper and produced a red bandanna handkerchief with which he wiped his mouth, leaving fragments of tuna and mayonnaise in the corners. He shook a small white pill from a box and washed it down with the last of the coffee. Then he folded the handkerchief deliberately and tucked it into his pocket, crumpled the paper over the remains of the sandwich, and dropped the mess into the wastepaper basket. Finally, he spread his hands behind his head and sat back in the high chair; he was still grinning at Richardson as he began to speak. He said, "I asked you here, pacifically, for a favor."

"I do favors for people, now and then."

"Not you do me a favor. Me do you one."

"Is that so?"

"That's so."

"I can hardly wait to hear about it, then."

"I kind of figured you might feel that way." The mayor shifted his heavy buttocks in the chair and grinned rapturously at the ceiling, as if the gift he was preparing to bestow were being lowered from there. In the hollows under his meaty arms dark stains were spreading in the nylon. "What are we going to do about your man Jack Walker?" he inquired at last, without removing his eyes from the ceiling.

"I'm going to keep him from being charged with a crime he isn't guilty of, as expeditiously as possible. I have no idea what 'we're' going to do."

Joe Edwards's expression was that of a man watching eventualities unfold precisely as he had expected them to do. "That is a matter I pacifically wanted to discuss with you, as his attorney."

Richardson thought: If he doesn't quit eyeballing the ceiling and beating around the bush and get what he would call pacific in a hurry, I'm going to turn his goddamn desk over on top of him. I'm going to trash his office and beat his secretary and throw every one of his lousy plaques onto the railroad tracks. Aloud he said: "Go right ahead. I'm like a kid at Christmas listening for reindeer hooves on the roof." He understood that he was expected to feel more like a spider: a sinner in the hand of an angry God.

The mayor removed his hands from behind his head and, leaning forward over the desk, placed them meditatively beneath his chin. His lips fell slackly away from the gums, but he was not grinning now and the ironic gleam was missing from his eyes. He said, "Has it occurred to you that you are representing more than a single person—pacifically, Mr. Jack Walker—in this affair?"

"You mean, the family?"

Mayor Edwards permitted himself a small deprecatory smile. "Oh yeah, the family of course. But what I'm thinking of, pacifically, is the community—the city of Fontenelle."

"The city?"

"Not being paid for it," His Honor explained patiently, "you probably never thought about it like this, but—as the chief elected official of the city of Fontenelle in Bridger County, Wyoming—I feel it my pacific duty to do so. On the one hand"— he gestured broadly—"you have the biggest oil company in the world building a plant costing three and a quarter billion dollars that's already brought millions of dollars into the community and six-seven thousand jobs. And on the other"—the mayor gestured again—"you have a fella that's the grandson of a former lieutenant governor of the state and a lifelong resident of the area, that just for no reason at all jumps a company hand and beats him to death—almost. And how," Mayor Edwards demanded, "do you think that makes the city of Fontenelle look? Like a bunch of goddamn red Indians," he answered himself.

Richardson said, "Do you think so? I haven't seen the

city fathers sticking their heads in the ground from embarrass-
ment."

"You think folks ain't embarrassed by what's happened?
Could be you ain't acquainted with the right people then." Along
with his manners and his grammar, the mayor's temper was
deteriorating rapidly. For the first time that afternoon, Richardson thought, he looked really nasty. "Look here, my friend,"
Mayor Edwards said. "You figured you were pretty hot stuff
blowing in here with your fancy Eastern law degree and your big-
city ideas and values (if values is the right word for what you got)
to beat all of us Western yokels over the head with, but they's
plenty of us has watched you figures you ain't so goddamn hot
after all. I promise you one thing anyway: You ain't going to find it
so easy this time like you did the last, you hear what I'm saying to
you? Just a little word to the wise, buddy."

Richardson, stuffing the last of the papers into the portfolio,
said, "You called me in here—at the taxpayers' expense,
incidentally—in order to say something, ah . . . pacific. Don't
you want to tell me what that is, before I go?"

The mayor took two cigars from behind the plastic pen-
holder clipped into his shirt pocket and placed them painstakingly before him on the desk blotter; after long consideration
he selected one of them. He peeled the wrapper from it and stuck
the cigar between his teeth and lit it from a nickel-plated lighter.
The mayor stirred the other cigar with the end of his finger and
took the finger away again. He said, "Get him to plead guilty to
involuntary manslaughter and the hell with it. The judge'll cut
him a good deal without giving them media assholes the chance
to make whoopee out of it."

"He isn't guilty of involuntary manslaughter."

"So what the hell? He *is* guilty of murder—I mean, attempted murder."

"That hasn't been proved yet."

"It will be proved, when the D.A.'s office and Judge
Thurlow are through with him."

"Does that mean you've discussed this with them already?"

"Not yet, I haven't. I wanted to hear how you would interface with the idea, first."

It occurred to Richardson that the mayor, motives aside, was offering something he could not responsibly dismiss out of hand. He said, "Let me pass this again by my slow, slow mind. The proposition stands that, in return for my client pleading guilty to the reduced charge, the state agrees not to pursue a case it has no particular—I mean pacific—desire to investigate thoroughly, owing to the possibility of further adverse publicity—"

"In order," the mayor interrupted from inside the bolus of blue smoke, "to pacifically get the community moving forward again, in a PR mode, in a positive way—"

"—even though the state itself, as opposed to the community, has no pacific reason to be concerned with PR, which presumably would mean less to it than the simple determination of the truth would."

The meaty hand clutching the cigar dropped with astonishing lightness onto the desk and the jowled red face peered around the cloud like a courtier peeping from behind a mask. "Come on, Richardson," Mayor Edwards said almost genially. "You know better than that."

He had to grin himself as he stood up, tucking the portfolio under his arm. "Just so I know which side I'm running with, the white hats or the black. Once the basic fact is established, I can usually—like most attorneys—play ball on either side."

"Yeah," the mayor said, grinning back at him without getting up from the desk, "we all had kind of noticed that."

It was vintage Joe Edwards, Richardson thought as he went out past the fat-dog secretary who, pretending to be engrossed in her forms, did not acknowledge his farewell: appealing with shameless effrontery to your worst instincts and throwing it up at you when you succumbed to that appeal. His boots, which had gone so stealthily over the vinyl carpet, struck out ringingly on the planking as the electronic lock fastened with an admonitory cluck at his back.

———————

For a while after the lawyer had gone Joe Edwards sat drumming with a pencil on a corner of the blotter. His lips, no longer stretched in a grin, made a flaccid circle like the neck of a sack from which the drawstring has been removed. Finally he picked up the telephone and, using the direct line, dialed Chief of Police Willard at his home number. The chief, with an efficient assistant to cover for him, was taking his Tuesday afternoons off for the summer. The voice answering the phone said, "Okay, this is a stickup."

The mayor said stiffly, "I'm calling to talk to your dad. Is he there?"

"You're the Masked Bandit, ain't you? What do you want to talk to him for?"

"Never you mind, young fella," he began, when a man's voice interrupted. "Hullo, this is Terry Willard speaking. I got it, Shane."

He waited for the boy to hang up before he said, "I just got through talking with Richardson, Terry. Looks like the sonofabitch may bite after all."

"Christ, I hope so."

"I put the fear in him real good. It's dollars to doughnuts he'll cooperate with us now."

"I sure hope so, Joe. If he don't come around to it himself, we'll have to take him there. It could get dirty."

"He'll come around, all right. You can count on me for that."

"You spoke with the judge yet?"

"That's step number two," the mayor said grimly.

For a while after he hung up the phone Joe Edwards sat drumming with a pencil on the corner of the blotter. His lips, no longer stretched in a grin, made a flaccid circle like the neck of a sack from which the drawstring has been removed. Finally he picked up the phone again and, using the office line this time, dialed Carol's number and sent her out to buy a cup of coffee from the doughnut shop next door.

I stopped the Jap in front of the apartments, leaving the motor idling and the lights on, and leaned to kiss her. "I'll call you in the morning. Not too early, I promise."

Candy said: "You mean you aren't coming up?"

"I can't, tonight. Better get on home and see how the folks are doing."

"You're going *home?* After the lovely day we spent together? What do you want to spoil it for, Sam?"

"I'm not spoiling anything. I have responsibilities is all. Get a good rest now, and I'll talk to you in the morning." She got out of the car without saying good night and banged the door. I watched her as she paused on the step to look for her key and shifted into first gear when the plate glass closed behind her. In the yellow light of the hallway her skinny body made a collage of rigid sharp angles. She did not look back.

We had taken a picnic lunch and spent the day at the lake, where I had swum in the clear blue-green icy water that only a couple of weeks ago had been a sheet of rotten snow slipping between steep red peaks and where we had both lain baking ourselves under a high white sun, watching a class of beginning water-skiers trying to get up on the broad flat boards and shrieking when they went under. There were many more powerboats on the lake than I remembered and the water had a roughened look, as if thousands of whirling propellers had permanently damaged its cobalt surface. After lunch a stiff wind had come up, blowing the napkins and papers along the little beach, straightening Candy's dry stiffened curls and making her more irritable than a mare in heat until we had to give up finally, pull our clothes on over our swimsuits, and go into the bar for beer and Crown Royal, which we drank sitting indoors out of the wind until the sun fell below the line of the brown treeless hills and campfires began to glimmer along the water's edge. We ordered ribs and baked potato, more beer and whiskey, and ate supper while four androgynous freaks called "the band" set up and tested their equipment, which hooted like a party of invading Martians. "We have to stay for at least a couple of sets," Candy said.

"I don't dance, remember? And I hate this junk they play now. Remember when we used to come up here and listen to Hank Williams, Waylon Jennings, Willie Nelson? People appreciated listening to real music, then."

"You're *old*, do you know that?"

"I've always been old—in that way, at least."

So we "danced." That is, we stood a foot and a half apart in front of an amplification system the size of a large refrigerator and wiggled like a pair of spastic arthritic cobras. The lodge was as I remembered it from twenty years ago, but the people seemed entirely changed; plenty of the men besides "the band" had long hair and almost nobody wore a cowboy hat. Once on the way back to our table I caught sight of Tom Studds with a blonde who was either not his wife or had had herself a repackaging job someplace; we ignored one another and passed on. Otherwise I recognized no one, although once or twice I was aware of vaguely familiar faces observing us curiously. It was as if that black semisolid cube of absolute sound—the scientific obverse of the absolute silence of deep space—had removed not only the ability to hear but the desire for any other sound; in the breaks between numbers the dancers—we included—sat numb and speechless at the little tables off the floor, drinking and staring at our fingernails. At a little past ten, with Candy too drunk to protest, I put her into the Jap and drove back to town, patiently enduring her heavy inconvenient head on my shoulder as I watched the moths swirl in the twin funnels of light the headlights made. Some of the moths were very large and struck with soft audible concussions against the hood and windshield. They swirled and slapped as I drove on through the darkness, feeling her weight pressing and subsiding with the motion of the car on the curves and thinking. I had been thinking all day and most of the previous night, when I had lain awake hour after hour until, with the coming of dawn, I had slept for a little while; I had been thinking when I left her standing, ruffled and insulted, in front of the apartments; and I was thinking now as the low pink slabsided bulk of the hospital slid silently into the headlights of the Jap. I was thinking that I could no longer live with the uncertainty, bear the not knowing; thinking that, sooner or later, I was going to have to know. Tonight liquor, combined with a peculiar feeling of desperation that had widened over the past several days from a pinprick to a perceptible black hole, had given me the courage to decide that later might as well be now.

I parked the car carefully between the yellow lines painted on the new asphalt and locked it. I went up the flight of shallow steps that mounted beside the concrete ramp and through the double plate-glass doors. The smell was like a gas, the chemical odor of mortality; a nurse in a white uniform and a crisp pointed cap glided soundlessly past me on soft white shoes, pushing a stainless-steel stretcher mounted on rubber tires and wearing on a pale and sexless face the expressionless solemnity of a professional pallbearer. I do not fear, and never have feared, death; but I have always been acutely in dread of hospitals.

The walls were painted a cold electric green above a floor composed of antiseptically clean linoleum squares, black and white alternating with one another like death and life. Through a window on my left I heard the whir of an electric typewriter; moving forward I caught sight of the rangy gray-haired nurse behind it. "Yes?" she said when she saw me. "Can I help you?" She had a long sour face like a sheep, and a sheep's rabbity gray nose above a gray beaked mouth. Her finger ends on the keyboard were stained yellow and her hair when she came over smelled of nicotine. Behind the thick lenses of her glasses her eyes had a magnified sharpness. I said, "I'd like some information, please."

"What kind of information?" Her voice was as dryly sharp as her expression.

"I would like to know what emergency admittances you've had—if any—in the last forty-eight hours."

Her sharp upper lip closed smartly over the lower one like a clasp. "You're not from the newspaper," she said.

"This is strictly a private matter. A friend of mine has been missing for two days."

"May I have your name—?" the nurse began, when a voice directly behind me interrupted. "Oh, Mr. Walker," it said. "Dorothy isn't allowed to give out information like that. But if you'll just step into my office, I'll be happy to do what I can to help you."

I turned, stricken, and there she was: a light-haired, violet-eyed girl, her trim small figure clad in the smart tailored skirt and classic blouse of Peck & Peck, Abercrombie & Fitch, L.L. Bean—the very model of the modern female sophisticate professional, confronting me with the poise and aplomb of a lady board chairman above the fat green file folder she held pressed against her breasts.

I don't open for business until six o'clock!" Fanny Mae Tuscher yelled at me from the door. "Or was you wanting to buy a hunting license?" she added in a softer voice. As long as I could remember the Doll House had been franchised by the Game and Fish Department, probably for the reason that it was in a sense a purveyor of sporting goods. Fanny Mae had been the proprietress longer than I had had need of, or interest in, those goods. She was an enormous woman with a dropsical belly that fell almost to her knees and a face composed largely of protuberances: nose, lips, wens, and an occasional long, coarse black hair. She had at one time been married, but had triumphantly buried her husband years ago. She was no different than my memory of her from a decade ago, except for being even stouter; certainly her voice had stood the test of time. I said, "I guess you didn't recognize me, Fanny Mae. I haven't been a state resident for more than ten years."

Fanny Mae clenched her hands on her elephantine hips and glared at me. "Sam Walker. I thought you was a familiar face. In

179

this business all men look alike. How long you been home, son? You got yourself a elk tag yet?"

"Like I said, Fanny Mae. I'm not a resident."

Fanny Mae trumpeted through her bulbous nose. "You get yourself a tag anyway. I'll sell you one. Piss on them game wardens—dirty sonsabitches. Just don't leave the meat lay, Sam."

I said, "Thanks for the offer, Fanny Mae. I'm looking for Chuck Richardson. Is he working down here this afternoon?"

"You're looking for Richardson, huh? I thought you come to get your pipes cleaned. Yeah, he's here. Out back eating his lunch, last time I noticed."

Chuck Richardson, in blue coveralls and heavy workman's boots, was sitting on a tar bucket with his lunch pail open beside him, eating a sandwich with tarry fingers. He had removed his cap to eat, and the springing afternoon wind lifted his black hair in a crested iridescent plume like a Homeric warrior's. I observed him with distaste and a renewed sense of my brother's appalling irresponsibility. "Hullo, Houston," the lawyer said when he saw me. "You're an eager sonofagun, aren't you? They don't open for business around here until six. Can I interest you in a cold antelope sandwich? Jenny made enough for two."

I declined the sandwich but accepted a beer and sat with it on a sawhorse a couple of yards away. I pulled the tab and took a long drink before I said, "I have some interesting news to tell you about."

"And I have some information for you. But you go first."

"I found the girl," I began—and stopped. To my astonishment, I discovered that Karen MacPherson was the last person in the world I cared to discuss with Mr. Chuck Richardson—or anyone else for that matter.

"The girl?"

"You know: *the*—"

"Of course." He caught up with me in a rush. "You think there *is* a woman, then?"

"There's a woman, all right."

"Meaning an attractive one?"

"Quite. In my opinion, at least."

"Does this local siren have a name?"

I told him her name.

"How did you find her?"

I described the first meeting outside the Railroader Café, leaving out the episode of the note. I explained how I had gone to the hospital the evening before for an Ace bandage to wrap a sore ankle with and found her in the director's office, working late. "I heard they hired a new director up there," Richardson said.

"She's the one." She had seen straight through my story about the missing friend, while being too polite to say so; probably she had assumed that she was herself the reason for my visit. But she had given me the information I wanted—no emergency admittances for the past seventy-two hours except for a rancher who had broken his neck herding cattle on a three-wheeler—and I had left in something under three minutes.

"Any mention made," Richardson asked, "of your brother?"

"No," I said, already regretting the impulse that had made me drive into town to tell him anything at all.

"Did Miss MacPherson strike you as the kind of girl that enjoys having affairs?"

I said, "Most girls do, don't they? How would I know?"—and felt my face glare like a flash fire under Richardson's surprised gaze. "Damnit, Houston," the lawyer said, "why the hell do I keep letting myself into cases where the client knows better than his attorney does where he's going, and how, and what he's going to do when he gets there?" From inside the Doll House Fanny Mae's masculine voice rose in a raucous outburst that caused him to smile unexpectedly. "How'd you like to be working for that?"

"She's probably telling you to get up off your ass and go back to work."

"She's already tried that. She won't do it a second time."

"Get out of the kitchen, you goddamn bitches!" Fanny Mae screamed.

I said, "They say her bark's always been worse than her bite, but if I were a dog I wouldn't let anybody talk to me like that."

Richardson's eyes twinkled. "I hear it every afternoon about this time," he said. "The girls don't seem to mind."

"I suppose not. It's probably the least thing in a girl's life."

"Room and board and a tight roof over your heads," Fanny Mae shouted. "Lay around all day sleeping, get fat on three square meals a day—ungrateful bitches!" she yelled.

The twinkle died suddenly in his eyes. "Let me tell you my news now," Richardson said.

"What's that?" The conversation was like a bad taste in my mouth; I felt strangely and inexplicably depressed.

"I was invited to City Hall for a levee yesterday afternoon. It seems the mayor is anxious to do a deal."

"What sort of a deal?" The real mystery, it occurred to me, was what a woman like this one could possibly have seen in my brother.

"In return for my persuading Jack to plead guilty to involuntary manslaughter, he wants to fix things with Judge Thurlow. All this is contingent upon Joad's actually dying, of course."

From the house came the clash of what sounded like hurled pans, punctuated by Fanny Mae's shouts and a brisk sequence of thudding noises. "That's odd. What do you suppose could be in it for him?"

"I have no idea. There has to be something, though."

"There has to be." I was thinking that there was something attractive about Miss Karen MacPherson beyond mere good looks; a demure quality that, in registering my interest, somehow suggested her own.

"What do you think?" the lawyer asked.

"You mean about Joe Edwards's offer? Christ, *I* don't know. It could just be the answer to everything, I suppose."

"What do you mean, the answer to everything?"

"The easiest way out for everybody. Including me."

"I see." Chuck Richardson balled the sandwich papers,

compacted the beer can between his hands, and dropped everything inside the lunch pail. "Did Miss MacPherson bother to mention how Frank Joad was doing when you spoke with her last night?"

I stared at him for what felt like a full half-minute before answering: The fact of the fellow's presence under the same roof had simply not occurred to me. "I didn't think to ask," I said finally, feeling foolish.

"Get out of here, you greedy twats!" Fanny Mae screamed. "And stay out!" We both turned to see her standing in the door gripping in one hand a small white poodle with a pink bow around its neck, while kicking massively at another, identical dog on the ground. As it fled with a yelp, she hurled its sister after it before closing the door with a bang.

"A classic example of what Freud called negative transference," Richardson remarked. "The poor woman probably always dreamed of running a finishing school for young ladies instead."

He replaced the cap on his head and stood from the tar bucket as the snapping sounds, flat and unmistakable, came in quick succession. I saw through the bracing of the sawhorse the lawyer drop to his knees and flatten himself on the ground behind the bucket, and splinters of wood flying from the fresh yellow boards. I stretched myself on my belly with my arms over my head, hearing nothing in the world but the quick carefully spaced shots that immediately succeeded the chip-chip-chip of the bullets and dissolved time into a calm and measureless infinity. The shooting stopped but I continued to lie flat until I heard around me the familiar sounds awakening like birds at dawn and lifted my head cautiously from beneath my arms. Behind the tar bucket Richardson lay in an identical position. We looked at one another. "Somebody just sent us a message," he said.

I stared at the high sagebrush flat behind the Doll House. "Whoever he was, he was shooting from up there."

"I couldn't be sure, but that was certainly my impression."

We stood warily and the lawyer picked up his hat, dusted it off, and replaced it on his head.

"If you'd only asked, I could have given you a little basic advice about getting involved with the Clemson Walker family in the first place," I said.

While Bette poured her drink Jenny surveyed discreetly the line of bent heads along the bar and the slouched dark forms at the little tables beyond them, without discovering the wiry unmistakable figure that—even when nearly unconscious from whiskey—never lost the furiously rigid posture that distinguished it among the other drinkers. "Your friend's been in here several times this week," Bette said as she put the glass in front of her. "With his girlfriend," she added maliciously.

"He has a girlfriend?"

"Can you believe it? She keeps him on a short leash, too. They were in for an hour yesterday afternoon and he drank nothing but ginger ale the whole time."

"Who is she?"

"I don't know her name, but she works at the hospital. I saw her there last spring when the kid had her tonsils out. She's kind of pretty, but she acts like a snob and dresses like my grandmother."

185

Bette went to serve a customer at the end of the bar while Jenny sipped whiskey and water through a straw and hugged the barstool with her knees as she sat brooding. Although she was aware that Jack Walker had never been more than an elaborate romantic fantasy, she felt that some part of her had nevertheless been crushed. By the time she finished the drink the early shift from the construction site was starting to come in and Bette's face was flushed and hectic-looking. "You want another of that or what?" she asked.

"No thanks. What time do they usually come in?"

"Who's that?" Bette's broad face was smooth and innocent.

"You know who, smartass!"

"Well, they've only been in twice. Yesterday it was about five, I think."

The revolving beer keg with the clock face in it said almost a quarter to three. "I'll have one more," Jenny said, "and then I have to run."

She nursed the drink while the clock hands crept forward and the fragmented shadows on the square touched, interpenetrated, and merged in a mat of solid blue. She was thinking that if Chuck were not successful and he went to jail, perhaps this girl, if she really were a snob, would have nothing more to do with him. She imagined herself writing to him in prison telling him that she loved him and believed in him and understood what he was suffering because she had suffered it too. She was mentally composing the letter line by line when through the window she saw a man approaching and slipped off the stool. It was Houston Walker, his face white as a sheet, looking as if he had seen a ghost. Jenny put down her money, snatched her purse from the bar, and made her way as quickly as she could without running among the tables and through the door at the rear of the building.

It opened into an alley which by late afternoon was already in shade, but the sudden access even of this attenuated light was like a hand laid across her eyes. When the hand was taken away, she saw the nose of the garishly painted hearse pointed at her and a long-haired man in blue denim slipping a hunting rifle behind the seat of it. He turned to face her, and Jenny stood staring at the familiar weak, ineffectual face with its watery pale eye, scraggly mustache, and receding chin, the rusty black eyepatch clamped tightly in place like a porthole. "Hello, Waldo," Jenny said. "When did they let you out?"

He grinned, showing blackened teeth in a gapped pink mouth. "Three and a half months or so. Not too long."

"They said you were up for life."

"I was. Some dick discovered what they called exterminatin evidence and my lawyer got the sentence overturned."

"Then you didn't really kill your wife?"

"Hell, Maggie was only a girlfriend. Sure I killed her."

"And you just walked out of that jail like a free man?"

"Not *like* a free man, baby. I *am* free."

"No," she said, "you're not. You never will be, either."

"I paid," Waldo told her. "I done my time accordin to what they had on me. It ain't my fault if what they had wasn't everthin they was."

"But it was a lie!" Jenny cried.

"Sure it was a lie. That's what the law is about is a lie. The law says it can hand a guy just so much punishment as he deserves, even though it knows it couldn't never punish him enough if he had ten lifetimes for it to do it to him in. It says it because it knows they ain't no way a guy can be punished unless that guy is ready and willin to punish his own self. I may be poor but I ain't stupid—not that stupid, anyway."

The air seemed to have chilled considerably while they were talking. Jenny shivered and hugged herself involuntarily with her bare arms. "You could try," she suggested.

Again he showed her the double row of blackened teeth as he rocked slightly on his heels in the scuffed and bulging running shoes. "I heard about Willie Munger gettin shot while I was in. Too bad, but them things happens. Looks like you come through pretty good though. Been tellin a few lies yourself, I bet."

Jenny fell back a step as if he had shoved her. "I have to go home now," she said in a breathless voice.

"Go on home then," Waldo said. "I ain't keepin you, am I?" He pointed above her at the rickety stairs rising to the rental apartments over the Bare Garden. "I'm number 2D. You're in town someday and got the time, stop up and visit."

She pressed her pocketbook tightly with her arm and started walking along the alley; when she had gone around the corner of the last building and had the square in sight, she broke into a hard run. The vinyl upholstery of the car seat seared the backs of her bare legs like a griddle, but she drove fast for several blocks before she stopped in front of the supermarket to roll the windows down and get her breath back.

Finally, her pulse and lungs restored to normal activity, she drove on out of town past the cemetery where the coveralled caretaker with his rake and spade stooped solicitously on the greensward above the negligent and patient dead.

From ten thousand feet Skull Creek Ranches looked not just insignificant, it looked negligible. The tin roofs of the trailer and the two houses burned amid the sprawl of the surrounding outbuildings with a fierce irreducible glare; directly below us the creek meandered through thick willow beside the road that exactly replicated the pattern, and I saw the livid red scratch on the meadow from which my father had taken off in the blue-and-white Maule on his last flight almost twenty-five years ago. Then the houses slid behind us and I saw where the creek chuted down through the black timber from the overgrown lot with the Homestead like a large gray stump at the middle of it. Tom Fuller's own Maule, painted red and white, flew with a smooth threshing sound of its single engine, the blur of the propeller less substantial beyond the nose than a thumbprint on glass. "Of course my biggest mistake was to respond to that telegram in the first place," I said.

Tom Fuller gazed through the Plexiglas window and shook

his head. He was in his early sixties now, an even six-footer, lean and taut-muscled, with fine silvering hair trimmed close over the ears and skin the color of cured tobacco leaf. He had on a tan aviator's shirt, creased white slacks, and polished yellow cowboy boots. "I don't see as how you had much choice, Sam. This family business has got a guy cornered, most of the time."

Tom Fuller had been for me, a boy of eighteen, the father I never had. Handsome, dynamic, and entirely worldly, powerful, and exuding a sense of power and success, he had at the same time possessed a remarkable talent for making a raw, inexperienced, and lonely youth feel himself, if not quite a man, at least a budding equal. For thirty-six hours following the shooting attack on Richardson and myself I had considered the situation from every angle. Then I had phoned Tom Fuller. "You do a lot of flying still?" I asked him.

"Take her up every weekend, summer and winter, long as the weather's good."

"When I get back to Africa I want to take lessons myself. Knowing how to handle an airplane comes in pretty handy in my business." For ten years I had been talking about learning to fly, without ever having done it. Off the wing of the plane on the passenger side the long ridges patched irregularly with green and black were displaced abruptly by a dark depthless blue, and when I looked back to Tom again I found myself staring along the underside of the red-and-white wing on which the airplane appeared to pivot.

"So you're looking forward to getting back to Africa and chasing the critters some more, huh?"

"Damn right, just as soon as I can get my folks straightened away. I've got a bunch of money invested in the safari business and besides, it beats having to work for a living."

The Maule made a low pass along a ridge. I saw tall pine trees spoke by like matchsticks, and from a small high park a herd of elk broke and disappeared into the timber.

"About this shooting the other day," Tom Fuller said. "Where'd you get the idea there's drugs involved, Sam?"

"It's the only explanation that makes sense, isn't it? He's tied himself up with the bastards, no telling how tight. Now they're going to do whatever it is they have to do to see that he doesn't have a chance to squeal in court." Another explanation that had occurred to me was that the affair was in some way related to the man I had hit with my car the week before. Each night now that moth's face with human features floated before me like a gibbous moon and I would wake in a cold sweat and lie for what seemed hours under the thin covers, hearing the voices of my parents entwined in the endless nightmare of the half-awake.

"I've heard plenty of things said about your brother over the years," Fuller said, "but never that he was part of anything like what you're talking about."

We flew for a while without speaking across the parallel ridges, red along the talused eastern slopes and black with pine on the gentler ones facing to the west. "That sure as hell is fine-looking timber," Tom Fuller said at last.

"You're damn right it's good timber. The Old Man put me through the University of Virginia just by borrowing against it. Then when he got in tight ten years ago he got out of it again by selling off a few trees. The best stuff is west of Elk Creek, though. The timber company wanted to take that too but he wasn't selling at any price in those days. There's hundreds of thousands of prime board feet down there, worth two and a half or three million bucks, and easy access as far as Elk Creek where East Fork comes in. After that you'd need to build a mile and three-quarters or so of road, but it's a low pass, not too steep."

Fuller laughed. "Your grandfather always lands on his feet somehow, don't he? You know, Sam, there's been plenty of times in the past thirty years that I've felt downright grateful to have lost that case. Considering how bad he hates me just for trying to get him convicted, I hate to think how he'd feel if I'd actually succeeded in doing it."

"Hell, Tom, you were doing him a favor. He got some of the best publicity of his career out of that trial. There isn't anything folks in this state like better than to see a rancher run some federal pen-pusher off his property with a shotgun, except seeing the guy get away with it afterward."

"I don't mind taking credit for that, then. I was just a pup in those days, Sam—hardly knew my way around a court of law. I *will* tell you I've improved considerable since then, though: I was a fairly efficient county attorney by the time your granddad helped Bull Humbel throw me out. Not that I blame him for that, of course—never have, All's fair in love, war, and politics, you know."

The plane was climbing again now. In the middle distance I saw sharp mountain folds receding westward under layers of heat and summer haze, and the long crystalline glitter of the enfolded lake. Tom Fuller said, "Let's do a flyby over Lake Adeline."

"Why not, as long as we're up here."

The Maule descended short of the lake and flew low above the water between raw-looking purple cliffs crested with black timber. An outfitter led a string of pack mules and several dudes on horses along the trail at the water's edge, and in the middle of the lake somebody was fishing from a raft crudely constructed of driftwood logs. I knew that raft: Clarice and I had built it together in the summer of '63 and used it for many summers afterward, always remembering to take it from the water and drag it into the trees when we were through with it. At the end of the peninsula where the lake forked, a helicopter squatted on the open shore at the water's edge. I glared down at it as the Maule swept upward again.

"What the hell is that doing there?"

"Seismographers," Fuller said. "The Studds brothers have had their choppers in here all summer, shooting holes."

I saw a million bright points pricking through from behind

the sky and the narrow orange path the fire made across the black water. I smelled the heat of it in the worn flannel of her old shirt and on the warm flesh beneath it. As children, Clarice and I had considered Lake Adeline to be our lake. We would swim and fish all day, at evening build up a fire and have a fine fish roast, and at night zip our bags together and sleep under the stars, hugging each other for warmth until dawn. "Those dirty sons of bitches," I said carefully.

"Everybody got to eat, Sam," Tom Fuller answered me mildly. "By the way: Candy tells me you two have a dinner date tonight."

"That's right, we do."

"I sure as heck am glad to see you and her buddies again. Just between us, her mother and I have been kind of worried about her the last couple of years."

"Seems like she's doing fine, to me."

"Prettier than ever too, ain't she? I tell you what now, Sam: Of course, I'm her father and a real stud-proud sonofabitch and all that, but for my money anyway, that little gal just gets skinnier and sexier with every birthday, even if the no-good bastard she married didn't notice it." The Maule banked steeply, dipped a wing, and leveled out toward the southeast like a homing pigeon. "Well, anyhow: Here's to a red-hot date tonight, Sam!"

"Thanks."

"It's just really great to see you two friends again."

"As far as I'm concerned, we never quit."

Tom Fuller nodded. "Let me tell you a father's secret: I don't think she ever did, either. But what the hell, Sam, you know how it is. When one of the families is dead set against a marriage, it kind of makes a girl think twice, naturally. Not to mention her parents."

"Naturally."

"I run into the Old Man two, maybe three times a year at political functions around the state. When he sees me coming he glares like George Crook meeting up with an entire Apache war party—or maybe like Geronimo meeting up with George Crook. Offhand, I'd have to say Clemson Walker is the best hater I've known in my lifetime; and, believe me, I've known some good ones."

"My brother's no slouch either."

"Sam, you got to do something about that one—and darn quick too. Otherwise, when he goes down, he's going to take what's left of the Walker family with him."

"I'm trying, aren't I? Incidentally—he's not taking me, I can promise you that. I'm planning on being back in Africa by the middle of September at the outside."

"Well, you're a young fella yet—though not that young. To tell you the truth, I sort of always figured you for a natural, Sam. Assuming you don't fool away too much of your life chasing the critters over there, you could have a big future ahead of you in this state. The name of Walker's got almost as much clout in Wyoming as the name Kennedy has in Massachusetts. If I was standing in your boots, I'd give it some thought."

A light chop had developed over the mountains, and the iron thunderheads superimposed themselves above the western peaks as if to invoke a matter of precedent. "So you're interested in learning to fly?" Fuller asked.

"I've been thinking about it."

"It ought to be a piece of cake for you, with your nerves and reflexes. One of these days when I'm not so busy with politics anymore I'll maybe get my instructor's license and give lessons. You ever been in a stall situation?"

"*Christ no.*"

"It scares the living daylights out of beginners, but actually it's a simple procedure. Would you enjoy a demonstration?"

The sun emerged from behind the clouds to throw the shadow of the plane on the green matting of trees that stretched beneath us like a safety net. I felt the perspiration spring cold along my hairline and set my teeth before I answered him. "If you like."

"It's a thrill, believe me. Here goes then."

For what seemed like a very long time nothing happened. Then the nose of the plane came up, there was a sudden absence of vibration as the engine cut out, and we were falling: lazily as a leaf but endlessly, as if there were not only no ground to catch us but no time passing us on from one moment to the next as we dropped through space. I saw Tom Fuller, his face cheesy and damp, struggling with the stick and, through the windscreen, the forest spinning like a slow green maelstrom with what looked like the Homestead at the center of it. I felt a lift, and then I was staring once again into the clear blue between drifting small clouds and fighting back wave after wave of nausea.

Tom Fuller said, in a voice that was a faint approximation of his ordinary one, "It's really quite a simple procedure, if you remember to keep your cool."

———————

Tom Fuller set the Maule down gently on the landing strip and taxied across the grass apron behind the house where, holding our hats secure against the wind, we guyed the wings. "Come in and have a drink, Sam," he said. "You look like you could do with a stiff one, and I know I damn well can."

The house had been built in the wide lawn-hugging style of the fifties and retained a shiny new appearance, as if it were polished each weekend like an expensive car. We went in under a low tinkle of wind chimes through a sliding glass door that made part of the west wall of the big living room and across the pile carpet to the maple-wood bar curving smooth as ribbon candy against the off-white-painted wall covered with signed portrait photographs of politicians half-obscured behind the relucent glass. "Now then, Sam. What's yours?"

"Whatever you're drinking will be fine."

"I'm having Cardhu. It's a fine single-malt whiskey, very hard to come by in this neck of the woods. The only way I can get it is through a good buddy of mine on the State Liquor Commission."

"I'm familiar with it, of course. I'll have the same, on the rocks."

He filled two highball glasses with ice and poured the whiskey over with a generous hand. He set two cocktail napkins on the bar, arranging the corners carefully to make a diamond shape, and placed the glasses at the exact center of the napkins. Then he raised the nearer one. "Welcome home, Sam! Don't make it so long next time. Going a tad gray behind the ears, aren't you? It'll be on your chest next, then in the short hairs. That's when a fella knows it's time to settle down, quit chasing the girls, and start running after another kind of whore."

I tasted the drink while I studied the framed photograph, its colors a little faded now, of Candy looking moonfaced, healthy, and pink, with wheaten hair; I guessed it had been taken when she was about sixteen, which would make it the year before I was smitten. For years I had stared straight through her before bursting, suddenly and without warning, into flame, like a bottle of nitroglycerin put away on a shelf. The truth about women is that they themselves so rarely have a thing to do with it, knowing which gives a man the advantage—women, unlike politicians, becoming whores less through lust than through vanity. I said, "To get back to this incident the other day: Do you think I ought to have reported it to the police?"

"Hell no. They're too busy shaking down the city with the cooperation of the local pols."

"What do you suggest, then?"

"Keep a sharp lookout. And buy yourself a good sidearm."

"I did that already this morning."

"Well, I wish I knew what else to tell you, Sam. Ready for another of those? Mary'll be home anytime now. She works out at the rec center from three to four every afternoon to avoid the after-five crowd. I know she'll be tickled pink to see you."

"I'll have one more." I would drink this one fast, I was

thinking, and take off. There were plenty of things you could discuss with Mary Fuller, among them golf, bowling, contract bridge, Hawaiian beaches, bad detective fiction, diet, aerobic exercise, and breeding golden retrievers, none of which happened to be a conversational specialty of mine. Tom Fuller refilled our glasses and we toasted one another again, solemnly. He said, "How would you feel about me having a word with the governor concerning your brother?"

"The governor?"

"It just might be I could talk him into leaning on Bull Humbel a little. Humbel is a stubborn booger but he might jump at the chance to do the state Democratic chairman a favor—even if he happens to be me—let alone the guv. Because Bull is the kind of fella that at his age is sooner or later going to want something for himself. As a matter of fact, I've been hearing rumors lately that he already does."

I had heard the pop of gravel in the drive as he finished speaking, and now Mary Fuller was fumbling around two brown-paper bags at the handle of the sliding door. Even at almost forty a man is not too old to feel a certain sinking feeling at sight of his girlfriend's mother. "I suppose it couldn't do any harm," I agreed, taking a fortifying slug of the whiskey.

Well," Jenny had remarked significantly as he tucked the legal portfolio under his arm, "here you go again." In the clear, almost Grecian light the diaphanous smock revealing the firmness of rounded breasts, waist, and thighs had given her the appearance, as she stood behind the threshold supporting Bret on the pad of her hip, of Andromache bidding Hektor farewell as he departs to meet the Achaians in battle; while the child, a product of his last significant legal foray, snatched with chubby hands at his father's face and hat. Still he felt very little heroic—the opposite in fact—as he climbed the courthouse steps and strode across the parquet floor on which his boots rang out in the familiar warning uproar at which he imagined apprehensive faces starting up above typewriters and computer consoles, behind each one of them a single shared thought: *Here comes Trouble again.* Because he was Trouble, Richardson admitted: Trouble (as it so often seemed) without particular or coherent motive, Trouble without a grudge to nourish or an ax to grind, but Trouble, with a surfeit of natural talent, nevertheless. Joe Edwards had implied as much and more when, one evening recently, he had called to decline the mayor's offer. Though himself in agreement with his client's decision, he remained fundamentally perplexed concerning the logical processes by which it had been reached. If Jack Walker, Richardson thought, wished above everything for a quiet and undramatic settlement out of court, surely Edwards's offer had been his best opportunity. If, on the other hand, it wasn't his highest interest, then what—in the name of God—was?

He hastened across the rotunda, hearing the familiar mocking applause issuing faintly from the shadows and poignantly aware of a powerful feeling of *déjà vu* as he made for the stairs which, in his impatience, he would have used even in the absence of the OUT OF ORDER sign hung on the elevator door. And yet, he thought, breasting the wide steps two at a time, it was all in a larger sense so different from the last time, when he had acted on a mere hunch that developed only later into belief; while in the present case he believed implicitly in the moral innocence of Jack Walker as a respecter of human life, if not of the sanctity of another man's marriage bond.

He reached the third-floor landing on a rising pulse and went on at a lope along the linoleumed corridor between doors of polished golden oak inset with panes of pebbled glass to the wider door at the end of it, sternly lettered in black. With his hand already on the knob he paused to listen to the gasping voice, lifted weakly in what might have been protest, anger, or even laughter, on the other side. While it was no fault of his own that the old man lacked both common sense and good grace enough to step down from an office he had not for years possessed the mental or physical stamina to execute, still simple human decency suggested that this was an inappropriate moment to confront His Honor the justice of the peace. It was unlikely he would be with Judge Thurlow for long, since he had nearly as much difficulty in talking for two or three minutes at a time as in keeping awake for twenty. Three doors down on the right was the men's lavatory, a spacious, high-ceilinged room with a tall embrasured window giving on the courthouse pines and the sharp blue mountains to the north. Now his boots barely whispered as he made a stealthy retreat and slipped around the heavy oak door. He paused at the washstand to remove his hat and slick down his back hair with his pocket comb. Then he set the portfolio against the leg of the toilet stall and crossed to the open window where, resting his arms on the high sill, he lit a cigar and stood puffing on it while he contemplated the sleek white side of the county jail, visible in patches through the trees. It struck him suddenly as comic that they were—the three of them— inextricably connected by the fact of having each one been temporarily lodged there.

He thought of her seated—only two years ago!—on the cot bed with the drawing pad on her knees, plump and budding in gray jailhouse pajamas; and of Jack Walker the evening before, gray-faced and woodenly upright in the dilapidated Barcalounger. He loved his wife—as, he was beginning to realize, he had always loved her—without believing in her; while, in the case of Jack, he believed in him without loving him. But could you really love, he wondered, and not believe; or could you truly believe without loving? He didn't know the answer to either question, and right now he didn't care. His interest in both of them was no longer grounded upon either caring or feeling, but upon curiosity—the clinical interest of the scientist. It was why, he thought, he was able to go on confronting the situation day after day without coming a little apart. He got out Old One Eye's latest letter and read it again. Then he refolded it and, with the delicate precision of a lepidopterist handling a rare specimen, put it back in his pocket.

Someone on the other side of the door rattled the knob impatiently and he shouted, "Just a minute!," before removing his elbows from the sill and giving a final lick to his hair. The knob sounded again, peremptorily this time, and he crossed quickly to unlock the door, which swung inward from the very frail figure of a bent old gentleman with clotted blue eyes in a brown face like an old half sole, wearing a red nylon windbreaker and an enormous Stetson hat and leaning feebly on a pair of aluminum canes. "Good morning, Your Honor," Richardson said. "Sorry to have kept you waiting."

The J.P. gave him an unexpectedly keen glance from his watery and cataracted eyes. "Howdy, young man. You back here on another one of them DWI charges?" His Honor's memory, though mostly a ruin, could be embarrassingly accurate at times.

"No, sir, I'm not. I'm here to deliver some papers to Judge Thurlow's office."

The justice continued to glare at him with slowly fading suspicion, as if to say, Well, you look up to no damn good to me. Then, without further remark, he shuffled four-leggedly through the door Richardson held respectfully for him. When the old man was well clear of it he stepped out into the hall and was nearly around the corner when he heard the clatter of metal on tile, followed by a dry rustling sound like that of a scarecrow falling and a thin howl of rage. Richardson turned on his heel and went back to the lavatory, where His Honor Jake O'Connell lay on his back on the floor with his feet inside the stall and his canes about him. His shriveled little eyes glittered with fury when he caught sight of Richardson. He cried weakly, "Get me up outa here, you young sonofabitch!"

Richardson helped the old man to his feet and picked up the canes for him. When His Honor was properly braced again he handed him the Stetson, after brushing it off with a solicitousness that seemed ostentatious even to himself. "Is that thing *yours?*" O'Connell gasped, pointing a trembling claw at the leather portfolio, one end of which barely protruded from the adjoining stall into which it had been kicked.

Mortified, he bent to retrieve it. "I apologize, Your Honor. I forgot—"

But the old man brandished the cane in his face. "Don't apologize!" he screamed thinly. "Just—wait on me! Sonofabitch elevator busted half an hour ago. Help me down the stairs, gosh durn it! Can't make it by myself."

He stood once again by the window, watching the pair of horned owls that came every year to drowse among the pinecones bobbing above the courthouse roof. Their flat round eyes were yellow and unimpressed, and it seemed to Richardson that one of the birds winked at him as he looked at them. When the old fellow was finished he held the door for him once more and guided him along the corridor to the stairwell, where he offered his arm for the descent.

Nearly half an hour later he released the thin arm and watched the bent figure shuffle stiffly away beneath the enormous hat that was like a small pearly cloud hanging just above his head. Jake O'Connell was said to have been sharp as a tack a quarter of a century ago, and Richardson, as he turned again to the stairs, felt that it was a shame to do the old man as he was about to do. But a lawyer, he reassured himself, had to start somewhere; which was in the present case the fact of His Honor's neglect, on the day of Jack Walker's arraignment, to swear in one of the investigating officers, as well as the accused himself. But not, he thought, with his hand already on the newel post, not before he did the other thing which, until this moment, he had not even known that he was going to do.

Crossing the parquet floor to the telephone booth in its darkened grotto he was aware only of the rhythmic chink of silver against his striding leg. The hinged door folded smoothly back at his touch, and the nickeled slot accepted the coin without hesitation. He dialed the number from memory and stood waiting in the closed-up booth for the call to go through. O.K. Pickett answered on the third ring. "O.K."

"Chuck Richardson. I was just fixing to give you a ring."

"Does that mean you have some information for me?"

"I got something. Not a whole bunch yet."

"Let's hear what you've got, then."

"This Joad fellow seems to have hung out with some pretty shady company when he was around here."

"Shady meaning what?"

"You know. Them druggies and such."

"Is that a fact."

"He had a wife living with him for a while, but she split. I ain't been able to find where to yet."

"I see. Anything else?"

"That's all for now, Chuck. I'll give a holler when I got anymore to tell you."

"Thanks, O.K."

"You bet. Anything else I can do for you?"

He drew a long breath and expelled it, before he heard himself say, "As a matter of fact, there is."

"Okay."

"It's about my wife," Richardson told him, and paused to await the reaction. He never got it.

Nilsa Martinez called again—collect—as we were finishing supper. This time she was querulous. She had not received, she said, the money for postage plus fifty-five seventy-five for the day's wages. Didn't Mr. Walker want his book back? Mr. Hemingway was a very famous writer writing a regular sports column for the *New York Times,* read every day by millions of people. Certainly fifty-five seventy-five plus carfare to and from the post office was not asking too much for a valuable book worth many times the amount? The friend with whom she lived was starting to complain: There was no space for books in the apartment except on top of the TV. Also she was afraid the roaches were going to eat it. If Mr. Walker wanted his book back he must send fifty-nine seventy-five, plus thirty dollars for the inconvenience, by money order *now* to her, Nilsa Martinez, at the Ravenswood Arms, 19 East Thirty-third Street, New York, New York. When she shut up finally I was able to explain to her that the mail stage out of Fontenelle had been attacked and robbed by bandits and the m.o. I had sent the week before presumably stolen. I promised that if she could hold off the roommate and the cockroaches for a week or ten days, I would send another order as soon as stage service was restored. Her voice by the time she got off the phone sounded satisfied, and I immediately dialed the Forty-fifth Precinct in New York and spent thirty-five minutes making a detailed report to an Officer Chavez, whom I tried unsuccessfully to cajole into paying a visit to the Ravenswood Arms. Then I went upstairs to my room to drink half of a fifth of whiskey, reread *Heart of Darkness*, and stare at the spreading water stain on the wallpaper. At last I capped what remained of the bottle, changed my shirt, and drove into town in the little Jap, which had developed an irritating hesitation. After checking the fuel filter for dirt and the fan belt for slippage, I had telephoned the company in Salt Lake, where they recommended that I drive the car to the Toyota dealership in Rock Springs or wait for a replacement to be delivered to Fontenelle. Having chosen the second option, I was prepared to wait a long time.

In town I drove directly to Al's Supper Club, where I learned that Candy had left early feeling ill. Candy sick was not my idea of a pleasant evening; also I was beginning to be bored with her. Perhaps twenty-one years can actually change a person that much, or perhaps it is impossible to see a person for what she actually is when you are a callow romantically minded youth of eighteen in love with the most popular girl in school. I ordered whiskey and water and stood at the bar with my foot on the rail and my arms folded on the padded front, watching the replay of the afternoon's ball game on the television until an unsteady voice spoke my name from behind. Most Likely to Succeed had been drinking heavily. He clapped a trembling hand on my shoulder and lurched a little from the perpendicular as he asked, "You goin to be up to my clearance sale, Sam?"

"You're having a clearance sale?"

"You mean you didn't see the notice in the paper?"

"I don't read the paper."

"Well, me an the old lady is sellin everthin: house, furniture, vehicles—everthin. Them sonsabitches has got me by the short hairs, Sam. I got to sell off all I own just to avoid goin bankrupt, and even then it's goin to be close. You wanna buy a twenny-three-foot boat with a one-fifty-one Evinrude an a boat trailer, I'm sellin em dirt-cheap on Saturday. You wanna buy a nylon hot-air balloon, never been used, I'm sellin that off too— dirt-cheap, like I tole you. That's what happens anymore to a guy that tries to live the American Way."

I took my foot off the rail, excused myself, and went around the end of the bar to the pay phone and the battered directory hanging on its chain. I opened the book to the M section, found the name I was looking for, and jotted the address onto a scrap of paper I found in my wallet. Then I slipped out the back door of the place and into my car.

The address was for one of the trailer parks on the northern end of town; I drove there in under four minutes. Gravel popped softly beneath the tires and the lights of the Jap slashed boldly across the darkened windows as I cruised the separating lanes searching for number 12. The car clock said 9:57 but I was assuming that, with her schedule, she was still up. Number 12 was painted white with a green belt around it, an older model but trim-looking in a well-kept yard with a new fence of yellow boards separating it on one side from its neighbor. The lights were on in the forward end of it and the vehicle parked by the gate was the little white Bronco I had last seen outside the Fontenelle Café. I slipped the Jap in beside it and stepped out; a woman's figure moved across a square of lighted window and back again. I pushed through the gate and went on over the lawn and climbed the flight of wooden steps to the front door. The bell when I pressed it made a faint chiming sound within.

"Good evening, Mr. Walker," Karen MacPherson said when she opened the door. "I couldn't think who'd be stopping by this time of night. But won't you come in anyway?"

I stepped across the threshold and paused just inside the

trailer, feeling awkward as well as—I realized suddenly—very drunk. "Can I get you a cup of coffee?" she offered. "I just made a fresh pot."

"Coffee at this time of night?"

"I have paperwork to do in the evening," Miss MacPherson explained. "I drink a lot of coffee. Far too much coffee. Coffee at night is what I have instead of inspiration."

I sat on the edge of the couch, cracking my knuckles and looking about the room, while she brought the coffee. The place was furnished and decorated in perfect taste highlighted by accents of the Southwest. There were serapes and small Indian rugs on the walls, and choice bits of Indian pottery on the side tables. There were potted cacti and yucca, and spider plants hanging in macramé in the windows. The effect was that of a carefully designed home in an expensive residential section of Taos or Santa Fe. Karen MacPherson had on clean blue jeans and a silk blouse with a rounded collar and a Jaeger sweater over it that set off her eyes, which I noticed were cobalt blue rather than violet, very dark, unshaded, and direct. Her ash-blonde hair was cut below her ears and simply styled, her skin was a delicate pink-and-white, and her figure belonged to the class that makes a man feel that whatever it was he ever wanted in life, he hasn't got it yet. "How do you take your coffee, Mr. Walker?" she asked.

"Black will be fine, no sugar. The name, by the way, is Houston."

She served it to me in a cup and saucer, which she placed on a napkin on the coffee table. "Can I bring you anything else—Houston? I don't keep much around the house, I'm afraid. I have some cookies."

"Just coffee is fine."

She brought a mug for herself and sat on the other end of the couch with her legs crossed, holding the coffee balanced on her knee. "You two really could be twins," Karen MacPherson said, "except for his beard and your looking more . . . mature. Well, couldn't you?" she insisted.

"Some people have said so." Her accent had a trace of the Southwest in it, not enough for a lethal effect. I remembered the Marlboros and withdrew them and the matches gratefully from my pocket. "Is it all right with you if I smoke?"

She shrugged. "It's your funeral, not mine."

I struck a match on my thumbnail, applied it to the end of the cigarette, and sucked defiantly. "Hell, that's the least of my worries."

She looked indignant. "You mean, death is?"

"Not death as such, but that kind of death—the long, lingering, peaceful kind."

"You think lung cancer is *peaceful?* I've seen—!"

"Compared to the alternatives, yes."

"What alternatives?"

"Getting trampled by an irritable buffalo. Having your scalp pulled over your face by a flirtatious lioness."

"My God," Karen MacPherson said. "What is it you do for a living, anyway?"

"I'm a professional big-game hunter in Africa. He didn't tell you?"

"You shoot dangerous animals for a living and he rides bulls for fun. How did the two of you learn to be so violent?"

"I rode bulls too, until I was only a little younger than he is now. Actually, I don't think of what I do as being particularly violent." And when I saw her eyebrows lift, "What I mean is, it's not essentially a physical encounter."

"What it really is," she said, "is anger."

"Who's angry?"

"You are, of course, and so is he. All of your family are angry, all of the time."

I said, "You seem to know my folks pretty well. How well exactly do you know *him?*"

"He's a friend."

"How good a friend?"

She set the mug down firmly on the coffee table. "I don't believe that's any of your business, is it?"

"Anything's my business, if I want it to be. He is my brother, after all."

"Then I suppose that makes me your business, too?"

"Girls who hand notes to strange men on the street usually do wind up being somebody's business."

She flushed and looked at her lap. "It honestly didn't occur to me to wonder what you would think. I'm not really much of a self-conscious person."

"Do you want me to tell you what I thought?"

"If you want to."

"I thought: Good for him, at the precocious age of twenty-nine he's finally found himself a woman, and a damned attractive one at that."

She flushed again as she reached for the cup and saucer. "Some more coffee? And then I have work to do."

"Please, sweetheart."

"I'm not your sweetheart!" the girl flashed.

I caught her before she could get off the sofa and pulled her down with one arm about her shoulders and the other around her waist. Her mouth parted in astonishment, letting me feel the hardness of her little teeth as I drew her against me, her body flopping and jerking with the firm muscularity of a fish's. Then like a fish she was out of my arms and away, her cobalt eyes dilated and her teeth still showing. "Get out!" Karen MacPherson said. "Get out now, and don't ever come back."

She held the door for me and I went past her and through it into the night, where I stood for a moment, breathing in the thin cold air. Almost overhead the Great Dipper swung; idly I traced the distance from the point star of the cup to Polaris, which appeared too wavering and faint to bear the burden of its navigational centricity. In that instant, as I started down the wooden steps, I had forgotten all about the girl.

The concussion occurred as an interval of sharp pain between blinding light and a more brilliant darkness. I fell, irretrievably, through a vertical tunnel whose invisible walls dissolved abruptly to eject me into the shining void beyond which, as I lay staring, the silver pinpoint of the North Star appeared winking, beckoning me to come in closer, closer. . . .

---

*id been watching for weeks to see would he do it or not and of
course being my brother he finally did and i left him stretched there
on the ground to wake up looking at the stars*

*theres a kind of knowledge a man can live with like what his
father was and what his mother and his sister actually are and a
kind that he cant such as that his own brother is willing to destroy
not only him but the woman he loves for no better reason than what
he really hates is not me myself but him in me and me in him
because we all of us once me him and clarice together loved the
same things and hated the same ones too until he being the oldest
understand first and let me take the rap for the train because he
said i was still young and that was when i began to understand
also realizing for the first time that it doesnt matter what you are or
who it is you are descended from in this world where honor bravery
and sacrifice are just labels nobody even bothers to stick on the
package anymore and where like pablo told me when i was still a*

boy the best you can do is hold your own against the time and try and do your duty including finally the one you owe yourself

i love my quote sister unquote but i dont respect her not because of what she has done and is doing but because she is the only one of the three of us never even to begin to understand for the simple reason that she never wanted to and doesnt now if you cant freeze time you can at least freeze the human heart which at a temperature of thirtytwo degrees looks exactly the same whether it belongs to captain uncle jo my brother or my sister or even mayor edwards since in this world today businessman politician rancher or brother we are all liars and politicians now and the frontier is really closed at last and it looks as though it means to stay that way forever

IV

The motor was not much bigger than a lawnmower engine and she saw at once that they had fitted it into the car wrong in Detroit; the amazing thing was that it had run as long as it had. It looked solid, compact, and squat, like a grubby recalcitrant child, and she wondered, furiously, how Chuck could have been so careless as to have overlooked it when he bought the car for her secondhand at the dealership in Rock Springs. She stared under the hood at it for a minute, then cautiously extended a finger toward something that reminded her of a switch, extending the upper part of her body across the engine block and pressing the tender inside of her bare arm against the cowling. She jerked the arm back with a squeal of pain and brought the top of her head up hard against the underside of the hood, jarring it free from the brace which immediately collapsed sideways, causing the steel panel to fall upon her shoulders and the upper part of her back, pinning her beneath its weight. Still squealing, she fought clear of the hood and flung it back against the windshield.

215

Then she kicked the tire hard and stood pressing her clenched fists against her thighs and calling him every bad name she could think of. She had spent the afternoon in town being whirled round and round the square on a wheeled bed propelled by two muscular youths who were friends of Bette's and wanted a girl to push in the bed races at the annual Labor Day carnival. Now—sweaty, hot, and impatient, with her hair still to be washed and Bret fed before driving back with him to Fontenelle for their second anniversary dinner—she had had a breakdown six miles short of the turnoff to Black Butte. And it was all his fault. She kicked the tire again, vowing to give him five dollars and send him into town to celebrate alone at that awful Mexican restaurant where the waitresses put their hands in the food like nursery-school brats.

On every side the brown sunburnt plain swept away from her toward the broken horizon, while in the middle distance the abandoned railroad depot and the two empty frame houses that fifty years ago had been a town stared at her from their blank windows with the dumb incomprehension of cattle. Far up the asphalt ribbon of the highway a car appeared, coming from town and traveling fast, and she stepped away from her own vehicle and waved her arms at it as it approached; without slowing, it moved into the center of the road and flashed past with unabated speed, the proud sunglassed profile of the pretty blonde driver maintaining a forward position behind the wheel. Jenny gazed after the automobile with an expression of rapt outrage, and kicked the tire a third time. She opened the glove compartment and got out a clean diaper, which she knotted onto the radio antenna. Then she sat behind the wheel again where, in the rearview mirror, she could watch the westbound traffic topping the last low hill. She had to wait only a minute or two before the second car appeared.

In the distance it looked like a determined pink worm crawling on the black downslope of the road. The painted eye on the front of it loomed larger and wider in the mirror, and then the hearse groaned to a halt beside her with a clatter of dying tappets and idled there as Waldo smirked at her through the rolled-down window. "You got to put gas in them things sometimes," he said. "They don't go by themselves."

Jenny stared at him contemptuously. "I put gas in it, smartass."

"What's the trouble then?"

"They put the engine in sideways. It never seemed to make any difference until now."

Something huge rushed at them from behind and passed on a long thunderclap of air with a warning blast from its horn; with misgiving, she watched the blunt gray stern of the trailer hurtle into the distance. "Lemme pull this crate out of the way," Waldo suggested, "and I'll have a look at her for you."

The hearse made her think of the gaudily painted vans Paoli Brothers had used to transport the circus in. She watched it pull ahead and lumber onto the shoulder of the highway, and then Waldo walked back and thrust himself under the back-flung hood. Jenny climbed out of the car and stood at a distance from him as he felt among the hoses and wires, untightening and rescrewing parts. "Can you make it go?" she demanded impatiently. "It was running fine until a few minutes ago."

Waldo stepped back and wiped his hands on his pants. "Got to let her cool down a couple minutes," he said. "Then I can fix her up for you in a second."

"You mean there's nothing wrong with the engine? Why did they put it in that way?"

"That's how they do with them little cars anymore. All's that's wrong is a radiator connection loose. We can go set in my truck till she cools down a little."

"That's okay," Jenny told him quickly. "I guess I'll just wait here instead."

"Why stand around when you can get comfortable? Anyhow, there's a thing I been wantin to talk to you about."

She glanced back at the little car standing lonesome at the side of the road as, clutching her pocketbook tightly in both hands, she climbed in beside him in the hearse. A pile of old clothes and greasy rags lay between them on the seat and the floor was covered with road maps, old skin magazines, and discarded fast-food containers; a wood-and-brass pipe filled with ashes and a gluey residue protruded from the tray drawn out beneath the dashboard. "Lucky it was me that come along instead of some sicko," Waldo observed. A pickup truck with a young ranch wife wearing a straw cowboy hat at the wheel and three small children in the bed went by, the children waving and screaming at them as they passed. "I been hopin you was goin to stop up and visit," Waldo said. "What you been up to since I seen you last?"

"Staying home mostly."

"That ain't healthy for a pretty young girl, layin off in the country that way."

"It doesn't bother me. I like it."

"How about your friends?"

"I don't have any friends."

"Hey, that's bullshit. You got a bunch of them."

"No."

"Sure you do. You got me and Bette for starters. And another guy."

She told him, "You're not a friend. I don't know you. I don't know anything about you."

"Yeah you know me," Waldo said. "Same way as I know you—like a open book." His left hand came up and fingered the eyepatch as he spoke, as if he were preparing to slip it aside.

"Can we go back and take care of my car now?" Jenny asked.

"Better give her a couple more minutes. After we've had our little talk."

His teeth showed in a blackened grin as a Highway Patrol cruiser leaned into the curve ahead of them and rushed past, its barlight flashing, the driver's face a pale smear behind the windshield. "They say the law don't never sleep," Waldo said. "Well, they's other folks don't never neither." He extracted a toothpick from his shirt pocket and stuck it into a face that reminded her of a grinning mask. "What did you do to my car?" she demanded suddenly.

He did not answer or even look at her, while the toothpick moved up and down in front of his mouth like the slow exploring tongue of a patient snake. "Are you going to kill me now like you did your girlfriend?" Jenny asked.

Waldo chuckled. He said around the toothpick, "Killin never was my way of having fun with chicks. But it looks like we maybe have somethin to talk about after all, don't it?"

"If you have anything to say to me, tell me. Then go back there and fix my car."

Waldo removed the toothpick with two fingers and flicked it into the road. Then he took from the other pocket a letter envelope folded once over upon the contents, and handed it to her. "Everbody likes lookin at pictures," he remarked. "See what you think of them ones."

Jenny unfolded the envelope and removed the four Polaroid snapshots. She sat holding them gingerly between thumb and forefinger, staring. "You know who the girl is?" Waldo asked. She nodded. "You reckanize the other one?" And when she shook her head, "That there's Frank Joad," he told her.

She gave the snapshots a long last look before replacing them in the envelope. Waldo took it from her and stuffed it back into his shirt pocket, which she noticed he was careful to button. "What do you want for those?" Jenny asked finally.

Waldo put a fresh toothpick between his teeth and moved it ruminatively up and down. "That's what I been wanting to talk to you about, sweetheart," he said.

In the old days," Pablo explained, "your grandfather never had to bring me nothing in the summertime and fall. I'd cut me a willow branch and tie on a piece of string and a hook to catch trout with and in the evenings the deer would step out of the woods and graze along the edge of the meadow as gentle as if they hadn't even been named yet and ever two-three weeks I'd shoot me one and have fresh venison to eat. In September before we started down with the sheep I'd kill an elk and salt him down good and he'd last through almost to spring. The woods was full of fool-hens too in them days and I'd shoot them roosting or on the ground with a .22 pistol. Sometimes I'd get a shot at a coyote before he could carry off a sheep or a lamb he'd killed and then I'd have mutton for a week or two. So it was like a paradise then and I used to set out on the step with a cup of coffee and look acrost them hills and thank the good Lord for putting me up here in the mountains with the elk and the bears instead of down there in Sodom and Gomorrah."

"And Clare and I wanted to be up here with you and the sheep all summer."

"And shoulda been, too." Pablo hooked a finger inside the dirty bandanna he wore loosely knotted around his skinny neck and jerked it. "No harm ever come to nobody, man, woman, or child, in the mountains."

"How about the time that bear scared the horse out from under you and almost chewed your arm off before you could get your knife into him?" As children we—Clare and I—had liked to lie on the grass outside the wagon while Pablo retold that story.

"That wasn't no bear," Pablo said. "That was the Lord Hisself done it after I filthied myself with a woman in town the week before." He unbuttoned his shirt cuff and rolled the sleeve back on a thin muscular arm in which the pale deeply bedded scars ran parallel to one another. "I been chastised all my life," he added proudly, rolling down the sleeve, "and ever time it's been the Lord that done it—not any man, never no woman."

We were sitting opposite one another across the pulled-out table in Pablo's wagon, which was a soup can laid end to end in a wagon box with slots cut in it for windows. Pablo's bed was a bunk set across one end of the wagon; beneath it was a small built-in refrigerator, a cupboard, and the slot into which the table fitted when you were finished with it. To the left of the door in the front end of the wagon was the enameled cookstove where an ironware pot simmered beneath the pipe going up through the roof. Each of us had a mug of coffee and a hard roll in front of him and Pablo had produced a can of sweetened condensed milk to fortify the coffee and spread on the bread. I had told the Old Man what the herder had probably surmised: that I was riding up to sheep camp to check on Pablo, who my grandfather was worried might be getting whiskey from a nearby construction camp where they were building an access road into a drilling site on the West Fork of Badger Creek. In fact I had no interest whatever in Pablo, drunk or sober, but it seemed a good time to be away, with the Jap being looked over in Fontenelle and drug hoodlums sapping me cold in the middle of the night. My first action after waking up under the stars with my head resting on my rolled-up jacket and the new .38 lying stripped on my chest had been to drive to the police station, where I had parked and waited around the corner for a quarter of an hour before deciding not to go in. Even assuming that they were not already bought, there wouldn't have been a thing the cops could do besides make out a report, which struck me as a poor exchange for the questions they would be certain to ask. "You couldn't give me one of them goddamn rice-burners," the mechanic had said sourly, shaking his head as he surveyed the car, and I had agreed with him.

Pablo kept the pair of heavy Army field glasses beside him on the table; every twenty minutes or so he would heft them ostentatiously and duck outside to have a look at the sheep, whose plaintive bleats mingled with the lost sound of their distant bells. The pungent odor of sheep covered the sidehill like an old blanket, and the droppings lay everywhere in close piles among the cropped and trampled grass. The brim of Pablo's black, greasy, and nearly shapeless hat was pulled low enough over his eyes that he had to knock it back each time he fitted the glasses into the sockets of his eyes. "Even Adam," I reminded him, "got screwed by a woman."

"He didn't know to keep a good lookout in them days," Pablo explained. "Anymore a guy don't have that excuse."

"Anymore, most guys don't want it."

"That is the trouble," Pablo agreed, "with nowadays."

I drank coffee and looked through the window at the farthest mountains where the yellow tumuli of smoke stood, as they had stood for weeks now, above the forest fires burning uncontrolled to the north-west. "Have you ridden over to have a look at the road construction yet?" I asked him in a casual voice.

Pablo shook his head. "It is too far to go, Sam. I cannot leave the sheep alone for so long." His dark face had a sober expression of conscientious regret.

We heard from outside the sudden solid thump and slap of heavy leather. Pablo rose quickly on his hands behind the table, and, turning, I saw that the paint horse had dislodged its saddle and blanket from the open wagon box where it was snubbed, and where a pile of green glass bottles lay exposed now to the afternoon sun. Pablo's eyes darted at the bottles and then away again. "Goddamn sonofabitch horse," he said on his way out. He replaced the blanket and saddle over the bottles and led the paint around to the opposite side of the wagon, where he carefully retied it. "I thought you said you hadn't been over to the road construction," I reminded him when he got back.

"And I ain't been, neither, Sam. Though I am a sinner like all men, I am not a liar, as you know. I been carrying them bottles for over a year to haul water in."

"Firewater, you mean."

"You can believe me or don't," Pablo said with dignity. "The Good Lord Who hears me knows I speak the truth."

"I hope He does."

Pablo reached the coffeepot from the stove and refilled our mugs. Then he pushed the can of condensed milk across the table to me. "Put some of that in it now, it's good energy."

"I will, seeing as how you haven't anything stronger to offer me."

The afternoon wind was rising, whistling in the window slots and lifting the wagon gently on rachitic springs; from several ridges over, the dull boom of a seismographer's charge sounded. Pablo took his hands from around the mug and got out a box of the handmade cigarettes he rolled at night. He kneaded one of the crudely tapered cylinders to a more symmetrical shape and lit it with a wooden match he fired against the stove. Pablo removed his hat and flung it up onto the neatly made bed and fitted the back of his narrow skull into the curve of the wall; the hat had left a ridge in his hair that went around from ear to ear. He closed his muddy eyes, inhaled a lungful of smoke, and held it for a long while. Finally he expelled the smoke, opened his eyes again, and stared at me with an expression of weary patience. "How is your brother making out down there?" Pablo inquired.

"Not so good, I'm afraid. The whole business looks hopeless to me. He couldn't have got himself a more incompetent attorney if he'd advertised specially for one."

"That is all horseshit, Sam. Your brother is a fine boy. He never wanted to hurt that fellow Joad."

"He came that close to killing him, though."

"That is what the cops say, Sam. The cops are horseshit too."

"The cops are totally beside the point. He admits himself what he did."

"Who but the Lord in Heaven knows all that a man in his heart admits to?"

"I certainly don't. And I sure as hell don't want to either."

"You ain't the Lord, neither," Pablo said.

"No, I'm not. Also I didn't ride sixteen miles up here to listen to any sermon."

"And I ain't wasting my time and breath giving you one. I been around Walkers long enough to know they don't have no more religion than a bunch of dirty Indians."

"We're agreed on that much, then."

Pablo lifted the stove lid and dropped the end of his cigarette into the maw. "Time to have a look at them sheep again. Slide on out of there and stretch your legs, Sam. Living in this wagon's like living in your own coffin."

On the hill the two thousand head grazed peaceably amid the forlorn music of the scattered bells. Pablo pushed his hat back and studied them for a while through the glasses, while I looked northward to view the heavy stands of healthy blue-tipped trees and reflect upon the plan I was formulating to persuade Tom Fuller to guarantee a second mortgage on the North Section, offering the nearly 640 acres of prime timber as collateral. It was by no means an ideal scheme, but it was the best thing I had been able to think of so far to prevent my entire patrimony from being sacrificed to my brother's legal defense.

"There was a man," Pablo was saying, "who owned a flock of forty sheep and them sheep was the apple of that man's eye. Thirty-six of the sheep was white, and four of them was black. This man kept a close watch of his sheep so nobody would disturb them or carry any of them away. But one day he had to go on a long trip, so he paid a sheepherder to look after them while he was gone. This man was away for a long time and when he come home he found the herder laying asleep with the sheep grazing around him, and the man was very angry with the herder and shook him hard to make him wake up. But the herder said to the man, 'Count the sheep and tell me is any of them sonsabitches missing.' And the man counted the sheep and found that there was forty-one sheep, thirty-six of them white and five of them black. And the man was angrier than ever and he kicked the sheepherder's ass for him, good and hard."

"What nonsense are you babbling about now? You and your goddamn Bible stories. Remember, we agreed: no sermons."

"I ain't said a sermon," Pablo told me. "That was all a long time ago, anyway."

I took the glasses he offered me and stared through them above the sheep to the tilted red points of the distant peaks. The wind rose again, and the sound of it in the treetops was like the sough of raised opposing voices in the night. "Someday," I said, "somebody has got to find that airplane. Haven't they?"

"Look," Jenny said, "if what you really and truly want is to leave me, then for God's sake just *go*. Bret and I will manage, somehow."

"You can live on the ranch until you remarry. I promise you twelve hundred fifty bucks a month until then."

"I don't want to get married again, ever," she said. "Not *ever!*"

"Then I'll give you two grand a month for the rest of your life—period. I can afford the money." Liar, he told himself. And she knows it as well as you do. He drew the long green bottle with the elegant French label pasted on it from its icy immersion and held it poised above her glass. "Some champagne?"

She looked at the bottle as if it were a loaded weapon he were pointing at her, and shrugged. "Why not? The only way we can talk to each other any more is to get drunk first."

He poured for both of them, and they touched glasses.

"Happy second anniversary."

"Many happy returns of the day."

Jenny looked into his eyes and away again. She took a sip of champagne and set the glass down carefully. She picked up her fish fork and speared a piece of lobster and chewed for a long time before swallowing. Pretty girls wearing scanty aprons tied low on their hips passed and repassed the table, quick lithe bodies pirouetting gracefully beneath the loaded dinner trays. Bill Gerhardie stood by the door that communicated with the bar, rubbing his hands and rocking genially on his crepe-soled shoes. Having seated them cordially at the best table, he had retreated immediately and kept a discreet distance since. "Is that what you *really* want, Chuck?" Jenny repeated, leaning to him as she spoke. "*Is* it?"

"Maybe."

"What do you mean, maybe? What kind of answer is maybe?"

"Just—maybe."

"*I'm asking you, Chuck: What is it that you want to do about all this, anyway?*

"I don't know," Richardson said. "I don't know what I want to do."

The ensuing silence had the lapidary stillness of a boulder in a torrenting stream around which foaming waters pour, disturbed only by the click of knives and the crack of lobster shells. It was worse by far than the fighting: Within its envelope worlds could be felt to rend themselves and hang by threads. Lovers fought, he reflected, but final silence is the reward reserved for silver anniversaries. In another seven—or was it eight?—years he and Christine would have been celebrating their twenty-fifth, even if he could no more believe in silence as the ground of existence between himself and his first wife than he could imagine an electrical storm without thunder. It was here, he recalled—in this very room, an incredible twenty-six months ago—that he had confessed this girl to her. What was it, Richardson wondered, about women that they seemed to offer no middle ground, compelling you to choose between loving and despising them, fleeing either to them or from them?

Covertly, from under the brim of the pulled-down hat, he watched her eat with that stubborn indomitable appetite that seemed always to smolder within her like a banked fire. Never trust a Dutchman with your aqua vitae or your wife with herself— was it George Bernard Shaw who had said that? In the soft light of the flame that fluttered below the font of melted butter her bare arms and throat had a voluptuous glow suggesting the virgins in the paintings of the Italian Renaissance. Now Bill Gerhardie was approaching them, grinning his leprechaun grin. He asked, "How is your dinner? Everything going okay here?"

"It sure is. Everything's just great."

"How about you, *madame?* Are you enjoying your dinner this evening?"

"Oh yes, Bill. Everything's just wonderful. I'll have to diet now the rest of the week."

Gerhardie slipped the bottle from the ice bucket and poured the rest of the champagne, concluding with a graceful turn of the wrist. He replaced it bottom-up in the water, rubbed his hands together briskly, and glanced from Jenny to Richardson and back to Jenny again. "Many happy returns of the day," he said. "You deserve it, you two. Louise!" he called, gesturing at the prettiest of the waitresses: a tall long-necked beauty with black hair, luminous eyes, and the unruffled grace of a swan on smooth water, whom Richardson had been eying lustfully all evening. "The house would like to buy Jenny and Chuck another bottle of Mumm's, if you please."

"I don't know—" Jenny began, but Gerhardie cut her off politely.

"Oh, *re*-lax, Jenny. After all, it keeps him off those Molotov cocktails, doesn't it? And, if you don't mind, I'll drink a glass with you to help you celebrate. —And three glasses!" he told Louise at the service bar.

She came with the tray and set the smoking bottle, wrapped in a linen napkin, on the table while Richardson took inventory of her proximate charms: A man needn't go thirsty the rest of his life because he no longer keeps a cow in the barn. Bill Gerhardie raised the bottle as reverently as if it were a Gobelin vase and poured a splash of the liquid into a glass, which he proffered Richardson with a bow. It was excellent champagne, exquisitely dry and chilled, the effervescence bursting like a thousand tiny golden grapes on the tongue. Following his marriage to Christine at the Greenwich Episcopal church, they had uncorked a flood of Mumm's at the Yacht Club, where marriages—a few of which actually proved unsinkable—were launched like luxury liners. "Wonderful," he pronounced.

"Oh, it's great stuff," Gerhardie agreed, filling all three of the glasses. "Here's to both of you: long life and much happiness together!

"You know," he added confidentially, "it's so good to me to see two people who get on so great together, have so much in common with one another; people who know how to be happy." Then, as a young couple appeared arm in arm in the door of the restaurant: "Excuse me," he said as he put down his glass, and left them.

"Are you going to have dessert, Chuck?" Jenny asked. "I'll let you have *one* after-dinner drink if I can have a piece of mint-chocolate-chip pie."

It struck him suddenly as astonishingly bold, this dance of hers along the precipice, so that even as he caught his breath at her impudence he found himself reluctantly admiring her nerve. Whether she intended it for outright mockery or not he couldn't be certain; more likely, he thought, it was simply an expression of that addictive impulse toward risk that seemed characteristic of the compulsive adulterer.

"The lady would like," he told the lovely, respectfully hovering Louise, "a piece of mint-chocolate-chip pie, and I want a Tanqueray martini up, very dry, with an olive. Make that a double, of course."

———————

When they left the Last Chance Saloon and Restaurant the August night was like a knife blade laid across the throat by a street thief. Already there had been frost: Summer was about to be torn from him and replaced by that season to which he turned every year as from the warm, loving, maternal girl with whom you will always be safe to the cool seductress with whom you risk uncertainty and even danger, but with whom also you will never be bored. Fall was the season of stiletto cold and smoking blood, sparking pine logs within a fire ring of stones and an inch of ice on the water bucket at dawn; the woodsmoke flavor of good whiskey and the sharp lingering odor of cordite; the nicker of horses in improvised mountain corrals and the bugle of elk along the ridgelines; the heavy tug of a fat feeding trout and the thump of lead through the heart of a bounding buck; a powder of fresh snow over granite cliffs beneath a climbing white sun in a blue enamel sky stretched above the yellow aspen, green pine, and purple willow; gun oil, horse dung, old saddle leather, sourdough hotcakes, elk-heart stew, and the bitter black bite of hot coffee in an ironware mug clutched in a mittened hand. Tonight Richardson felt his nostrils dilate to the scent of fall, yet for the first time since he had come West—perhaps for the first time in his life—he was unable to respond to it. He felt impotent. Suddenly it was as if nothing would ever come to him again, as if the best of life were already over and he were worse off than dead, with only the long downhill road ahead leading through the staggered small deaths of the senses to senescence and the final oblivion. Between the earth and the stars a silver skim of vapor was being drawn across the night like a sheet. "Let's go have a drink at the Bare Garden," he suggested.

Her look of horror was supremely satisfying. "*Absolutely not*, Chuck! I want to go home—*now!*"

"Be a sport, Jen. It's our anniversary, after all."

"But the sitter!" she wailed. "I promised her we'd be home by eleven."

"It's just nine-thirty now."

"No," Jenny said in a definite voice. "Not tonight, Chuck. I don't feel like drinking. I'm not in the mood. You know perfectly well we'd end up trying to kill each other."

"For Christ's sake, Jenny, quit acting like an old woman. What's the matter with you tonight? We haven't had that much to drink. And it isn't like you to turn down another one even if we had."

Her face as he drove through town was a mask of misery in the cold aura of the streetlights. He parked across the square and she followed him like a cringing dog over the grass and into the bar. Thank God Richardson prayed, surveying the smoky interior, for places such as this where a man could degrade himself according to the depths of his innate depravity and the strength of his talent for self-destruction. And if I make a really good job of it, he promised himself, I'll spend the night on a cot in a nice comfortable taxpayer-paid-for jail cell, and serve the little bitch right, too. He was discovering that he was a great deal drunker than he had realized upon leaving the restaurant.

He chose a table at the center of the room and signaled to the cocktail waitress, a redhead with coppery skin and wicked green eyes. "Dry martini, Tanqueray, up with a twist," she said, writing it down on her pad before he could get his mouth open.

"Usually I prefer an olive to the twist, but you've got a great memory anyhow for a girl your age, Fran."

"Jan. It isn't memory, it's association." She glanced with sly curiosity at Jenny, who sat leaning on her elbows with her hands clasped on her pocketbook, staring at the table.

"Only you forgot to add, 'Make that a double.' "

"I didn't say it," Jan told him, "but I wrote it down."

"You're a great girl, Fran—I mean, Jan. You really are."

"I recall you telling me something of the sort one evening; about four years ago, I think it was."

"Is it really four years ago already? How time flies when you're having fun."

"And how it flies when you're not," the girl said, moving on to the next table.

"You forgot to order," Richardson told his wife. She was hunched over her pocketbook, her face and neck a livid red, not looking at him.

"How many times do I have to say it—*I don't want anything more to drink!*"

"Suit yourself, then."

"You know what?" she said. "I think the trouble with you is you've been spending too much time with that Houston Walker. You're starting to behave exactly like him."

"Christ, am I? Maybe I should try being more like his brother then."

He lit a cigar and sat smoking it, ignoring her. When Jan brought the drink he finished it almost at a swallow. He had decided that they would sit here, the two of them together, until closing time or until Jack Walker showed up, whichever was first. Across the table Jenny sat cowering, in mute but obvious terror and anticipation. O.K. Pickett had called that afternoon to report that Frank Joad had had dealings in Fontenelle with a man named Waldo, a former associate of Willie Munger's, but that Joad had apparently double-crossed Waldo, who had threatened revenge. He had no idea what, if anything, this information signified, but the connection with Munger had alerted every one of his senses. "Hell yes, I'll have another," he told Jan when she came by again with her pad and pencil.

Bob Pulasky came into the bar, followed by Bruno Bellini. They spotted Richardson from the door and began making their way heavily over between the crowded tables. Like a hunter holding his sights on a pair of marauding bears, he gauged their approach. "Hi Jenny, hi Chuck. How's the boy?"

He lowered his head threateningly at them but did not speak.

"He sure looks growly tonight," Bob Pulasky told Bellini. "Think we ought to kind of lay off him, Bruno?"

"I don't know," Bruno said. "He's growly all of the time, ain't he?"

"Look at his face," Pulasky said. "Christ, Jenny, what did you do to him—put his bed out in the backyard or what?"

Richardson told them, "Cut out the clever stuff tonight, you clowns. I'm not in the mood."

"Is that right?" Bob Pulasky asked. "Well, in that case, Chuck—*excuse us!* I guess we know when we're not wanted. Don't we, Bruno?"

From beneath the hat he watched them as they went on to the bar. "Can we go now, Chuck—*please?*" Jenny asked in a stricken whisper. She looked to Richardson as though she were close to tears.

"Not yet."

"Then let me have the truck keys now, before I have to fight you for them."

He fished the keys from his pocket and pushed them across the table at her. "It is upon this rock that I will build my bordello." Funny, he thought, how a Catholic education comes in handy at times.

"*What?*"

"Nothing. You sure you don't want a toddy, for a nightcap? Fran is on her way back over here."

"Absolutely not. *No.* And if she gets any closer than three feet of me, I'll scratch her damn eyes out—I promise you."

"Well, I'll leave the two of you to fight it out while I pay a

233

visit to the little boys' room." He stood unsteadily from the chair and placed a hand on the table to balance himself; it rocked slightly beneath his weight and he pushed away from it like an inept boater shoving off from a dock. The go-go dancer was wriggling on her platform, and it occurred to him as he went that, of all created things, woman was the ugliest. In the rest room he locked himself carefully into the stall and sat on the folded-down seat, holding his head in his hands and fighting back nausea. So she had returned to her old ways, like a dog returning to its vomit. What, after all, did it really mean to him? Beneath the interfacing panel a pair of boots with the pantlegs down around them showed, and from the top of the stall a column of sweet smoke rose, spread, and gently lowered in separating layers. *Tremble, ye women that are at ease; be troubled, ye careless ones; strip you, and make you bare, and gird sackcloth upon your loins.* When the nausea had passed he stood and urinated. Then he unlocked the stall and washed his hands in the greasy sink, pausing afterward to contemplate in the cracked glass the glowering face that appeared to him for an instant as he gazed upon it to belong to his client and mortal enemy Jack Clemson Walker. When he returned to the table, Jenny was gone and Jan was taking away the dirty glass with the piece of olive in the bottom of it and the crumpled cocktail napkin. "Where'd my wife go?" he asked the waitress.

"Home—she said."

"How could she—?" Then he remembered the truck keys.

The girl took a neatly rolled wad from the pocket of her apron and held it out to him. "She asked me to give you this before you leave."

He took the money from her and unpeeled it: three five-dollar bills rolled inside a ten.

"She said to tell you to call the cops when you're done and have them drive you to a motel," Jan said. A ghost of a smile barely touched the corners of her mouth. "Do you want me to bring you another martini first?"

"Why not? I'll be up at the bar with Bob and Bruno."

They grinned sardonically at him as he approached. "Oh-oh," Bruno Bellini said, "it looks like Chuck got stood up tonight. I guess Jenny's going to put his bed in the backyard after all."

Richardson pulled out the stool between them, sat on it, and spread his elbows wide on the bar. "Nobody's putting my bed anywhere. I'm buying the next round, and then you turkeys are going to help me drink to Liberation Day—you hear?"

I had not cared for Tom Studds when, as captain of the Fontenelle Flyers and senior class president, sporting around town in a cherry-red pickup with the muffler cut out of it and a silver stallion mounted on the hood, he had made an (unsuccessful) bid to rush my sister off her feet. Now, looking hopelessly middle-aged in a tight-fitting lime-green cowboy shirt in which his paunch protruded over his belt like a ripe melon, his eyes bloodshot and bulging under the bill of the dingy baseball cap, he moved heavily forward with a bushel sack of potatoes in one hand and a paring knife in the other. He was being cordial this weekend but not overly so, as if to suggest that, while he respected our mutual gestures of goodwill in token of the past, I no longer belonged to the sodality of Search and Rescue, and both of us knew it. I was there because, having remained for ten days in the mountains, I had seen smoke rising from a couple of ridges over and ridden across finally to investigate.

For ten days I had ridden along trails and across country I

had explored as a boy, carrying in my saddle-bags only a canteen, matches, the .38 revolver and a collapsible fishing rod, a bed-roll, and an old canvas duster belonging to Pablo. Each morning the sky was an unearthly blue, broken in the afternoon by the clouds that formed above the mountains in ethereal approximation; at night the constellations were spread through the heavens like a gas, and I lay on my back among the wildflowers looking up at them while the coyotes whooped and barked on the surrounding ridges. I caught trout in the creeks and little lakes and baked them on a flat stone over the campfire; one evening I shot a doe at water and ate a little of the meat and smoked the rest and carried it in the bags. Often I tied up and went on foot among the canyons, parks, and saddles, where even after twenty years I had need of no maps, and one day I climbed the crimson talus to the summit of Mt. Sublette, where I sat in the abandoned fire lookout the Forest Service had left there after packing it up by muleback sixty-five years ago, drinking water from the canteen and chewing venison, looking due north to the Tetons and northeast to the Wind Rivers. On a lower elbow of the mountain an elk herd lay bedded in a field of snow, nothing between us but the empyrean and a pair of eagles riding the thermals five hundred feet below. The guy wires holding the structure in place were still secure, and among the planks, beams, and broken glass that littered the floor I discovered a joist with the names E. James and P. James cut in it—the James brothers, Eddie dead years ago of lymphatic cancer, Paul killed more recently in a car crash—and a section of shutter with the initials SHW and CSW inscribed on it. Clarice and I had carved them with the point of my old Bowie knife on July 22, 1963, and afterward unrolled our bags and spent the night at just under 11,500 feet of elevation, stretched together on the floor beside the overturned coal stove.

After forty-eight hours in camp I was ready to admit that I had made an error by accepting the invitation to join the rendezvous; still, my mistake was venial by comparison with Pablo's.

The herder's horse stood snubbed to a pine tree behind the big sidewall tent while its owner sat a short distance away at the card table, playing cribbage and drinking red wine from a gallon jug that he hoisted with monotonous regularity in the crook of his arm. Pablo had been gambling and drinking since the previous evening, when I had returned from hiking into Lake Adeline to discover him drunk in camp and two thousand head of sheep wandering everywhere—and then, as it had seemed, suddenly nowhere. It was going to take plenty of time to round up two thousand head, but Pablo was not worrying about time, or money. He had lost approximately five hundred dollars already—four hundred more, I suspected, than he had to his name—but losing was not cramping his style any. Now and again he picked up a few dollars, and when that happened he would jerk the ancient .30–'06 lever-action Winchester from under his chair and squeezed off a few rounds into the air, bringing down a shower of pine twigs, cones, and needles over the cardplayers. There were complaints, but too many people were getting rich— theoretically at least—off Pablo to want to get tough about it. "You're an old Army grunt," Studds said as he offered me the sack and the knife. "Peeling spuds is all you need to feel like twenty years old again."

"I'm not doing one damn thing else around here until some-body gives me a hand getting that sonofabitch sobered up and out of this camp. I don't care what order that happens in."

"What's the trouble? He's your man, ain't he?"

"He isn't anybody's man now. For Christ sake, Tom, don't you guys know any better than to give a dago sheepherder a drink? He hasn't been out of the mountains since early July. By tomorrow morning there's going to be two thousand head of my grandfather's sheep scattered between here and eternity. It'll take until after Labor Day to get them rounded back up again, even after the bears and coyotes have had their share."

Tom Studds showed me a fishy eye. "He come riding in here

about three o'clock yesterday afternoon while you was away jogging. Said he was thirsty and lost his canteen. Somebody broke down and give him a beer, I guess." He shrugged and lowered the potatoes onto the ground. "Ain't our problem if you folks don't hire sober help."

I looked over the scattered tents surrounded by the sprawled snoring figures, the hunched cardplayers swearing and slapping at the mosquitoes, the horseshoe tossers lunging unsteadily at the stakes. "Don't be a prig, Tom. This isn't exactly a temperance meeting, is it?"

"You ain't enjoying yourself, Sam, the trail you come in on is still there."

"I'll be using it as soon as those sheep are rounded back up. Not before."

Tom Studds said mollifyingly, "We'll get him sobered up first thing in the morning. Hell—too late to do much about it tonight, Sam."

I reached for the sack. "How do you want these things cut up?"

"Peeled and sliced is all. The guys are cooking home fries to go with them T-bones. We's going to eat like fucking kings tonight, Sam."

I carried the sack to the fire, sat down on one of the logs they had felled for benches, and began peeling and cutting potatoes. I finished three of them before I laid the sack against the log and went over to my bedroll for the bottle of whiskey I had bought off Tom and the tin cup he had lent me. I had been wanting a drink all day after waking with the mosquitoes at dawn after a disturbed sleep to lie watching clouds swim like pink salmon in a green sky that stretched behind the indigo spikes of the trees, recalling fragments of departed dreams that seemed in retrospect more like hallucinations. The voices were the ones I had been hearing in bed at home, but clearer now, louder, more distinct—more insistent. I had watched the pink clouds ease themselves across the jade sky until I could no longer bear the whine and stab of insects, then carried the tin plate and cup to the firepit where they were already preparing the six dozen eggs and forty pounds of pork and putting the five-gallon ironware coffeepot to boil. When I had eaten breakfast I had watered the horse and retied it, and then slipped quietly into the pines in the direction of the hogback that separated camp from the southeastern shore of Lake Adeline.

I struggled up on all fours on the waxy needles, snatching at snowbent trunks and the lower branches of trees beneath the indignant chatter of squirrels, to the spine of rock from which the lake below appeared as a blue slot in the sharp red folds of the mountains. It looked smaller and less imposing than I remembered it, but also more significant in some vague indescribable way. In those days of our early adolescence, when we had packed in the tent, the blankets, the fishing gear, and the food, my sister had not been the cripple she was so soon to become. Stripped naked, we had swum together in the breathtaking water and afterward lain on the rocks feeling the sun reheat our long white bodies; at night, we had lain huddled together under the blankets for warmth as we listened to the heavy trot and startled snort of large animals passing on their way to water. I had sat for half an hour on the hogback, watching the lake and the mountains behind it: There was a faint haze of smoke from the north, giving the sky a leaden quality. Then I had started downhill, sliding and skidding on the pine needles, while the muffled opposing voices swelled, echoed, and finally diminished in my head.

I finished peeling and cutting the potatoes, while Bill Sawyer raked inch-thick steaks across the hissing grill with a long-handled fork and Tommy Mason restrung the electric lights over the card tables and cranked up the gasoline generator. Pablo had finished the wine and was drinking whiskey now; the sclera of his eyes were red and his swarthy face had deepened to a liverish color. Tom Studds scraped the cut potatoes into a dutch oven and put them on the grate to boil while I poured myself a fresh drink and moved over on the log beside Big Mac McGhee, who sat drinking half of a fifth of scotch from a plastic tumbler. " 'Lo there, Sam," Big Mac rumbled moistly over the rim of the tumbler.

"Hello, Mac."

"It's sure been a great weekend, ain't it?"

"I've enjoyed it."

"I bet you don't have great times like this with them junglebunnies in Africa, do you?"

"Different, anyway."

The air was chill now, but Big Mac still had on the leopardskin suit he had gone bathing in the creek in that afternoon and that fitted him the way a rubber band fits a beer keg. In his enormous fist the tumbler looked no bigger than a cocktail glass as he rested it on one of the huge knees spread wide to accommodate the hanging paunch. Big Mac had a farmer's tan and a red sunburned face that was both coarse and sensitive, jovial and profoundly melancholy. He asked, "Ain't it about time you stayed back in civilization, Sam? Seems to me as how a guy could get kind of funny in the head after a while, living off in them underdeveloped countries like you been doing."

"A guy can get funny in the head living anywhere, Mac."

Tom Studds banged on a cookpan for supper and the card and horseshoe players started to drift over with their plates and cups. Bill Sawyer forked the steaks around, and after stretching my boots toward the fire, I balanced the loaded plate on my knees and began to eat. The fire on my face and legs and the hot food and whiskey in my belly created a warmth that retied me to these men, the acquaintances and, in a few instances, even the friends of my youth. When we were through eating we scraped the plates into the fire while Bill Sawyer put the coffeepot back on the grill and Big Mac, his naked torso glistening in the firelight, played "Red River Valley" on a small nickel-plated harmonica. Big Mac finished the song to scattered applause and poured the second half of his fifth of scotch into the tumbler. He drank deeply, wiped his mouth with the back of his hand, and began another one as the men squatted down on their heels with their bottles against their legs and stared into the fire. Goodwill and affection rose within me and seemed to flash like electricity to the surrounding figures; I was aware of having to resist an impulse to rise and go from one to the other, embracing them. The music came winding down like a river flowing from some lost and infinitely remote place, whose regaining it seemed to speak of with sweetest promise. Shadows staggered among the straight gray trunks of the fire-lit trees, and from over by the tents came the noise of retching and the sound of bodies falling heavily. Big Mac continued to play on the harmonica, but the men were already drifting back to the tables, where Pablo sat by himself with the rifle propped against his leg and his head tilted on the chairback. I sighed with real contentment and poured myself another drink, which I finished while Big Mac played several more songs. At last I stood awkwardly, stiffened by cold and the hard ground, and waded unsteadily into the trees, where I relieved myself against a log. I was fumbling ineffectually with my fly buttons when a burst of gunfire sounded from camp and I turned, still groping, to look. Pablo stood at the cardtable with the .30–'06 pointed above his head, while around the table people were getting to their feet. Leaving the final buttons undone, I hurried from the woods toward Pablo and the gesticulating men. "You dirty raghead bastard," someone shouted. "Put up the goddamn gun or get the fuck out of the game."

"Take it easy, Pablo," I said. "What's the problem here, Gus?" I asked.

"The goddamn trigger-happy sonofabitch almost blew my fuckin head off—that's what's the matter!" Gus shouted, but Pablo interrupted him. The old man's eyes glittered, unfocused with drink. "They don't want me to play anymore, Sam. Them sonsabitches is tryin to cut me out of the game. Says no goddamn sheepherder was ever good for more'n three hundred bucks."

"Are you?"

"That ain't the point, Sam. I need money, I know where to get it. The point is, I been winning off of them dirty bastards, and now they want me out of the game."

I turned to Gus again. "Pablo stays in the game."

Tom Studds pushed his way through the bunched men. His eyes were hectic and bright, his face the color of a fighting cock's. He said, "Pull your man out now, Walker, or we'll do it for you."

"Keep out of this, Tom. You haven't been captain of anything for twenty years."

A hand from behind fell on my shoulder, but a single step forward put me just in range of him and I swung hard and connected cleanly with the point of his jaw. Then I was down, rolled beneath the massed weight that was like a breaking wave through which I caught glimpses of light and snatches of thick unsatisfying air, while Tom Studds's voice echoed distantly in my ear like a conch shell: "All of them crazy . . . totally insane . . . dirty son of a whore . . ."

sell it just sell it for gods sake and well move to california
i dont give a damn anymore sell or dont sell all i want to
know is is it mine or isnt it

A constellation of brilliant stars, arranged in vaguely coherent pattern but partly obscured by the black points of the trees, emerged against the dark; a shape, shaggy and indistinguishable, bent itself directly above me. "You wanted a fight it was me you ought to of give it to, Sam," the voice of Pablo said. "The fight your old man should of let me have for not calling him home from Korea like I ought to of done, 'stead of boozing it up with the whores in town. For almost forty years I been waiting for you or your brother—one or both—to give it to me."

My focusing eyes located and fixed themselves on Polaris,

still wobbling high in the sky like the wheel of a speeding car about to break loose. What in God's name, I wondered, is the drunken old fool blithering about now? I must have been still semiconscious then, because the fact that Pablo was actually crying seemed completely unremarkable to me.

W hen she answered the telephone in a drowsy voice at
the ninth or tenth ring, he told her, "Go on to bed when you're
ready. I'm not coming home tonight."

"What do you mean, not coming home?"

"Just what I said. So don't wait up for me. All right?"

"I don't understand," Jenny said. "Is there something the
matter, Chuck?"

"Nothing is the matter."

"You aren't drunk, are you?"

"No, I'm not drunk."

"Where are you?"

"In town. It doesn't matter where."

"You *are* drunk!" Jenny cried.

He said, "I have to go now," and added in a gentler voice,
"I'll be seeing you." He hung up the receiver, folded back the
door of the telephone booth, and went along the corridor past the
bar, where the party of Japanese engineers continued to sit

straight and stiff in their chairs with their neckties carefully in place and the uniform black-framed eyeglasses high on their noses, to the front door through which he slipped unnoticed to his truck.

Outside the only sound was the sad chirp of crickets mourning summer's impending death and their own. A veil of shadow interpolated itself between him and the stars and the air was sharp and faintly acrid in his nostrils; shifting winds during the past week had brought the smoke drifting down in a southeasterly direction from the spreading fires in the north. Richardson drove slowly up the steep dirt road from the Doll House to the flat, where the town showed as a galaxy of lights arranged in patterns of arrested motion against a huge and universal darkness. A city patrol car waited with its parking lights on at a right angle to the road so that his own lights raked it, glinting on the door emblem and picking out the white expressionless face of the officer seated stiffly behind the wheel. Fanny Mae rarely had to call the cops, who nonetheless monitored her customers as they came and went, more likely from prurient than from professional interest. At the intersection of the road with the highway he self-consciously signaled a right turn and coasted down the long grade toward town. All he wanted now was oblivion, purchased in the anonymity of a cheap motel cell.

He had understood from O. K. Pickett's voice on the telephone that it was trouble. The private eye had called him late in the afternoon from Fanny Mae's place, where he stayed on his visits to Fontenelle, and Richardson had irritated Jenny by making her hurry supper before he drove back to the Doll House, after having spent the afternoon putting the finishing touches to the extension roof. In the twilight, the house had an air of cloistered activity, like a church in a Moscow side street, that the parked cars and antique carriage lanterns beside the door failed to demystify. "If it isn't Dr. Richardson, the famous cardiologist, himself," the Spanish girl had said when she saw him, and led the way through the front hall past the bar, in which a large party of Japanese engineers wearing suits and ties but who had apparently checked their Nikons at the door were ritually waving cocktail glasses at one another, to a curtained sitting room at the back of the building where O.K. sat perched on a Victorian love seat behind a small marble-topped table with a tall glass of whiskey in his hand. The Doll House was decorated and furnished in the Gay Nineties style; the girls—including, after six o'clock, Fanny Mae herself—appeared in period costume, as if sin itself were a quaint artifact of the historical past.

O.K. Pickett was a man just below middle height, spare and muscular, with a round balding head and round bloodshot eyes that were otherwise quite colorless. He wore—as he always wore—blue jeans doubly supported by red clip-on suspenders and a tooled Western belt, and a cowboy shirt in a loud pattern with red gaiters at the biceps. He placed his hands on his knees and sprung himself from the love seat as Richardson entered to offer the lawyer a horny palm. "Chuck." "O.K." No question about it, Richardson thought; he's setting me up for some bad news.

"I'm having a drink."

"I'll have one with you."

"Whiskey be okay? I got a bottle at the bar."

"Whiskey is always fine."

"Tell them to send in another glass," O.K. Pickett told the dark girl. "Hell, have them set up another bottle too." He refolded himself like a pocket knife into the love seat and Richardson drew a ridiculous gilt chair up to the little table. "The girls here are like my own family," O.K. said. "Coming back to Fanny Mae's place is always like coming home to me."

"For me, it's like coming to work."

"When I was a kid my daddy used to drive up here every Saturday night from Green River. Fanny Mae, she was just one of the girls in them days. She was always his special favorite."

"She must have been quite attractive, years ago."

"Fanny Mae," O.K. Pickett said proudly, "has always looked exactly like what she looks today."

"Is that so."

"Her and my daddy were like husband and wife until the day she married Bob Tuscher," O.K. said. He added confidentially, "The booze killed my ma a year later. In my whole life, I never saw that woman draw a sober breath."

The girl brought the filled glass for Richardson and set it down with the bottle on the table. Then, after giving Pickett a sisterly smile, she left.

"In my business," O.K. said, "I seen life in the raw, but never no rawer than what I seen in my own home."

Richardson, being unable to think of an appropriate comment, said nothing as he tasted the whiskey. O.K., he noticed, had almost drained his own glass.

"Women are the best thing in life there is," O.K. Pickett said, "so long as a guy knows just exactly what it is he's getting."

Richardson said, "I don't want to spoil your evening, O.K. Maybe you ought to go ahead and tell me what it is you have to tell me and get business out of the way." He was watching Pickett's hands now; the fingers kept knitting themselves, coming apart, and reknitting. The detective's eyes darted away to the corner of the room and back to his employer's glass. "Better drink up, Chuck, and let me pour you another one."

Richardson reached for the bottle and set it on the floor beneath the table. "I want it straight now, O.K. And I don't mean whiskey, either."

O.K. Pickett breathed deeply and clasped his hands between his knees. He said, without looking at Richardson, "You know this Waldo feller I was telling you about?"

"What about him?"

"He's bragging it around that he's been sleeping with your wife," Pickett said. "Could be bragging is all he's doing," he added quickly.

Richardson was aware of a sudden swell of relief, followed by sensations of an overwhelming lightness of being of which his own brief laughter seemed a wholly inadequate expression. "Is that all, O.K.? Everybody else in town is."

———————————

He drove from one NO VACANCY sign to the next, past motel lots crowded with out-of-state licenses. He considered following a jeep trail into the desert and sleeping out in the back of the truck, but he had brought no bag or blanket and the nights were cold now. Perhaps, he thought, I should just swallow my pride and go home. Instead, he drove back through town and up the hill to the dirt turnoff where the cop still waited in the parked cruiser, his face a nonjudgmental blank under the headlights. Probably he had concluded that Fanny Mae's roofing engineer was taking it out in trade.

Fanny Mae was not in the bar, nor in the large front room in which she liked to spend her evenings flirting heavily with the newly arrived customers and drinking gin on the rocks. Richardson cornered the dark girl and was taken by her to the kitchen, where Fanny Mae on huge knees was giving the dogs their vitamin pills. She had hold of one of them by the scruff of the neck, while with the other hand she tried to force a ball of raw hamburger down the animal's throat. The dog threw its head from side to side and humped its back like an inchworm, its claws scraping and skittering on the linoleum. "You nasty little twat!" Fanny Mae screamed. "Open your gullet before I tear your goddamn head off." When she saw Richardson she let go the neck and sat back on her haunches, roaring like a sea lion. After she had her breath again she said, "Well, look who's out on the town tonight. You come to take it out in trade? That way I don't report it to them bastards at the IRS."

Richardson said, "Can you put me up in a spare room tonight, Fanny Mae? I don't feel like driving out to the ranch and the motels are booked solid."

Her efforts with the dogs had left runnels of sweat in the lines of her heavy face and spittle in the corners of her mouth. She leered bawdily and said, "You want a room for the night, do you? How about a rubber dolly to go with it?"

"No thanks. A little peace and quiet will be fine."

"What do you think I got here, buster? A goddamn AAA-approved hotel?"

"If it's inconvenient, I can sleep in back of the truck."

Fanny Mae grabbed the poodle suddenly by the tail. "Get over here, you little bitch, and take your medicine."

Richardson said, "You hold her, Fanny Mae, and I'll get the pill down."

Fanny Mae swept up the dog in her wide flippers and pressed it to her belly as though it were an infant in tantrum. Richardson took the pellet of meat from the floor, inserted it on the back of the slavering tongue, and clamped the champing jaws shut until it was swallowed. When he released the muzzle the dog whirled instantly, snapping about itself like a barracuda, and bit him in the fleshy part of the hand. The wound bled profusely, and Fanny Mae, cursing, hurled the dog against the refrigerator. The Spanish-looking girl, whose name was Marita, brought a bowl of warm water and soap, tincture of iodine, a towel, and bandages, and washed and dressed the hand under Fanny Mae's direction. "It was anyone but you, Mr. Richardson," she said, "I could count on them suing me for everything I got, the dirty sons-abitches. Marita, take Mr. Richardson upstairs and give him room six on the third floor. That mattress is shot; the last time I put a girl in there I had to pay chiropractor bills for a week. It ain't so bad sleeping singles, though."

"Yes, Fanny Mae."

"Anything else he wants, run a tab."

"Yes, Fanny Mae."

Richardson followed Marita up two flights of stairs and along the hall to an end room directly beneath the gabled ceiling. The room had a narrow iron-framed bed with a deeply troughed mattress, a bedside table with a china lamp and an old-fashioned bell alarm clock on it, and a Japanese screen in the corner; the scrap of rug on the floor was ragged where it had been cut from a larger piece. "You have a heart attack, you can call the ambulance yourself," Marita said, and left him.

He sat gingerly on the side of the bed and slowly removed a shoe. He thought of the bar and put it back on; then he remembered the Japanese engineers and took it off again. He removed the other shoe and tucked the pair under the bed and lay back on the counterpane with his arms folded beneath his head. From below came the woolly thump of a jukebox, while around him the walls seemed to breathe with the passions of love; he wondered briefly in which room they had put O.K. Pickett. He lay absolutely still for what seemed to him a long time, thinking about nothing, until he heard a quiet knock at the door. He took his arms from under his head, swung his legs off the bed, and padded on sockfeet to open it. A tiny girl with soft brown hair and a plain-pretty face stood on the runner carpet, shyly staring at him from soft doe's eyes. She said, "Fanny Mae told me to come up. She said to tell you I'm compliments of the house."

Richardson drew the door back farther and stepped aside to let her enter. "Come in, Compliments. I'm afraid I can't offer you anything to drink."

"I can bring you anything you want from the bar. Please don't order anything for me, though." She had closed the door and stood before him with her hands clasped in front of her, looking like a child waiting for a reprimand by the teacher. "Do you want me to go behind the screen," she asked, "or would you like me to get undressed out here?" The Gay Nineties tart costume, which he imagined would be extremely difficult to take off, underscored his impression of a radical innocence that seemed almost irreducible.

"I don't want you to do anything anywhere," Richardson said. She had, he observed, a shapely little figure, round-hipped and surprisingly full-breasted, and a sweet small face like a wood sprite's. "Is it something the matter with me?" she asked in a tiny voice, giving him a stricken look.

"There's absolutely nothing the matter with you, my dear. The opposite, in fact."

"Then why don't you want—?"

"I don't know why. Maybe because I'm old enough to be your father."

"Oh, I've been with *lots* of men older than you."

He remembered the turkey-necked geriatric sitting up fiercely in the bed with his look of invincible triumph. "I suppose you have."

"*Much* older!"

He wondered: *Is* there anyone older? After a certain point, age becomes just a matter of years.

"I've been watching you at work all summer," the girl blurted. "You couldn't tell, could you?"

"Watching me?" He gave her a long look, without being able to remember having ever laid eyes on her before. "No," he said.

"I'm glad you don't want to," the girl said. "I've felt like every day, all summer long, what you were really coming here for was me. I don't want anything else except what I have now."

He thought about that for a minute. "How old are you—if you don't mind my asking?"

"Twenty-one and a half. I've been working at Fanny Mae's almost exactly six months."

Richardson said, "You're a very intelligent girl for your age, Miss—"

"My name is Fawn," she said. "That's a funny name, isn't it?"

"I would say pretty. Mine is Chuck—that's an ugly one."

"I knew what your name was," Fawn told him. "I asked Fanny Mae weeks ago."

"You did?" Richardson said. "In addition to being intelligent you're also rather impressionable, Fawn."

"If your wife died, could you ever even just *think* of marrying me?" she implored him.

"Probably I could. I'm a very selfish man. But my wife is not going to die."

"I love you," Fawn said simply.

Richardson sat at the head of the bed and patted the foot of it with his hand. "Sit down. Do you like champagne, Fawn?"

"I don't know. I don't think I ever tasted any."

"I'll have Marita bring up a bottle and two glasses," Richardson said.

W ell, why *not*, Sam? If they say anything to you about it, all you have to do is tell them I'm your guest, not theirs. It's your home too, isn't it? Why can't you invite whoever you want? I certainly would never let *my* folks tell *me* who I could bring and who I couldn't."

She sat with one leg drawn up on the sofa, her skinny brown thigh exposed through folds of the dressing gown. The Sunday paper lay disheveled between us under a scattering of toast crumbs and fragments of egg yolk congealed in drips of bacon fat. I smoked a cigarette and considered mixing a pitcher of Bloody Marys as an antidote to the whiskey I had drunk the night before, "dancing" with Candy. "It isn't a matter of principle," I explained. "It's a question of why make trouble when it isn't necessary?"

"I know," she said, "you don't have to tell me. It's your sister you're thinking about, isn't it? Why don't you just admit to me you wouldn't dream of doing anything to offend her? Sometimes I think it's too bad you were born brother and sister, you'd be absolutely perfect for each other."

"As a matter of fact I don't give a damn what Clare thinks or doesn't think. If I'm worried about anyone's feelings, it's Ma's."

"Your mom and I have always gotten along fine," she protested. "I don't see what her feelings have to do with anything."

"Listen, Candy, it's *my* folks we're talking about. You're just going to have to take my word for it it would be disruptive, and that's that." I lifted my bare feet off the coffee table and fumbled on the floor for my slippers. "I'm going to mix us a pitcher of Bloodies now."

"Go on if you want to," Candy said. Her blue-shadowed eyelids snapped shut like the halves of a Venus flytrap, then open again. "Just don't kid yourself that you're going to buy me off with a few drinks, Sam, because I have news for you: This time, you're not."

I mixed the vodka and the tomato juice and was squeezing the first lemon when the telephone rang. "Hello, Sam?" Tom Fuller sounded bright and chipper as a brush salesman. "How are you this fine morning, my friend? Can I talk to Candy for a sec? Or isn't she awake yet?"

"She's awake. I'll get her."

She came quickly despite the dragging hangover, her bare feet whisking across the linoleum, and almost snatched the receiver from me. "Hi, Daddy, what's going on? . . . That's okay, we've had breakfast already. . . ."

I worked deliberately finishing the drinks as I strained to interpret as much of their conversation as possible. It was really obscene, the old goat phoning every morning as if to cheer us on. The thresh of the electric blender covered her voice for several seconds, and in the silence that followed I heard her say, "He doesn't want me to go to the Walker barbecue after the rodeo, but I just finished telling him I was going anyway, whether he likes it or not. . . ."

I removed the glass from the frame and set it next to the

vodka bottle before turning to confront her. She stood with her back to me, holding the receiver cradled between her cheek and shoulder.

"He says he's afraid of upsetting his mom. . . . I don't know, it doesn't matter, I guess. . . . Well, I'm going anyway, whether he likes it or not. . . . Search me, Daddy. Why don't you ask *him?*" She faced about then to present me with the receiver and a blankly innocent expression. "He wants to say something to you."

"You bitch," I told her, with my hand over the mouthpiece. I took the hand away and said, "Yes, Tom."

"Sam!" Fuller's voice was plummy with hurt amazement. "What's this about you not wanting to take Candy to your granddad's barbecue? Why heck, boy, my daughter's as good as any of your folks—and a damn sight better than a couple of them I could mention, if you don't mind my saying so! Look here now, Sam: If I was a good-looking young buck like yourself I'd be just as proud as punch to take a gorgeous gal like my daughter home to meet my folks, and you can bet on it. Maybe you haven't noticed, but I damn well have: That little lady's even skinnier and sexier than when—"

I took a deep breath and cut in on him. "It isn't that, Tom. But Jesus Christ, my folks are going through hell right now, and—"

"Oh hey, about that: I been meaning to tell you, Sam, it looks like we finally might be getting some action in that department. I talked to the guv day before yesterday and he was just getting set to give our buddy Humbel a call and really talk business with that turkey."

I glanced at Candy, who was nonchalantly decanting Bloody Mary into a pitcher partly filled with ice cubes, and pressed the receiver closer to my ear. "Is that so?"

"You goddamn betcha! The guv talks a good game about bringing the energy companies into this state, but when you get right down to it his heart's with the old-time ranching families that made Wyoming what it is today."

Cautiously I asked, "When did the governor say he was going to call Humbel?" Seated at the kitchen table, her legs slimly crossed to expose a pair of sharp kneecaps, Candy watched me coolly through curls of cigarette smoke.

"Well, he didn't say exactly, but I kind of understood it would be some time in the next day or so. Could be he's talked to him already and hasn't got around to telling me about it yet."

"And you really think it will help?"

"Do I think it will help? Jesus Christ, boy, where you been living all your life? And don't act smart and tell me Africa, either! Of course it'll help. Bull Humbel is the kind of guy that when you say jump he asks how high on the way up."

"I hope so."

"I know so. Now if I was you, Sam, I'd just set back and wait now, 'cause you're going to be seeing some results in the next few days—after the long weekend, anyway. So you just relax and forget about everything, you hear me? And quit giving my little girl a hard time and go on to the rodeo and the barbecue and enjoy yourselves. Life's too damn short to worry about the other crap, you can take it from an old sucker that's been there himself and knows all about it. Oh, and Sam, about me guaranteeing that mortgage on your granddaddy's land: I had a talk the other day with my accountant and he didn't seem to feel like I had anything to lose. We'll set down and pow-wow about it after the weekend, okay? So long then."

She was still at the table, watching me like a cat with a mouse. At last she lifted the pitcher, poured two glasses of Bloody Mary, and passed one of them to me. "Here's to us," she said, raising her own.

"To be perfectly frank with you," I told her, "I don't think my brother's really worth it. The sex has been okay, though."

She drank, her eyelids dropping with pleasure like a scratched cat's. "Actually," Candy said, opening her eyes and looking past me at the ceiling, "I've always hated sex, to tell you the truth."

She stood at the curb with the child under one arm and a beer can in her hand, waiting her turn in the bed races and feeling conspicuous in the scarlet-and-black costume of a lady of the night *circa* 1890 made for a woman at least one size smaller.

In the brightly painted booths around the square people were buying hamburgers and beer, message T-shirts and pizza, Indian dolls made in Taiwan, and fake Mexican jewelry. On the outdoor stage where rock bands performed at night and contest awards were presented during the day, three small girls, looking smug, did an unscheduled tap-dance routine to the accompaniment of music broadcast from loudspeakers hung in the patient gray cottonwood trees. Across the street files of men in gaudy shirts and cowboy hats the size of steak platters went through the propped barroom doors, closely observed by the Central Americans who crouched on their haunches along the sidewalk, their eyes bright and feral in their dark impassive faces. A shout went up from the opposite side of the square where the first two teams had just crossed the finish line, and Jenny turned away from the street to watch for Bette working her way back through the crowd to the starting point. In less than a minute she appeared, wobbling painfully on stiletto heels and grinning out of the red whore's mouth painted on her face. "We won!" she yelled when she saw Jenny.

Jenny put Bret carefully into her arms and set the can down on the curb as two young men impatient as racehorses, stripped to the waist and impressively muscled, maneuvered her bed on its ball-bearing wheels into the starting position. She climbed onto it, fastened the safety belt, and took hold of the steering wheel, which came almost to her chin, while Bret wriggled and grinned in Bette's arms and waved his fists at her. Jenny called, "Mommy will be right back, lovey!" as the men put their shoulders against the frame and braced their running shoes on the asphalt. She had just time to wave and smile once more before the starter fired his shotgun.

The next twenty-one seconds were a blur, or rather a constellation of blurs among which she was expected to dodge while the wheel leaped in her hands and the only sounds of which she was aware were the slap of rubber-soled shoes on pavement and the hard stertorous breathing at her back. Cheering crowds lined the street, which was split suddenly by a tall wedge of red brick facade; Jenny threw the wheel over and they made the corner with a lurch, yawing badly but still going fast. Jenny gripped the wheel harder and tried to hold it steady as they came to the next corner; they were around it before she knew what had happened and into the home stretch. Beyond the finish line the street was full of people and she was already wondering could they stop in time when suddenly a figure appeared directly in front of her, its arms outstretched like a scarecrow. She heard—felt—a thump as the figure disappeared, and then they were across the finish line among the spectators. Jenny, looking behind herself, saw a child stretched on its back and surrounded by kneeling people. A man came running with a first-aid kit as the police moved out from the curb holding their nightsticks drawn and motioning at the crowd to get back.

Feeling that she was about to be sick, Jenny slid from behind the wheel and stood beside the bed; then she sat down suddenly on it again and started to cry. A girl she didn't know came and put her arm around her but she went on crying. The girl was talking to her, telling her it hadn't been her fault as the ambulance arrived with flashing lights and began to back toward the victim. Jenny was vaguely aware of the young men behind her reassuring themselves in unsteady voices that nobody was to blame, and then she saw Bette step forward from the crowd. The attendants were beside the boy now, taping his ribs and slipping a brace onto his neck. "It wasn't you guys' fault," Bette said. "The little twerp asked for it. Kids that dumb don't deserve to live to grow up." She added, "By the way, you won." Except for Bette and the strange girl, nobody was paying any attention to her. Jenny tried to get up from the bed again and found that she was able to stand this time without feeling sick. The attendants slid a board under the boy and strapped him to it. "How about a drink?" Bette offered. "I'll bring you a whiskey from the Bare Garden." Jenny said, "Please," in a weak voice, and looked gratefully at her friend. Then she went rigid all over. *"Where's Bret?"*

A blank expression moved over Bette's painted face. *"Where's my son?"* Jenny cried.

Bette said, "We were standing there beside that tree to watch you finish. I put him down when it happened. . . ."

She was through the crowd in seconds and at the foot of the cottonwood; Bret was not there. For an instant she felt paralyzed by a blinding panic that was succeeded almost instantly by a rush of galvanizing, superhuman energy. She heard a man's voice say, "You looking for a lost kid, ma'am? Some guy just come and got him."

"Somebody took him? What did he look like?" Her own voice sounded completely disembodied; it might have come from the sky, or out of the tree itself.

"Kind of a tall guy with long hair. Looked like a biker—one of them hippy types—to me. "

She had left Chuck's pickup truck parked on the cutbank above the freightyard, half a block from the square. She reached it gasping and jerked his big revolver from the glove box; then she was running again up the other side of the street and along the shabby low buildings toward the alley behind. The hearse was there, nosed against the wall like a basking shark beneath the flight of unrepaired steps. She soared against them like a hawk, and plunged into a shabby corridor unlit except for the diminishing wedge of light between the wall and the closing door. In the twilight she could just make out that the door immediately to her right was marked 2A, the one opposite 2B; at the end of the hall were two more doors, which she approached silently over a strip of disintegrating carpet. Apartment 2C faced a gray blank in which a set of worn screw holes traced a vague outline; she bent to it and put her ear to the keyhole. For almost a minute there was no sound. Then, as distinctly as if she were in the room with him, she heard Bret's cheerful gurgle.

Afterward she did not remember shouting or knocking; the door, which must have been unlocked, had simply dissolved in front of her and simultaneously she was inside the apartment, tracing large and threatening gestures in the air with the gun. Bret sat cross-legged on the floor, surrounded by girlie magazines: He was holding one out to her in his grubby hands, wanting to be read to. The room was dark, with cracked and faded walls and a single small window covered on the outside with opaque plastic. There was a pullman kitchen at one end filled with unwashed dishes, and at the other a card table with bent legs and a scarred top supporting more magazines, a cheap-looking stereo system, and an ancient manual typewriter with dirty keys and a badly dented platen. On the filthy unmade bed that had been shoved against the wall on the opposite side of the room Waldo sat, also cross-legged, clipping his toenails. Jenny advanced to the center of the floor and snatched Bret into her arms. Then she pointed the revolver steadfastly at Waldo. "Give me my child," she demanded.

Waldo, who had been watching her with what appeared to be amusement, suddenly grinned. "You got him, ain't you?"

"Do you know," she asked, "what they do to kidnappers? Do you know what they'd do to *you*—a convicted murderer?"

In the semidarkness the black patch stared at her like the eye of a gigantic insect. "I'm a exterminated convicted murder," Waldo corrected her. "And they ain't any law I know of against helpin lost kids. They was, ever Boy Scout in America would be in reform school."

"If you ever help my son again," Jenny said, "I'll kill you. Do you understand now? I couldn't have killed the Collinses, but I could kill you. You couldn't die hard enough to suit me."

"Not with that you won't," Waldo told her, smirking. He indicated the gun with the point of his chin.

She looked at the weapon in her hand as though it were some kind of trick. "What do you mean—not with this?"

"You got to put shells in them first," he explained, and when she looked again she saw that he was right: six empty black holes, devoid of the saving glint of brass. "You got what you come for anyway, didn't you?"

"Listen," she said. "If you really thought I was going to go for a perverted deal like that, you're crazy. If Jack Walker needs those pictures that badly, he can buy them from you himself." Her view of the door was blocked by the floppy magazine Bret continued to wave, but she found the knob with her hand and grappled with it around the gun. Less than a minute later she was out of the building and on the ground, a white-faced young woman fleeing in full daylight across a city street with a child on one arm and an unloaded horse pistol in her hand.

At the truck she strapped Bret into his car seat and went around to the passenger side to close the door she had left open. He had dropped the magazine, after tearing several explicit four-color photographs from it, and was attempting with difficulty to

262

extract a fresh diversion from the kangaroo pocket of his sunsuit. He began quietly to fuss when his mother, impatiently and with hands that were only now tremulous, reached inside the pocket and withdrew the contents: an envelope, familiar-looking but now soiled and dog-eared, folded into a packet around what appeared to be $3^1/_2'' \times 4^1/_4''$ snapshots.

Jenny said, "Bret, how many times do I have to tell you *not* to touch what doesn't belong to you?"

T

hey sat, the three of them, surprised by the early twilight brought on by the shortening days and the pall of smoke through which the sun rose like a red greasy ball each morning. "Would anyone other than myself," Richardson asked, "care for a shot of something before we try to figure this one out?" Receiving no answer, he proceeded anyway to the kitchen where Jenny was giving Bret his supper, took the glasses down from the cupboard, and rummaged a bottle of whiskey from under the dry sink. His eyes met his wife's across the table; she lifted her eyebrows in question, but he merely shrugged at her as he cracked the ice cubes. When he returned with the tray to the parlor, Houston Walker remained seated as far along the couch as he could get from the MacPherson girl, who sat bent forward above the coffee table holding her hands clasped between her knees and staring at the bloody hole in the sky where the sun had passed through like a bullet. They looked, Richardson thought, like two wallflowers at a high school dance with no one to turn to but each other, yet stubbornly unwilling. "Thank God," he said, "for Mr. Jack Daniel, who understood that man's best friend was never supposed to be a dog. Say when, both of you. Karen?"

"To *here*," she agreed, scratching her glass with a manicured nail. He poured to the mark and a little over, whereupon she snapped, "That's enough!" in a voice that caused him to bring the bottle up with a start.

"Houston?"

"*Christ yes!*" Beneath what was left of the equatorial tan, Walker's face was drawn and gray, his eyes pithless like those of a man who has just witnessed his wife and family being flayed alive by savages.

He poured stiff drinks for both of them, and they all three drank in a silence relieved only by the pop and tinkle of thawing ice. "I don't know what I was thinking about, not telling you before," Karen MacPherson said finally.

"It was no responsibility of yours to tell me what he had made it none of my business to know about in the first place." Whatever comfort her eyes expressed seemed to Richardson to be entirely theoretical.

"I guess what I really feel guilty about is not telling him right away after I heard him that night in Jackson, bragging about the nine sections of land and the two thousand head of sheep he was going to marry—just like, when I first knew him, he was going to be president and chairman of the board of Ameroil before he was forty and it all seemed so plausible, for the first two years of marriage anyway. Maybe I even thought— oh, damn!" she cried, covering her face with her hands and swaying from side to side on the sofa. "Maybe I even thought, Well, let her find out for herself, then I can say I wasn't the only fool to be taken in by the arrogant conceited bastard." She took her hands away from her face, killed half her drink at a swallow, and dabbed at her eyes with the cocktail napkin.

"How would that have done any good?" Houston Walker

demanded brutally. "The only difference would be that we'd have a May murder on our hands now instead of a June one."

"Goddamnit, Houston," Richardson told him. "You've been talking murder for the past two months now, and I for one am getting tired of it. Isn't the reality unpleasant enough as it is?" And when the man ignored him, merely running his fingers together and cracking the knuckles as if to express his own endless and immitigable resentment, "The question is not what any one of us here should, or should not have, done. The question is—what are we going to do with *these?*" He stabbed the pile of turned-down photographs on the table with his finger, and reached for and uncapped the whiskey bottle.

"Burn them," Walker said, unlacing his hands abruptly and letting them drop between his knees.

"Burn them?" the girl almost screamed.

"You heard me."

"But don't you understand what Chuck can *do*—?"

"Of course I understand." Walker's voice was cold, almost insulting. He turned his back ostentatiously on Karen and said to Richardson, "Forget about those damn pictures, Chuck. I have a better way. You know who Tom Fuller is, don't you?"

"I know of him. Never met the guy in person. He's some kind of local political mugwump, isn't he?"

"He's chairman of the State Democratic Committee and a close friend of the governor's. There's a good chance the governor is going to ask him to head up his reelection committee two years from now. I was crazy in love with his daughter when I was a pup of eighteen or nineteen." He paused, and Richardson thought that within that pause he saw him throw a quick look toward the girl. "I've been discussing this business of my brother with Tom for the past few weeks. He and my folks have had their differences, but Tom and I have been friends for more than twenty years. I got a call from him this morning around eleven o'clock. He'd just got off the line with the guv, who said he was going to call Humbel this afternoon and lean on him good and hard."

Richardson asked, "What is there that Humbel can do now? We've already turned down their offer to a plea-bargain."

"I don't know, but we'll find out in the next couple of days, I imagine."

"Longer. It's a three-day weekend coming up."

They were silent again for a while. Finally Houston Walker said, "On second thought, Chuck: Whatever it is you decide to do, don't burn those photographs."

"Oh, you mustn't!" the girl cried, and snatched them up protectively.

"I want to confront him with them afterward," Walker continued in a furious voice. "I want him to know that even if he beats the rap in the end, we all of us knew about it: his attorney, his girlfriend, and his brother. I want him to have to face up to what it is he's become, what he's made of himself. I want him to admit to himself that he's a sick, sick man. I think he owes that much, at least, to the truth."

He set the empty glass on the table with a loud affirmative rap as he finished speaking, after which all three of them lapsed into an embarrassed silence in which they assiduously avoided looking at one another. There seemed to be absolutely nothing left for anybody to say.

Houston Walker, whose car was being looked at in Fontenelle, had caught a ride out to the ranch that afternoon with Karen MacPherson. Richardson watched the lights out of sight before putting up what was left of the whiskey and washing and drying the glasses. Then he went back to the bedroom where Jenny sat in undress at the vanity table, brushing out her hair. She smiled at him in the mirror as he bent to place his arm about her shoulders, drawing her to him until at last her arm relinquished its stroke and the brush hung immobile in her trailing fingers. She allowed her head to fall back on his, and for several minutes they remained in tableau, contemplating their image that reminded him of a Mormon wedding announcement. Presently Jenny said, "Houston Walker is, like, the most awful person I've ever known. Isn't he?"

"He works hard at it. But he's spent half his life running away from the devil he knows, only to fall into the clutches of the one he didn't know and probably never even dreamed of. Since he isn't the kind of guy to go away and hang himself, I'd say that whatever it is that's kept him going these last twenty years, he's going to go on needing it for a while yet."

With his free hand he drew the packet from his shirt pocket and propped one of the snapshots face forward against the bottom of the mirror so that now two couples faced them, one inset against the other. In the smaller picture Frank Joad's furious face as he drew back from the punch wore an involuntary expression of astonishment; while Clarice Walker, exhibiting the bared teeth of a lioness at bay, strained in the man's grip and covered one eye with her hand. Behind them, the neon facade of the Strawberry Fields Club in Rock Springs glared against a classic Western sunset of purple, green, and gold.

"Saving the family farm," Richardson said. "It's still one of America's oldest and noblest ideals, even if you have to marry the head of a drug ring to do it. She got smart almost—but not quite—in time."

I sat on the hard paintless bench under a sky tarnished by the smoke of the consuming fires to the north, while the loudspeaker over the announcer's stand ground out harsh unintelligible music and the Grand Entry Parade, like a Chinese dragon, wound through the arena in a succession of glittering sinuosities. Soon both the music and the parade would cease, the pimple-faced trumpeter would once again strangle the national anthem, and the angry old man in the Garibaldi shirt and silver hat would deliver the invocation and opening remarks; finally, we would all be seated once more, and I could pull my pants out of my crotch. I needed to keep reminding myself that with the one-way air ticket between Salt Lake City and Pretoria reposing safely in the inside pocket of the safari jacket, I was capable of enduring whatever horrors the remaining three days might have in store for me. Four seats below us in the bleachers two women sat with their shoulders pressing lightly together: my mother rigid with that clenched and furious willing that in women of her age usually finds expression only in church, my sister severely upright in a position conveying her customary public hauteur. Caught now and again by a stiff wind, the fall of blonde hair between her shoulder blades lifted with the nervous excitement of a filly in heat. My father's yellowed note with the faded brown stains on it, entrusted to me by Pablo less than forty-eight hours before, was folded tightly into the lining of my wallet as a kind of talisman ensuring my own survivability.

"My father's waving at us," Candy remarked, tugging at my sleeve. "Over there by the team-roping chute—him and my mom together." I gave her a cold look in return and gazed pointedly in the opposite direction. Her eyes were a rabbity pink color and the sunlight striking through to the dark roots of her dried-out hair gave her the ghastly appearance of a porcelain doll left outdoors for a season. I saw Chuck Richardson and his pretty, fresh-looking young wife standing by the ambulance with Karen Mac-Pherson, who was in conversation with one of the white-coated attendants. "Are they coming to the barbecue too?" Candy asked jealously.

"Richardson and his wife are invited, of course. I don't suppose the MacPherson girl is." It struck me that her face, at the mention of the name, went suddenly blank, as if she was holding it out in front of herself on a ribboned stick in the manner of an eighteenth-century courtesan. It's amazing how intuitive even the dumbest of them can be at times.

"Your sister," Candy whispered, "just looked at me."

"Did she? That was sweet of her."

"You didn't see the look."

"I wouldn't worry. She'll be polite."

"I'm not worried, stupid."

"That's good," I said. "I wouldn't want you to be worried about anything."

To keep her from worrying, I lifted two more beers from the cooler and gave her one. I was drinking absentmindedly, keeping my eyes on the fence where the cowboys lounged near the chutes.

My brother stood apart from the rest, his arms extended along the center rail from which his lean body slumped above his crossed boots in a defiantly negligent attitude. He looked both entirely familiar and entirely not, like a close friend who has just won the Nobel Prize or been diagnosed as having terminal cancer.

"I need to pee," Candy said in a tense whisper that brought me back to myself with a start.

"Well, better go now if you're going, then. He's fourth up after the next guy."

I saw her eyes dart at the two women below. "I can wait that long, I guess."

"Sure you can. Just lay off the beer for a few minutes."

"*Me* lay off? *You're* the one that's half crocked already."

"Maybe so, but I can hold mine."

"Go hold it in your hand then," she snapped in a fit of alcoholic temper. Her eyes had a varnished look like those of a drugged person or a somnambulist. As far as Candy was concerned, nothing that was happening today was actually real. Nothing was ever real to her, unless it arrived in wavery distorted color broken periodically by commercial breaks.

The clowns retreated as the cowboys sprang away from the chute through which the plunging double figure—man-beast, beast-man—exploded. "Three more and I get to go pee," Candy remarked. Across the oval of yellow sand the black-hatted sardonic figure continued to hang; it crossed my mind to wave in its direction. Karen was standing at the fence now, between Richardson and his wife. Another rider exited the chute, and when I looked again the figure on the fence was gone. "Number eight!" the announcer yelled. "It's Jack Walker, ladies and gentlemen— four-time champion and winner of this year's July Fourth competition!"

I saw my sister, tall as an Amazon and proud-looking as a Roman consort, rise suddenly in the bleachers holding in her hand a large blood-red American Beauty rose which, as the cowboys leaped aside, she hurled into the path of the dark upended shape. Then I too was on my feet, waving my hat and yelling like a madman as Jack Walker—my brother!—flung up his hand and held it high above his head. While the buzzer sounded its harsh defeated rasp I saw the bull's heels go up as if in celebration of their mutual victory before the rider toppled slowly forward, supple and bending as a dancer, over the horns. The two made a single image still but now the symmetry was twisted, the positions reversed, and the roar of the crowd changed to a rolling groan as the cowboys leaped from the fence and the clowns ran in waving their scarlet rags. The trampling legs were wet and red now, the brindle belly spattered, but still the hooves went on striking and battering at the limp inert weight that encumbered them. Suddenly they parted. The bull, blowing hard and making a feint with its horns at the clowns, circled the arena and galloped through the gate they swung wide for it into the pens as the men gathered about the prostrate figure; some kneeling, others standing, but all of them with their hats off while the gaily painted ambulance advanced with the gray dignity of a hearse on wide silent tires through the muted dust.

It came to me as I struggled to drag one screaming hysterical woman down through the seething crowd toward two other screaming hysterical women: *It isn't that I ever believed, even as an angry rebellious kid, that You actually existed: It's that, deep down, one way or another, everywhere and every time, forever and ever amen, I've hated You as if You did!*

no matter how long youve ridden you get that same feeling in your gut each time but it dont matter once that buzzer goes and ole bull goes up under you like a blowed boiler this ones a good one looks like i drew good today after all wrap that hand tight now and give em a ride to make em stand up and yell funny how youre more scared thinking youre going to get throwed in two seconds flat than hung up in the rigging and stompled

god knows i wasnt meant to be a hero which is all right maybe because this aint a time for heroes no glory anymore but duty jim bridger bill ashley jedediah smith captain bonneville and captain uncle jo all of them made by the country they loved as much or more than they made it and made me too finally like it needed a hundred and fifty years to produce a guy not brave enough to fight indians or grizzly bears handtohand or pry open a continent like it was a tin can but just to take care of his own people and not by lies or politics but just by keeping his mouth shut like every true coward is born knowing how to do

Chilton Williamson, Jr.

*who knows whether if they hadnt sent my dad to fight in
korea or my mother hadnt met that dude in jackson or if pablo had
sent that telegram or my father hadnt let her come back from new
orleans at all all this would have been necessary but then life itself
is necessary aint it only five seconds to go now check that hand
before he blows the one thing that really scares me is getting locked
up id rather they just went ahead and dropped the pill and maybe
they will too if she can keep on keeping her mouth shut get them
heels up straighten that back you do what you got to do and they
call it courage sometimes but what hurts the most is knowing that
if something did actually happen to me she wouldnt understand
because even then she still wouldnt want to nobody in this dirty
rotten world knows if there is a god or aint but if there is all i would
say to him is this listen god i dont want to go to jail but if i have to
just say the word and ill go then without no fuss*

*get after it you stripeass sonofabitch get them heels up i
known whores buck hardern you hold that hand up and put a ride
on him oh the goddamn everlastin buzzer and im home free now*

*i wonder would captain uncle jo have had the courage to do
what he done if he could have seen how it was all going to turn out
anyhow*

274

At the Fontenelle Café they still had the linen cloths, good china, and heavy silverware—even the single red rose in the pewter vase—that I remembered from my boyhood. I was sitting at a reserved table for two, waiting for Karen MacPherson to appear; it seemed like a very long time since I had waited in a restaurant for a girl. She herself had suggested the café as being neutral ground, not knowing of the countless times I had eaten lunch there on trips to town with my grandfather.

That morning before leaving the ranch I had broken down the .30–'06 Winchester belonging to my brother and packed it, together with the red-and-white chaps, in my luggage. I had neatly arranged Jack's other possessions, packed them into boxes, cleaned and swept out the trailer, and loaded the garbage into the back of his old pickup truck. When I had finished the job I had made myself a drink and considered what to do with my father's note. My first idea had been to burn it, my second to return it to Pablo to keep along with the gyroscope of the blue-and-white Maule he had carried away with him from the "accident" out of the mountains more than twenty years before. Finally, I had folded it back into my wallet again, sat down at the shaky card table Jack had used for a desk, and typed out on his little portable machine a six-page account on notarized paper of the holdup of the nuclear-waste train at Greasewood Junction on May 23, 1973. I wrote how I had read of the scheduled transit in the *Fontenelle Fortune* and how (I did not mention Clarice's role in the conspiracy) we had decided not to allow it to proceed unchallenged across the state. I described how we had built the barricade of old ties near the top of the long climb where the train would be moving slowly, how we had camped overnight with the horses near the ambush and listened at daybreak to the four locomotives thundering against the grade; how we had pulled the tall black hats over our faces, tied the bandannas over our noses and mouths, and spurred the horses along the deep wash overgrown by sagebrush toward the tracks. I told how we had checked our revolvers and ridden forward at a lope, and how it had occurred to me, at the penultimate moment, that, if arrested, I stood to forfeit my honorable discharge from the Army and all my benefits as a veteran. I described how I had fallen back and let Jack charge alone up the embankment to the halted train, waving his six-shooter and yelling like a red Indian, while the heads of the train crew started in disbelief from the windows. I described how he had ridden for more than half a mile down the tracks beside the train, yelling and firing into the air, and how a local brakeman working a stint into Idaho had recognized both the boy and the big Appaloosa he rode. I told how a sheriff's deputy, responding to radio calls from the cab, had spotted the horse from the highway and through a bullhorn ordered Jack to stop. I finished by telling how I had assured Jack, at the jailhouse, that as a minor he had nothing to fear from the law, instructed him to describe the incident as a practical joke (leaving me out of the affair entirely), and how he had agreed to do that. Then I signed the letter, folded it, and stuck it into an envelope addressed to Bull Humbel, Esq., District Attorney for Bridger County, Bridger County Courthouse, Fontenelle, Wyoming. After placing the envelope in the inside pocket of the safari jacket on the side opposite the plane ticket, I had closed and locked the trailer and walked back across the turnaround to the house.

Indoors it was very still and cool. I crossed the parlor, went quietly upstairs, and along the hall to my room, which no longer resembled a museum but a storage room instead. I had removed the books from the shelves, the relics from the display case, the trophies and photographs from the walls and packed them into cardboard boxes, which I had finally made to go with difficulty into the closet with my mother's old clothes and the human fragments in plaster she had created through the inspiration (Grace, so to speak, under pressure) of Clarice's father in Jackson, whom I remembered only as a tall Swede with longish yellow hair and a beret over it who drove a red convertible, told me carnival stories about a place called New Oar Lines where he lived in the wintertime, and quit giving my mother art lessons and having picnics with her at the Homestead after my father came home from Korea. My bag, new-looking and shiny, awaited my departure beside the hardside guncase out of it I had left the dusty-looking book, bound between faded boards, that had arrived several days before by Express Mail and rested now on the bedside table. It had been accompanied by a note from Nilsa Martinez which read, "Dere Mr. Walker, Becose of taking so long yure book has been lossed becose of sercomstans beyound control, the man i tolk to at the bookstor say this one even more voluble than the other, it cost me lot of extra mony to by for you. Nilsa." She had sent *The Sound and the Fury* by William Faulkner, with the author's signature written on the flyleaf in suspiciously fresh-looking ink. In the corners of the room and along the window ledges dying flies crawled beside the desiccated husks of their brothers, but beneath the paper stain one blue cowboy continued to battle one red Indian to the death. After stopping in the bathroom to wash my hands thoroughly, I went

back along the hall to my mother's study, which I entered directly
without bothering to knock. The restaurant was already filling
with men wearing bolo ties and carrying Stetsons in their hands,
sitting to do deals over fried liver and bacon, when I caught sight
of her coming in from the street, trim and lovely in an off-white
skirt and pink silk blouse that perfectly set off her ash-blonde
hair. She saw me even before I waved at her and walked quickly
up to the table as I rose to pull out the chair, which she slipped
into with a lithe efficient movement, without looking at me.
"Thank you very much," she said.

"Would you care for something to drink?"

"No, thank you."

"Are you sure? I'm having one."

She said, "Perhaps I'll have a glass of wine. They serve a
nice dry white here."

I called the waiter and ordered wine for her and a double
whiskey on the rocks for myself. I said, "As a general rule I never
take a drink before five, but today feels like a day to beat all days
already." She had looked up as I entered from behind my mother's
leather-top desk on which a handful of freshly sharpened pencils
glittered in the ceramic holder, her hair drawn severely back
from her ears and tied at the nape with a black velvet ribbon. She
had my mother's heavy leather-bound appointment book open in
front of her on the desk: prepared, after thirty-seven years, to
assume full control at last. "You don't have to give me a reason for
what you do," Karen MacPherson said.

I said, "I asked you to meet me again because I wanted to
apologize."

She gave a dry small laugh. "You haven't done anything to
apologize to *me* about."

"I think I have." I raised my glass to her. "Cheers."

"*Cheers?*"

"It's only a saying," I apologized, blushing.

We touched glasses politely and an awkward silence followed, in which I heard Clarice's voice: "Why would God make

the world just to destroy it a little day by day? I wish I had been there when they nailed Him to the Cross. I wish I could have been the one to stick the sword in and make Him writhe. If there really is a God, then He ruined everything." I said, "I'm sorry about that night. I must have been awfully drunk."

"It doesn't matter," the girl said. "Could we go ahead and order now? I have to be back at the office in half an hour."

I watched her over the menu as she studied the daily specials. She was young still but not that young: Her hair had been definitely lightened and there was a slight relaxation apparent in the skin on her cheeks and neck. She was about the age I was starting to like them now. It all seemed vaguely unreal to me: this woman in her simple elegant business clothes, the tall rather formal windows, the good silverware, the pale rose with its fringe of delicate green leaves in the vase between us, the snow-white cloth with its sharply pressed creases. "I'll have the chicken-and-avocado salad, please," Karen MacPherson said, closing the menu and setting it aside. I noticed that her face was pale under the makeup and that the bones looked more prominent, as if in the past week she had grown thinner. Her aplomb appeared as strong as ever but also to be costing her a bit of an effort, and I wondered whether or not women of her type actually ever cried. I gave the waiter our orders while she toyed with the silverware, then took my great-grandfather's watch from my pocket and laid it on the table between us. "I had another reason for wanting to see you again. This belonged to my brother. I want you to have it."

She glanced at the watch and then quickly away again; watching closely, I observed the wineglass tremble between her fingers. "I don't need anything to remember him by. But thank you anyway."

I covered the watch with my hand and pushed it toward her. "Please, Karen." It was the first time I had addressed her by her name. She sat regarding it as though it were a poisonous spider, then snatched it and dropped it inside her pocketbook. "Thank you," she said, and dabbed with a handkerchief at the corners of her eyes. The salad arrived, and with it my cold roast beef. I picked up my fork and knife and began to eat, wondering as I did so what she and my brother had found to talk about; perhaps they hadn't needed to talk at all. The girl ate like a bird—a hungry bird. I was getting a little desperate: The chasm between us was widening rather than closing, and there was so little time; in eighty-four hours I would be home again in Africa. Life, I was beginning to suspect, was basically unfair. Karen finished her salad and checked her wristwatch as she drank the last of the wine. Around us the Rotarians, Lions, and Kiwanis were lighting after-the-meal cigars, while the waiters cleared the tables and took away the linen cloths. She seemed completely removed from me, and from the world at large; it was a way I had never seen her before, and suddenly it hit me: She really *had* loved him, whether as a brother or a lover was immaterial. "Well," Karen said, taking out her purse, "I have to run now. Thank you so much for the watch, and have a safe trip back to Africa."

"You're very welcome. Lunch, by the way, is on me."

"No, really."

"I insist."

"Why don't we just," she suggested firmly as she put down a bill, "make it a dutch treat? That way, everything will be absolutely fair and straight."

We left the restaurant together and stood facing one another on the sidewalk, where she gave me her hand in a formal gesture. The smoke from the fires obscured the dome of the sky; it was rather like saying goodbye in one of those huge opaque railway stations of Europe. Karen's little white Ford stood parked behind my faltering Jap—the mechanic had remained unable, after two inspections, to identify the problem—at the curb. "Goodbye," she told me, "and good luck. I hope you won't need too much of it."

I saw the car out of sight around the block before climbing into my own, where I sat with the key in my hand behind the wheel. "I'd sell my soul," she had said as I was leaving, "to save the North Section," and I had almost challenged her with it then. But what, after all, would have been the good? After thirty-seven years, even the death of my brother had not been enough to make her want to understand. Walking out of that room I had felt, for the first time in my life, completely free of my sister, and no need to argue it with her ever again.

A̲t the Bare Garden first, then at the Number One Pit, finally at the Stockman, they had bought me drinks. People tend to be generous that way—always ready to give the teetering boulder a friendly nudge and crane their necks over the precipice to see how far will it fall and how much rubble it draws after itself. After leaving the Fontenelle Café I had driven the fifty miles through the strange indirect light, like that from an eclipse, to the state mental hospital in Bear River, where I had delivered the medical insurance papers I had got that morning from Clarice and shocked the staff by refusing to visit my mother. It was a complete mental collapse, the doctors said, which might or might not be permanent. I had stopped off at one of the local bars for a whiskey and driven back to Fontenelle, where I sat in the Bare Garden drinking whiskey and soda and listening to the latest and apparently final chapter of the *weltschmerz* of Most Likely to

Succeed, who had sold his house and all his worldly possessions and to evade his creditors was moving with his family to East Africa, where he had taken a job with an international oil consortium. "A guy can't live the American Way anymore," he had explained, "the only thing for him to do is go to where there *ain't* no American Way." At the Number One I had switched to whiskey neat, and by the time I reached the Stockman I was feeling generous enough to assist the barmaid, an attractive well-built redhead, in loading a pair of unconscious Mexicans across the saddles of the horses they had ridden into the bar and secure them loosely with their own lariats. After leading the animals out of the bar, through a connection of back alleys, and safely across the railroad tracks, I had released them into the prairie with a couple of brisk slaps to their rumps. The herders were meager little men become unmanageable deadweights; they had kept slipping off the polished leather, first on one side of the saddle and then on the other, and one of the horses had defecated on the pool table while the girl and I were finishing our knots. After I had got rid of the Mexicans she bought me a drink, and before I had drunk half of it the idea of driving out to the trailer court was irresistible. I put down what must have been a twenty-five-dollar tip, got in my car, and drove very slowly, with impeccable manners, through town to the Mormon First and Second Ward building, where the Jap's engine gave one last spasmodic flutter and died like a broken heart. I pushed the car against the curb, locked the doors, and continued on foot across the bridge that spanned the railroad yards and along the highway to where the trailers gleamed in their ordered rows like pale uncovered coffins. "I suppose you're celebrating tonight," Karen said when she saw me. "Isn't that right?"

"Celebrating what?"

"Going back to Africa, of course. What else would you have to celebrate?"

"That's so." I hadn't thought about it before, but it didn't seem to matter either way.

"Well, you're doing a good job of it. I've seen passed-out Indians in Oklahoma City that looked better than you do."

I followed her to the kitchenette, where I sat in a molded plastic chair at the table while she poured ground coffee into the paper filter and water through the top of the automatic drip. "I must say you don't seem to me to be acting much in character tonight," Karen said. "Despite the bull-riding and the elephant-shooting, physical self-abuse—unlike the other kind—never struck me as being your kind of thing."

I said, "That business with the train: It was Clarice's and my idea, keeping them from bringing nuclear waste through. I chickened out at the last minute and let him take the rap, since he was legally a minor. I was afraid that if I got caught they'd take back my Purple Heart and maybe even my honorable discharge."

She stared at me uncomprehendingly. "What are you talking about? What train? I don't know anything about any train."

"You mean he never told you?" I sat back in the chair feeling foolish and at the same time relieved. Karen filled two mugs with the coffee and set the sugar bowl and a waxed container of milk beside them. She asked, "Would you be offended if I said I think you are the most completely divided person I ever met in my entire life?"

"I don't think so."

"Well," she said, "you are."

I added milk and sugar to the coffee and took a long drink. By the time I had finished the first cup I felt painfully sober and very sleepy. Karen refilled my mug and stood back against the counter, looking at me speculatively above her own. She said, "If it's your conscience that's bothering you, perhaps you should consider accepting your responsibilities here instead of running back to Africa."

"What responsibilities?"

"Don't play dumb. You know what I'm talking about."

"But this isn't my home any longer."

"It never was mine, but it could be."

I glanced quickly up at her and saw that here, sure enough, was a woman I might have. It would have to be for keeps, though, while I had always thought of myself as the kind of man who toys with the idea of marriage until the age of fifty and then goes out and buys a dog. Beyond that, there was the fact of her having been Jack's woman: the reward he had coveted and deserved and that it was not for me to lay claim to and enjoy in his absence. She was a woman I could have explained it to, of course, but I was conscious of having an extreme distaste for explanations at the moment, and besides, she was the sort that didn't require to have everything spelled out for her in block letters. Instead I asked, "It isn't any of my business, of course, but how could a girl like you have married a man like that in the first place?"

She said, "I was twenty-one years old at the time. Just a kid out of nursing school, looking for something more romantic to worry about than the latest catheterization technique. He was captain of the U. of Oklahoma football team and the girls were all crazy for him. Frank Joad looked like Betty Coed's dreamboat, and when you're twenty-one years old and your dream comes true it's like shooting yourself in the foot. Don't you remember what it was like being twenty-one, Houston?"

"I remember."

"I'm going to go to bed now," Karen said. "I'll bring you a blanket and a pillow and you can sack out here on the couch. It's too late to run you out to a motel, and anyway I'm exhausted. I feel as if I hadn't slept for a week."

I sat on the edge of the couch when she had gone and slowly removed my socks, pausing thoughtfully to rub between my toes. I set my boots together under the coffee table and hung my folded pants over the back of the nearest chair. I looked around for the safari jacket, remembered that I had left it in the kitchen, and went to retrieve it. It was badly crumpled and I tried smoothing it out with my hands as I stood by the partly open window, breathing in the dry cold air and admiring a perfect moon that drew me back to Africa, the giggle of hyenas in the bush while I sat with Patrick Roberts before a mopane-wood fire drinking carefully chilled martinis and smelling the sweet fry of eland steaks and buttered potatoes. Reflexively, my hand moved into the satin lining which, for the past five days, had obliged by releasing a soft and satisfying crackle. Now the absence of any sound whatever hit me like the click of a firing pin in an empty chamber.

The shock lasted a fraction of a second and was succeeded by the concentrated impersonal attention of a test pilot ticking off his options in a tailspin. The ticket in its paper wallet had been in the pocket when I had paid my half of the bill at lunch, and later in Bear River when I had taken out the insurance papers. It had been with me at the Bare Garden and at the Number One, where I had still been sober. I had not lain with any whore, nor fought with any man, nor been rolled in an alley. At the Stockman I had been very drunk. There had been an incident with a couple of sheepherders, and I remembered dimly the presence of horses also. A pretty redhead had helped me to load the drunks onto the horses, and between us we had had our hands full keeping them up there. The men had kept slipping off their saddles on one side or another and finally we had had to secure them like a couple of elk quarters. Various items had dropped from their pockets: pen knives and small change, a wallet on a leather cord, books of paper matches, tins of chewing tobacco, a letter or two which I had retrieved from the floor, folded, and thrust into the hip pocket of one of the men. . . .

Somewhere beneath the cold prairie moon a Mexican herder was being borne ploddingly along, denimed cheeks upturned to the disinterested stars; drunker than a waltzing piss-ant and poorer than Tom's turkey, but with an eighteen-hundred-dollar-plus airplane ticket good for one-way travel between Salt Lake City, Utah, and Pretoria, South Africa, bent against the bony curve of his blue buttock. Presumably, he was no more solicitous of it than the original bearer had been, since neither I nor the people at Pan American ever heard of it again.